C000172323

KINDRED SPIRITS

A NOVEL

Mary Hubble

Grosvenor House
Publishing Limited

This book is published by
Grosvenor House Publishing Ltd
Link House
140 The Broadway, Tolworth, Surrey, KT6 7HT.
www.grosvenorhousepublishing.co.uk

This book is a work of fiction. Any resemblance to
people or events, past or present, is purely coincidental.

A CIP record for this book
is available from the British Library

ISBN 978-1-83975-098-4

Chapter 1

When I finally plucked up enough courage to make a new start in a different town, my friends were impressed by my change of address:-

> 16, Salvin Street,
> Mill Hill,
> Rantersford.

"Sounds posh," they said.

I hastened to enlighten them, for although Salvin was an eminent Victorian architect and Mill Hill is also a nice area of London, Rantersford is a small rather rundown town on the East Coast main line.

"Why move there, then?" they asked.

"Because the houses are amazingly cheap and if I don't like it, I can easily get away by train," I explained bluntly.

This silenced them while they waited to learn how things turned out.

The day of the move did not bode well. A violent storm during the night felled trees across the whole country, and the removal firm said it wouldn't be safe to drive a high-sided vehicle up the A1. So I, and Orlando the cat, stayed with my close friend Maureen, and were taken to Rantersford a day late.

Number 16 Salvin Street was waiting to welcome me.

When my possessions are arranged to my liking, I go out into the narrow back garden which is in need of attention. The next door neighbour, a stout man with iron-grey hair, peers over the dividing fence and asks if I am stopping.

"Stopping?" I repeat, "Stopping what?"

"Staying," he translates, as if to a half-wit.

"Well, I've only just come," I rejoin, also as if to a half-wit.

He sighs. "Some people don't like it here. I was born and bred here, and I *do* like it."

I assure him that I expect I will like it when I have lived here long enough to make up my mind. This seems to satisfy him.

"Do you like beetroot?" he demands next. Is this some kind of trick question?

"Do you like cats?" I counter, fearing he might object to Orlando, not wanting to cause friction.

He moves aside so I can see a bench in his yard and indicates a beautiful long-haired tabby.

"That's my Dolly," he says proudly. "I'm Sid. I'll bring you some beetroot from the allotment tomorrow."

I return to the house and pour myself a glass of sherry. I do not habitually resort to alcohol when under pressure but neither do I habitually make life-changing decisions such as moving house on my own. I look at my reflexion in the mirror over the fireplace. Is forty-eight too old for beginning again? In some lights I can be taken for several years younger, but this has not always been an advantage.

I used to get very upset at being taken for nineteen when I was actually twenty-five. It happened frequently enough for me to question my dress-sense and general behaviour. Did I lack maturity? Had my mother suppressed my natural development for fear of me 'going to the bad', a phrase often used about some of my outgoing friends? Certainly I was abnormally shy, but that could have been the result of early teasing at school because of my slightly protruding front teeth. They could be concealed as I grew up if I didn't smile overmuch, and I was comforted to see the film star Zoë Wanamaker on screen expertly coping with a similar drawback to great acclaim.

Anyway, compared with some women, I can be described as quite good looking today.

My dear friend Maureen had advised me about finding new friends in Rantersford.

"Get a list of clubs and groups in the town which cater for your interests," she said. "You like art, politics, religion, music, literature and animals, so there should be plenty of scope."

As a qualified librarian, I have up till now had no difficulty in getting a job, so when I have washed my now empty sherry glass, I compose a letter to the Rantersford chief librarian, asking if he has any suitable vacancies.

I had noticed an imposing building in the town centre with the words Public Library and Museum over the door, so I put on my coat and walk down the hill to deliver the letter by hand. During my professional life I have had wide experience of library work so feel confident that I will soon be earning my living again.

However, when I enter the imposing building I am told that the library is situated in the shopping centre over a supermarket, and has not shared the museum building for several years. I presume that no stonemason is available to alter the wording over the door, and that the citizens of Rantersford have got used to ignoring it. A helpful man with his hair in a ponytail gives me the new library address, and I post the letter at the main office, which has unambiguous lettering over the door.

Suddenly lonely and discouraged, I go early to bed, allowing Orlando to sleep on my feet.

The next day is Sunday, and while I am eating my breakfast I hear a church bell ringing quite nearby. Maureen has told me to join groups which share my interests, so assuming that a church would make a good beginning, I put my head out of the front door to get the direction of sound.

After hastily combing my hair and donning my best coat, I run up the hill and arrive at the church of St Stephen just as the bell ceases ringing. Panting for breath, I enter the heavy door and sit down on a pew at the back next to a plump motherly woman who offers me her hymn book.

"I know all the words by heart," she whispers. As it so happens, I also know most of the words by heart, so we sing in happy unison.

The vicar is fairly young with a clear pleasant voice. Shaking my hand after the service, he asks if I live nearby or if I am just visiting.

Not wanting to commit myself to regular attendance, I mutter that I have moved house and am getting my bearings.

The members of the congregation chat to one another and smile at me in a friendly manner so I send a mental note to Maureen, telling her that I am following her good advice - literature, politics, art, and animals still to be investigated.

I let myself into 16 Salvin Street in a good mood. Already I am beginning to love the place. It is mine to decorate and furnish as I like. My ex-husband has been generous with furniture, telling me to take what I wanted, as he could manage with one of everything, and had never liked 'clutter'.

At first it hurt me to realize that the tasteful William Morris-type items I had chosen for our home over the years had meant so little to him, but now I am free, I can take pleasure in arranging my share throughout the high-ceilinged rooms.

The local street-map shows rows of terraced houses radiating from a main road leading to the railway station. Originally these dwellings had been built to house railway workers and opened straight onto the street. Most had three bedrooms and extended at the back with gardens or a yard. In my case, the third bedroom has been converted into a bathroom, and there is a shed in the garden.

Sid is mending a bicycle when I go out to do some weeding.

"Here's the beetroot," he says by way of greeting. "Doris doesn't like it. Says it takes too long to cook."

I thank him for the generous bunch of roots and soil which I put in the shed to deal with later.

An untidy woman bustles out with a basket of very wet washing which she hangs on a drooping line. It drips onto Sid as he works on the bike.

"Why can't you squeeze the water out before you hang it up?" he asks roughly.

"I would if we had a wringer," she snaps back.

"Hullo, I'm Clare" I say, trying to sound friendly.

"Ah," she nods. "Hope you don't mind me washing on a Sunday."

"No, of course not," I reply. "Better the day, better the deed."

They both look at me blankly, evidently never having heard my mother's maxim. She was full of appropriate phrases which she trotted out whenever the occasion arose, and I sometimes catch myself repeating them.

Doris returns to her kitchen and slams the door. Sid attacks his bike furiously with a spanner, and I hope they don't have loud rows, as the walls between terraced houses are often not insulated.

I walk down to the town centre before lunch and buy a local newspaper. The 'What's On?' page gives a list of activities which are planned for the coming week. They are mostly jumble sales and charity coffee mornings, and meetings of various interest-groups. I reject the Hard of Hearing Club, Knit and Natter, Dementia Drop-in, and Jogging for Beginners, but make a note of Rantersford Ramblers, Rantersford Writers, Painting for Pleasure, and a free piano recital in a church not St Stephen's. Local news seems to concentrate on parking

6

restrictions and the future of the hospital. As I don't have a car and am reasonably healthy, I have no need to worry.

A few letters have started finding me at my new address, delivered at various times of day. This means that I can never be sure till tea-time whether or not any mail is coming my way. There has been no reply from the chief librarian so evidently he or she is not eager to give me an interview. Perhaps I should write again or phone. Then at last an official looking envelope arrives with a local postmark. It contains a brief letter saying that the Rantersford library already has a qualified librarian. If I wish, I can go on the list for voluntary holiday work.

This comes as something of a shock. During my professional life, I have worked in various towns and always succeeded in securing a suitable job. Mostly these have been in public libraries but the most recent was in a school library, which fitted conveniently with my daughters' education. Must I now sign on at the local Job Centre?

I check my bank statement to see how long I can manage without an added income. My ex-husband has not been mean with his allowance but, apart from that and my own meagre savings, there is nothing in the 'paid-in' column.

By a miracle, Rantersford has a good Citizens' Advice Bureau and a kind lady sorts me out. I fill in a form for Unemployment Benefit and agree to attend regular meetings where my applications for suitable work will be checked. As librarianship is all I am actually qualified for, my applications will be few and far between, but the powers-that-be are reasonable enough, and as long as I keep to the rules, they will pay me sufficient to live on for a specified number of weeks.

At my first meeting I get to know several other unemployed people, but I am not a typical case. They are mostly men, sulky and discouraged. They exercise their rights in an aggressive manner.

"I'm not killing chickens," is their commonest cry.

The biggest employer in the area is a factory which prepares poultry for supermarkets, and no one can be forced to take a job there if they object on conscientious grounds.

I am put in mind of conscientious objectors in the Great War, and wonder if it feels the same killing chickens as killing people.

Before the expiry of my specified date, I find out about the Enterprise Allowance. This lasts for a full year and involves starting a business. It sounds ambitious, but is loosely translated by the Department, which uses it to reduce the actual unemployment figures. The application form suggests an occupation such as opening a flower shop or a café which could be managed with the grant.

I once toyed with the idea of writing a novel but never got round to it. Is this my opportunity?

"Can I get an Enterprise Allowance to write a book?" I ask. After a muttered conversation in a corner, an official replies that I can, as long as I apply straight away. There is a cut-off date, but there is enough money in hand to accept a few more applications. What luck!

Now I suppose I must set about writing the book. I have in the past written some poems which were published in small magazines. One even won a prize in an international competition, but of course you cannot make a living with a pen these days.

I wonder if there will be a penalty at the end of the year if the book doesn't get accepted by a publisher? Some books take several years to write, anyway. I buy a thick exercise book from Smith's and some biros. I haven't got a typewriter or a computer, being something of a Luddite where machines are concerned, so I call in at the public library over the supermarket to procure a membership ticket. Here I will surely find a book on authorship which I can borrow.

As I look round, it comes as a shock to find how things have changed without me being aware. My long years in the school library have cut me off from the transformation which has been quietly taking place in the mainstream.

Words like Society, The World, Mind and Body, Mystery and Myth, Entertainment and LARGE PRINT are used to label the shelves. With difficulty I find a book called 'Writing for Pleasure and Profit'. I take it to the counter and it is date-stamped by one of the few assistants on duty. It would appear that my many years of experience and paper qualifications count for very little these days.

The dreaded words 'Information Technology' flash into my mind and I am afraid. Maureen comes to my rescue. "Now you are a *Retired* Librarian," she tells me firmly. "There's no dishonour in that."

She is right. Now I am a Writer. I check that the exercise book and biros are safe in my bag, and make for the exit.

Chapter 2

Sid and Doris have begun to chat over the fence when I venture into the garden. Sid even offers to help with the weeding, but I gather that although he has an allotment for vegetables, he knows nothing about flowers and, as I don't want him pulling up the few good plants among the weeds, I refuse his kind offer.

Doris only comes out to hang up her dreary washing or take it in again. She is what my mother would have called a 'slut', not in the sexual sense, but in that of a bad housekeeper. She never seems to clean the rooms or comb her hair and, when she goes shopping, she struggles home complaining about her poor feet, bearing two large carrier bags full of white bread and unhealthy ready-meals. These she heats up at too high a temperature, and the smell of burning meat often issues from her open back door. Sid is an expert at scraping burnt toast, and makes frequent visits to the dustbin raging about wasted food.

By contrast, the neighbours on the other side are respectable and neat. They are called Veronica and Terry, mother and son.

Every week without fail they go to Mass at the Roman Catholic church, arm in arm. It is difficult to tell if Terry is supporting his elderly parent by taking this posture, or if she is holding onto him in order to control their walking pace. Certainly they make a sedate pair and seem to be devoted.

Whereas I sometimes hear Doris and Sid through the wall shouting at each other, as I feared I might, there is never any disturbance from Number 17. Terry works at the NatWest Bank so I'm rather surprised that they don't live in a better area of the town. Maybe his father died young and left him to earn their daily bread. We have passed the time of day, but no more so far.

I have been back to St Stephen's church on a weekday to find out the times of the regular services written on a board outside. There is an 8 a.m., a 10 a.m. and 6.30 p.m., or even a 10 a.m. only. I make careful note of these variations though I think they are to be found each week in the local newspaper, which I don't always purchase. Perhaps the vicar with the nice voice has to cover two parishes. His name is the Reverend James Thomas. I will go next Sunday at 6.30 p.m.

I have read 'Writing for Pleasure and Profit' but it really isn't much help. It goes on about grammar and style and subject matter. It is one of a series on various subjects ranging from lip-reading to shorthand. Another visit to the dreaded library seems in order, for I must at least return the book or I will be in trouble. Perhaps I should sit at home and think very hard about what kind of book I want to write. And then get on with it.

Choral Evensong at St Stephen's is a very pleasant experience. I get there in plenty of time, and am given a hymn book and a prayer book at the door. St Stephen's is Victorian, built when people attended church in large numbers. Seating is fixed pews. The altar seems a long way away, and there are choir stalls beyond a wooden screen. An imposing· organ with large pipes and a curtained loft looms up behind the pulpit which is balanced by a brass eagle lectern on the other side of the main aisle.

As a child I attended a very similar urban church so I feel at home here.

The choir, consisting of girls and men rather than the usual boys and men, is well-rehearsed, led by the organist from his loft. Indeed, I am so impressed by the quality of singing that I only stop myself just in time from applauding after the anthem. The vicar reads the service with obvious conviction,and it doesn't seem to matter that the congregation is rather sparsely scattered among the pews.

"Hullo again," says the vicar as I am leaving. "Have you settled in yet?"

"I think so," I reply. "Do you have any activities during the week?

"The Women's Fellowship meets once a month on Thursdays," he says promptly, and hands me a programme from a pile on a shelf. I thank him and sidle out.

Maureen would have said "Well done", but I am not so sure. I don't want to get too involved. After all, I am supposed to be writing a book. Fiction is my favourite reading matter, but my book doesn't have to be a novel. Perhaps autobiography would be easier. My life has been somewhat complicated with secret bits which I do not want to reveal. Childhood? Early married life? Job?

My happiest years were the early married ones, when we lived on a caravan site while my new husband studied for a degree and I worked at the local lending library. Then there was the school library. That might be the most interesting. I vow to get down to it tomorrow. Today the sun is shining and I need to do some gardening.

While I am pulling a deep dandelion, Orlando and Dolly come face to face on top of the fence which separates my patch from next door. Sid is tinkering with a bike. I have found out that he makes a bit on the side by mending other people's bikes, but I wouldn't have enough confidence to trust him with mine. At first I fear that Dolly is going to attack Orlando, so I get ready to rescue him, but she changes her mind and they sniff noses, balancing neatly. Then they both jump down on my side. Sid looks up from the bike.

"Your Dolly has made friends with my Orlando," I say, hoping he doesn't mind.

"Good," he grunts. "She's usually very choosey. Do you want any more beetroot?"

I haven't actually finished the last lot, so I say "No thank you".

"Lettuce?" he asks hopefully.

"That would be nice," I reply, not wanting to seem ungrateful.

Doris comes out with some wet washing so Sid moves out of range.

My little garden is beginning to look quite nice. The main bed is raised on a kind of brick foundation so I don't have to bend down too far. Terry tells me that it used to be an air-raid shelter during the war, but I find that hard to believe. Surely he and his mother didn't live here then? It's difficult to guess his age. He is tall and slim, and stylishly dressed in a modest kind of way.

This Saturday there is a CND group manning the charity stall in the market. Maureen put politics on her list of my interests, so although CND membership includes people of all political persuasions, I guess this lot are Labour supporters, which suits me. I pick up a leaflet and sign a petition, but don't get away easily. A small curly-haired lady in a multi-coloured skirt engages me in a conversation about the Trident nuclear submarine.

"It should be cancelled," she argues. "It makes us a sitting target and costs millions."

She's right but I haven't got time to help at the moment. I say I'll keep in touch and hurry home to start planning my book.

I have decided to write an account of my job at a school library in diary form. While I was working, I took occasional notes of things which happened. If I spread events over a whole school year with diary dates instead of chapter headings, I could end up with a proper book. Anyway, I will start by trying to recall enough suitable material.

I am beginning to notice some flaws in Number 16 Salvin Street. Nothing alarming, but it is nearly one hundred years old, and I guess things will start to go wrong and need replacing. The house in Hertfordshire was new-build and, apart from a burst boiler, caused no anxiety. But moaning wind behind the gas fire and faulty sash-windows are a different matter.

Today I make the mistake of opening the front room window. It slides down easily but when I want to shut it I can't. The sash-cord isn't broken but it doesn't operate properly, so the lock won't slide across. In desperation I go out into the street to try from there. A young man with a black dog on a lead is passing and I waylay him.

"Please could you help me?" I ask not in an OAP voice, but brisk and sensible.

He stops. "What's the trouble?"

The dog pulls to the nearest lamp-post.

"I need someone to hold this bit of the window up while I go back inside and slide the bolt across," I explain.

"Right. I'll just tie Nigger up," He wraps the lead round the lamp-post, and suppressing my indignation at the dog's name, I quickly nip inside. He valiantly holds the window frame while I climb on a chair and fix the lock.

This is an example of the general good nature of the locals which I had observed from my first day here. Political correctness is foreign to most of them but this makes them appear innocent rather than prejudiced.

A few days after the sash window incident, I am startled to see from my bedroom Sid and Doris having a battle royal in their back yard. He has one shirt-sleeve hitched up and is brandishing a wooden rolling pin, while she dodges his random swipes with surprising agility. Thinking I ought to do something but not sure what, I go outside and make my presence heard.

"Stop it!" I say loudly. "You're being very silly."

This has the effect of making them both blame the other and appeal to me to arbitrate.

Sid flaps his loose sleeve. "She poured boiling water over my arm," he accuses. "Look!"

Certainly his arm is very red.

"He pulled my hair," complains his wife, "and he tried to hit me with the rolling-pin."

"That's because she went for me first."

Doris, fearing that her case is being lost, demands that the police should be called.

"Don't be daft, it's only a tiff."

"Well, what do you want me to do?" I ask, feeling like Solomon making judgement.

"Call the police," repeats Doris, "I'm not going back in if he's there."

Sid leans on the fence and groans. His arm obviously needs attention. I tell him to give me the rolling-pin, so he does, like a soldier relinquishing his weapon. Who had won?

"I think Sid needs a doctor for his arm," I say, "I'll call an ambulance, not the police."

She snorts and retreats into the house while I phone 999. When the ambulance comes, Sid tells them he spilt boiling water while making tea, and they take him to the hospital for treatment.

Next day he returns with his arm in a sling and she lets him in. Later, she asks me for the rolling-pin back, as she wants to make some pastry. Against my better judgement I let her have it, but take the precaution of advising her to put it in a safe place when she's finished with it.

I am wondering if it would be better to set my book in Rantersford rather than the school library, as events are coming thick and fast.

Maureen would say I ought to join the church Women's' Fellowship and the CND group, and an interesting evening class, or I will get lonely.

True. Although I have met several Rantersford natives, I cannot honestly say I have yet found any with whom I have much in common.

There is a telephone number beside the name of the leader of the St Stephen's WF, so I dial it and get a brisk-sounding man. This confuses me for a moment, but assuming he is the leader's husband, I ask to speak to Mrs Johnson.

"She's at a meeting," he says in a rather resentful tone. I explain my reason for phoning and say I'll try again later.

"OK," he says and rings off.

Something makes me think that he is probably not a churchgoer himself, and I am proved right when I meet Lorna Johnson the following Sunday.

She was a teacher, good at organising events and taking charge. I guess James the vicar must have had a word with her about me, as she picks me out and takes me on one side after the service.

"So you've come to live nearby," she says, shaking my hand. "I hope you are settling in." This term 'settling in' seems to be used a lot by Rantersford people.

Sid was more blunt when he asked if I was 'stopping', but it carries the suspicion that newcomers might not take kindly to the place.

When I have assured her that I am happily established, she asks me what my interests are. I recite Maureen's list, and she seems impressed

"We have a nice mixture of people in the Fellowship. I'm sure you will make many friends if you join."

So I come away with a membership form which I promise to return.

Chapter 3

At last I have got down to writing my school librarian's diary. I find that I can clearly remember many of the children, and events which happened while I worked at the New Town Comprehensive come flooding back into my mind. I won't need to exaggerate or invent, as enough notable incidents occurred to provide genuine subject matter.

Both my daughters were at another similar school and the hours I worked fitted in well with theirs.

Although my husband had more or less left home, he did occasionally appear with shopping or conscience-stricken offers of help.

Anyway, I won't be including my domestic circumstances in the diary, as they would probably not interest my planned readership.

I notice that Terry goes to the Saturday 6 p.m. Roman Catholic Mass on his own this week. Unhampered by his mother's arm, he walks quickly down the hill, taking rather short steps for a man. I hope Veronica isn't ill. Perhaps I should knock on their door and ask.

As it happens, I do not need to do that. Bad news travels fast, and Sid informs me that "The old lady at Number 17 is kicking the bucket."

"You mean she's very ill?" I ask in alarm.

"Didn't you see Doctor Flynn at the house?"

"I don't watch the street all day, and I wouldn't know your Doctor Flynn if I did see him."

"Ah, if you were born and bred here you couldn't help knowing Doctor Flynn. Everybody here knows him."

"Well, I hope I never need to know him", I say. "What's wrong with her?"

"Dropsy," he announces. I search my mind for the modern equivalent of this complaint. At school I had been told that Queen Anne had dropsy.

"You mean kidney trouble?" I ask. "When your legs swell up?"

"That's right," he says admiringly. "She can't walk."

"Oh dear. Will Terry be able to look after her?"

"Doris says not. She thinks he's useless."

I waylay the object of Doris' scorn the next day on his way back from shopping. "Sorry to hear your mother is ill," I begin. "Is there anything I can do?"

To my alarm he bursts into tears and drops his plastic carrier bag. The contents spill out onto the pavement. (Brown bread, cheese, bananas, spinach, tissues, toothpaste.) We both grovel to retrieve it.

"Thank you," he sobs, "So kind."

"I hear she's had the doctor," I say, patting his arm comfortingly.

"Kidney failure," he volunteers. "She's not been very well for years. Maybe she'll have to go into hospital for dialysis."

So my definition of dropsy had been correct.

He blows his nose. "She mustn't see me like this," he mutters.

Such filial devotion is touching.

"Call an ambulance if you think it necessary, "I advise. "They'll look after her at the hospital."

He lets himself in with his key and I go to tell Sid and Doris the latest.

The are both of the opinion that Terry is gay. "He's never had a girlfriend," says Doris, "and he walks funny."

"That doesn't always mean what you say," I argue, but she's probably right.

I myself have several homosexual friends and find them intelligent and caring, and keen on art and music.

At about 2 a.m. I am woken by the sound of a heavy vehicle drawing up outside my bedroom window. I get up and look out. It's an ambulance.

Oh dear! Poor Veronica must have taken a turn for the worse. After a short wait, there is a tramping on the stairs, and Terry, followed by two paramedics carrying a stretcher, emerge from next door.

Looking down on the event as I was, it seemed unreal, like a picture by Stanley Spencer. Should I go down? Before I can make up my mind, Veronica is slid into the back, followed by Terry who is wearing a loose raincoat. Then they are away.

The street is silent and dark again but I can't sleep, so go downstairs and make a cup of tea. Orlando, wondering why I am appearing at an unaccustomed hour, stares at me like an orange owl. For the second time since my move to Rantersford, I feel lonely. What if I am taken ill one night with no-one to help? I hear Maureen say "Join the church WF quick."

"Right," I say, and find the form given to me by Lorna Johnson. It doesn't take long to fill it in and I go back to bed feeling calmer.

The following Sunday I attend the 10 a.m. service at St Stephen's bearing the WF membership form in my handbag. As it happens, Lorna isn't there but James the Vicar directs me to another lady called Pat who turns out to be the secretary. She informs me that the Annual General Meeting will be taking place this evening and I am very welcome to attend.

"It's at 7.30 after Evensong in the meeting room," she tells me, "Lorna will be there."

I spend the rest of the day on my book which is coming along well.

At 7.15 I stroll up the hill. From outside the church I can hear the choir. It really is very good. I wonder if they accept older women as members. I was in my school choir, so I know how to follow a score on the page.

After the final hymn, a group of ladies comes out of the church and goes into the hall. I follow. Lorna and Pat are arranging themselves at a table on the raised stage. They have agendas and reports and similar committee paraphernalia in front of them, and once the chairs in the body of the hall start to fill up, they hand round batches of papers for people to peruse. It is all very business-like. When she catches sight of me, Lorna waves and smiles, as does Pat.

I recognise the plump lady who had shared her hymn book with me on my first day.

"Hullo," she cries, and sits beside me in a friendly fashion. "I hoped you would come back. I'm Susan."

We glance down at the agenda and wait for things to begin.

As the clock strikes 7.30, the vicar hurries in and says a short prayer. He really has got a beautiful Welsh voice. None of the ladies seem to belong to him, so I presume he's not married.

"Has he got a wife?" I whisper to Susan.

"She's left him," she whispers back. Fancy that! He excuses himself before the business begins, and I imagine him going home to his lonely vicarage for a solitary supper.

The items on the agenda are gone through. They are mostly reports of various activities which have taken place during the year, and suggestions for a future programme are invited.

I surreptitiously count the ladies in the room. There are about twenty, which Maureen would have considered promising. Surely I can find some kindred spirits here? They are of varying ages and sizes.

I say sizes because Rantersford is noted for its overweight inhabitants. When I first arrived here, people wanted to know who the thin woman was who had come to live in Salvin Street? They meant me, but I have never considered myself to be underweight. I gather that in past decades there were various heavy industries in the town, and people ate a lot to stoke up and then burned off the surplus energy by working hard. When the industries died out, the habit of eating large meals continued, resulting in excess fat, particularly among the men.

I guess that the slimmer members of the WF are teachers or secretaries, and am proved right when I am introduced to some by Lorna over refreshments after the meeting.

"We usually have a speaker on the second Thursday of each month," she explains, "and sometimes go on outings or hold a quiz."

This all sounds fine and I am sure I will soon make new friends. I walk down the hill with Susan who lives in the next street. She is something of a chatterbox but good company.

"When the vicar's wife pushed off, all the ladies were after him," she prattles. "Some of them still are, but he keeps his distance."

My mind is buzzing by the time I get home. I even wonder if I should join the competition to win the vicar, but dismiss the idea as I know I am really best on my own.

Bad news from the hospital. According to Sid, who spoke to Terry in the street, Veronica must stay there for tests and treatment.

"That means they can't do any more for her," he gloomily predicts.

I do hope he is wrong. I go round to number 17 and knock. After a rather long delay, the door is opened by an almost unrecognizable Terry. His hair is in a mess and his pullover on back-to-front. So different from the usually stylish clean young man. He invites me in.

It is strange to walk into a house built as a duplicate of one's own, but furnished in a totally different manner. Number 16 has William Morris curtains and a G-plan unit, bentwood dining chairs and lots of books, while Number 17 is full of heavy Victorian furniture and religious pictures on the walls with palm crosses tucked behind the frames. The Roman Catholic influence is paramount – one almost feels obliged to genuflect before a little table which carries a coloured statue of the Virgin Mary.

Terry takes me through to the back dining-room and, without asking me if I would like a hot drink, puts the kettle on. He seems to be moving in a dream, lost without his mother.

"I can't bring myself to go and visit her," he confesses, "she looks so awful connected to those tubes."

"But you must go," I say, shocked. "She will be so upset not to see you. The tubes are only to change her blood."

He shudders and runs a hand through his hair. A few dirty plates lie in the sink but he obviously hasn't been eating properly. Some bananas lie in a bowl.

"You could take her some fruit," I suggest. "They don't supply much fruit in hospitals."

"Don't they? I've never been a patient in one."

Something has to be done.

"I'll go with you," I say firmly, "Comb your hair and put a coat on. We can easily walk there."

Then a thought strikes me. It is eleven o'clock on a weekday.

"Aren't you supposed to be at work?"

"They've given me a few days leave of absence," he mutters. "I couldn't concentrate."

We set off not exactly arm-in-arm, but I feel a kind of maternal responsibility for him. Sid and Doris see us go by but don't comment.

When we get to the hospital we have difficulty tracing Veronica as she has been moved to a different ward. The staff are very kind, and take us to Ward 2 where there are only four beds. She is lying flat with no tubes or frightening machines. Terry is relieved by this, but I fear that Sid was right and that treatment has been removed as being no further help.

When he speaks she opens her eyes and takes his hand. I put the bananas on the locker beside her bed and move discreetly away, to be accosted by another old lady who talks nonsense in a quiet monotone. She reminds me of my own mother who died a year ago in a similar institution. How miserable these places are, but how important it is that they now encourage visitors.

A tea-trolley is wheeled in and a cheerful volunteer offers me a cup. I take it though I know from experience that it will be tepid. This is general policy to prevent patients from scalding themselves.

Before we leave, a nurse has a quiet word with Terry. Veronica is asleep, still holding his hand, so neither she nor I hear what was said. He kisses her forehead and looks round for me almost as if seeking an understudy. Together we find our way out and walk home.

"Do you want me to come in?" I ask when we reach Number 17.

"No thank you," he replies, "I'll be all right. I'll phone Father Damian. They said she might not last much longer. I'm so glad you made me go."

Relieved that the Roman Catholic Church would be taking over, I pat his arm and let myself into Number 16.

Sid is in his back garden. "Is she dead yet?" he asks loudly over the fence.

I shake my head and put my finger to my lips. "Shut up," I say sternly, "He'll hear you."

Doris comes out. "Don't expect any kind feelings from him," she warns, glaring at her nearest and dearest, "He hasn't got any."

"Look who's talking," her husband retorts defiantly. They seem incapable of keeping their daggers undrawn.

I go into the house and pour myself what is becoming an almost habitual glass of sherry. Drinking alone is not good. I must find friends to entertain.

Chapter 4

For a start I call on Susan. She lives on a street parallel with mine, linked by a short passageway. Gradually, I am getting used to the layout of this area, and am finding that not having a car is an advantage, as parking is awkward and the town centre is very close on foot.

Susan opens her door promptly and seems pleased to see me. She is wearing curlers and a pinafore like someone in a television situation comedy.

"Are you coming to the Women's Fellowship tonight?" she asks over a mug of tea. I have neglected to look closely at the handouts for the AGM and admit that I have forgotten the date.

"A lady is coming to talk about 'Wildlife in your Garden'," she informs me. "It should be interesting."

I don't think there is any wildlife in my garden to speak of, but I agree to go.

"I'll call for you about quarter past seven, shall I? Then you won't feel strange," she says kindly.

So it is arranged, and I go home wondering what to wear.

My clothes usually come from Charity shops, for I've learned that if you don't mind wearing things which someone might have died in, you can pick up really posh garments priced within ordinary reach. I rummage through my built-in wardrobe and extract a smart jacket and skirt in blue wool. That will do.

Susan calls promptly at 7.15 and we set off.

"You do look nice," she comments. In all honesty I can't say the same of her, as the buttons on her red coat are straining to fasten across her plump tummy, but I say I like red as it cheers me up.

"Do you need cheering up?" she asks, taking me at my word. Serves me right. Not wanting her to think I am in need of sympathy for a hidden grief, I tell her about poor Terry's mother being so poorly.

By this time we have reached the church hall where Susan introduces me to several lades whose names I immediately forget.

I hear Maureen whisper "Don't be shy, be outward looking."

I try but am relieved when Lorna and Pat, whose names I do remember bring a tall lady in green trousers on to the stage. We all go quiet.

I quickly realize that not many members of the audience have small gardens like mine. These ladies live a car-ride away. I guess that they have moved away from the Mill Hill area to the more prosperous private estates which grew up when the town expanded. Susan and I are among the minority who still reside in the original parish of Stephen's.

Nevertheless, I listen to the green-trousered lady as she goes into raptures about urban foxes and pond-life.

My father was a pharmacist whose hobby was gardening. He spent every spare moment digging and planting in the sizeable plot behind our suburban semi, but his attitude to wild life would have shocked the green-trousered brigade.

Slugs, green-fly, and even rabbits were attacked with chemical weapons, and he used to bribe me to collect caterpillars from the gooseberry bushes for one penny per full matchbox.

Questions are invited after the talk, and several people want to know what to do about rats.

At the very word there is a general exclamation of disgust. Actually the only wild animal I have so far seen in Salvin Street has been a rat. It was a fine specimen which sat up and cleaned its whiskers. I advised it to go under Sid's shed and it did just that. I decide against telling the ladies this as I fear they might turn against me, but I mention it to Susan on the way home

She laughs.

"Snobby lot some of them," she remarks.

Well, I have made an effort to mix with people of my own background, but can't claim to have found a bosom pal yet. Perhaps I should seek the local CND or join an evening class.

There is no light in Terry's house when I let myself into Number 16. Could he have been called to the hospital? What if he had needed me?

"Don't be silly," Maureen scolds, "Father Damian will see to him."

So I go to bed with a clear conscience, vowing to get on with my book tomorrow.

True to my word, I concentrate on writing from 8 a.m to 11.30 a.m., when I stop for a cup of coffee. This brings my mind back to the present and Veronica's precarious health.

I recall the dark house next door, close my exercise book, and hurry round to check.

Father Damian answers to my knock. He is dressed in his full-length black cassock.

"Ah," he says in a solemn tone. "You must be Clare from next door. Terry has told me how kind you are."

"Not at all," I murmur. "How is Veronica?"

"I have given her Extreme Unction at the hospital. Terry is having a rest on the settee." He steps aside to let me in. "I'm sure he will be pleased to see you."

I enter on tip-toe, but Terry has roused himself and is standing beside the coloured statue of the Virgin Mary. I suspect that he has been praying rather than resting but he seems calm.

"Father Damian brought me home from the hospital in his car," he tells me. "I'm going there again this afternoon if they don't phone."

"I'm so sorry," is all I can think of to say, but that is apparently enough. After all, I hardly knew Veronica. She seemed to dominate her son, so her absence will affect him deeply. I don't think he has 'come out' even to himself, but I foresee conflict when he has to reconcile his sexual orientation to his religion. Father Damian doesn't seem to be one of the enlightened priests who speak out on the subject but I could be wrong.

The phone rings, making us all jump. Terry bravely answers it. "I see. Thank you. Yes, of course."

He put the receiver down. "She's departed this life," he announces.

At this Father Damian smiles and pats his shoulder. "She will be happy in the next life you can be sure. I will take you to see her now and help with the arrangements."

Let's hope the hospital staff will have had time to lay her out in the chapel attached to the main building. I have no desire to view a corpse, so I melt away to my own territory. I will, of course, keep an eye on Veronica's bereaved boy, and try to sort him out.

Sid is eager for news. "I saw the Father bring him back. Has she gone?"

He sounds genuinely sorry and respectful. Doris wipes her eyes with a grubby handkerchief and says she will find out the date of the funeral and send some flowers.

I return to my writing. Using the diary form is currently fashionable, and it seems to suit the subject matter. The idea of heading each entry with a date, taking school holidays into consideration, divides the text into manageable chunks, so readers will be able to dip in anywhere.

I am surprised how amusing some of the incidents are. They often involve misunderstandings.

Take the day when I decided to tell the twelve-year-olds about the childhood of Charles Dickens. I said his father got into debt and was locked up in prison till he could pay the money back. So young Charlie was sent out to work in a factory sticking labels on jars of boot-polish.

Also, his mother sent him to the pawn-shop, which made him very embarrassed.

Here there was a general unease among the class and one or two sniggers.

"Do we all know what a pawn shop is?" I ask, getting ready to explain about the three balls sign. No-one put up a hand except brave little Wayne Wilson. "Please Miss it's where you buy dirty movies."

How could I have been so behind the times? Another day I misheard a question from an anxious third-year girl. I *thought* she said, "Miss, what's loose living?"

The phrase isn't used much these days, but thinking she must have read it somewhere, I did my best to outline a few vices which might add up to an answer.

She looked puzzled. "I only asked because Julia Walsh says her brother does it," she admitted.

"Well, it doesn't actually do you any harm," I assured her.

A bright fifth year joined in. "Yes it does, Miss. People do it on the tops of buses. It turns you mad."

Out of my depth, I turned the tables.

"What exactly?" I asked.

"She told you. Glue sniffing."

I was saved by the bell for the end of Break but decided to invest in a hearing-aid.

I will call the book 'My Granny's got a Handbell'.

This seems original and intriguing and will attract readers if it ever gets published. It was said by Dean Harcourt in reply to myself when I first started work at the school. During the morning break and the dinner hour, the library always got overcrowded by genuine researchers and those who sought refuge from bullying or inclement weather. When the electric bell went for resumption of lessons, I had to chivvy the reluctant pupils out. This led me to remark to Dean, who was one of my 'helpers', that what we needed was a handbell which we could ring loudly. Two days later, Dean produced a gleaming brass handbell from his satchel and placed it on my desk. "There you are," he said proudly.

"But does your Granny know?" I asked, fearing the wrath of a robbed old lady.

"She doesn't want it," he assured me.

"Well, please thank her very much," I said, and as it was the end of Break, I gave the bell an energetic swing.

In response, everyone packed up and left the library without delay. From then on, I rewarded my helpers by allowing them to do 'bell-duty'. It always worked. No one can ignore a brass handbell.

A folded leaflet marked 'Urgent' has come through the door. It is from the local CND branch about a meeting to discuss the cancellation of the Trident nuclear submarine. I suppose I will have to go. Maybe the small lady with the curly hair and bright skirt will prove to be a suitable new friend.

In the early days of our marriage, my husband and I had been active members of the Nuclear Disarmament movement. I had supported the Greenham Common women, and he had considered joining the committee of 100. Willing to suffer for his beliefs, he was indignant when the police refrained from arresting him for sitting down at a big demonstration. Our two daughters have followed in our footsteps, which pleases us, as teenagers usually deliberately disagree with their parents. Now they are at University, putting the world to rights. Their slogan is 'If it's wrong change it.'

When we split up they refused to take sides, and have kept in regular touch with both of us.

At Christmas, they celebrate by visiting us in turn. This year they will go to him, so I will be on my own for the festive season. Will I be lonely? Perhaps I should invite myself to Maureen's'.

Chapter 5

Veronica's funeral mass is to take place on Thursday next at the Church of the Good Shepherd. Father Damian will of course officiate. Although I am Church of England, I am not unfamiliar with Roman Catholic worship, and will support Terry if he needs me. Rather to my surprise, he has been managing well so far. He returned to the bank after his compassionate leave, and has been shopping for food on the way home from work. I gather there are some Irish relatives who will attend, but no kith or kin live nearby.

Usually there are local people who go to R C funerals as a mark of respect, and because Veronica was a very regular worshipper, she must have had friends in the congregation. I wonder if Terry will wear a black suit and a clean white shirt. I go round to check, and find him at the ironing board, making quite a good job of collar and cuffs.

"You must look smart for her," I say and then feel foolish.

He smiles. "I intend to. She set great store by appearances, and I am sure she will be watching."

I recall his words when he was told by the hospital that his mother had died. "She has departed this life." They seemed strange to me, but as a devout RC he evidently thinks of her as being up there looking down on the rest of us.

I hope she soon goes quietly into the afterlife and doesn't haunt him for long or he will never have the courage to come out and start a real life of his own.

Sid and Doris are sending flowers to the undertakers, but they aren't going to the service. "Can't stand funerals," says Doris with a shudder, and Sid mutters something rude about the Pope.

It's Sunday again, so I call for Susan at 9.45. She is wearing a different coat but it fits her no better than the red one. There is an item in the church newsletter saying that any ladies and gentlemen with good singing voices who would like to join the choir are welcome to come to an audition on Friday at 7 p.m.

"The organist won't have boys in the choir," Susan informs me, only girls, ladies and men. Some of his girls have gone to University this year, and he needs replacements. He's very particular, so he won't have me. You try if you want."

"If he's very particular he won't want me either," I reply. "But I might go along."

The service starts, and I regard the choir members through half-shut eyes. They wear impressive blue robes with white collars, and stand neatly in the stalls like obedient ponies. The organist conducts them from the loft by observing them in a mirror and waving an occasional arm. They certainly make a harmonious sound. I imagine myself standing at the back, keeping up as best I can, but I suspect that, if I joined, I would have to attend regular practices and that would take too much of my time.

The day of the funeral has come. The RC church is in the town centre and serves a wide area. Father

Damian works on his own, but seems dedicated to his large flock. An elderly housekeeper lives in the presbytery doing the cooking and cleaning and answering the phone. Her name is Peggy, and she is very strict about his mealtimes. At least he uses her as an excuse for getting away from prolonged engagements. "I must hurry back or Peggy will say the dinner is ruined," is his catchphrase.

He has been very good to Terry, treating him like a troubled teenager in spite of his real age, which I have discovered is thirty-five. Veronica's influence has certainly arrested his development and I have taken it upon myself to sort him out 'come hell or high water', as my mother would say.

The Irish relatives are sitting at the front, while several of Veronica's friends are scattered round the semi-circular range of seats. A few years ago, the Victorian building was re-modelled on modern lines with stained glass windows and a striking version of the Stations of the Cross.

Terry catches my eye, rather like a frightened horse needing a reassuring pat, but the Irish contingent looks steady enough to see him through, so I smile and take a place near the organ.

The coffin stands in the aisle, decked with several floral tributes. I can't pick out the labels bearing messages, but Doris and Sid's offering will be among them.

There is a lot of standing and kneeling and singing. Most of the people know what they are doing and why, and although much of it is similar to what I am used to, I don't want to go wrong, so I follow the special handout.

There is a picture of Veronica on the front, looking much younger and pleasanter than she was, but we must remember her at her best.

Half-way through, I offer a polo mint to an elderly man who remains seated when everyone else is standing. He takes it gratefully and perks up. I recall that in my childhood my mother made us go to church on an empty stomach, as that was the unspoken rule even with the C of E. Every week someone fainted and had to be taken out. I'm sure God would not have wanted this, but God's opinion can never be known for sure, can it?

When the service is over, we all file out, shaking hands with the Irish lot at the door. Food has been arranged in a hall adjoining the church, and Terry begs me to partake. I'm not really hungry, but allow myself to be tempted, and am introduced to various uncles and aunts with Irish names which as usual I can't remember.

I explain that I am the next-door neighbour just in case they are curious about where I fit in. I don't want them to assume that Terry has at last found a nice mature lady friend. It seems to me that they think he needs taking back with them to the Emerald Isle, and I pray that he doesn't agree to go. That would condemn him to a miserable future of subterfuge and sin. He has been booked in with them for one night at the only classy hotel in Rantersford, so I leave him to their mercy.

"See you tomorrow, Terry," I say firmly as I go to walk home.

To my great relief, he comes home next day before lunch, having bidden his relatives goodbye with what I gather was mutual relief.

"They wanted me to go back with them," he reports," but they aren't really my sort."

"Good, But won't you be a bit lonely on your own?"

He shuffles his feet. "Father Damian has an idea which I am considering."

"Goodness me," I think. "Surely he's not going to be trained for the priesthood!" But I say nothing, and hand him his milk which I had put in my fridge. He lets himself into Number 17and is quiet for the rest of the day.

Most of the houses in Salvin Street have milk delivered to the step by the Co-op Dairy. I have one pint on alternate days and pay on the Saturday morning. Our milkman is very reliable and has been on the same round for many years.

His customers treat him as a friend and confidant so he is sometimes delayed. By the time he gets to Number 16 he is in a rush to catch up and usually jumps from his electric float, plonks my bottle down and climbs up again with the empties, all in one sweeping motion. Doris tells me he is due to retire soon, and people will miss him.

I bump into Susan in the supermarket when I go for my weekend shopping.

"Are you going to the choir practice tonight?" she wants to know.

As usual I had not taken proper note of the date on the church newsletter so had to make up my mind quickly. "Yes, I expect so. Are you?"

"No, I can't really sing," she admits, "but you've got a nice voice, and they do need new members."

So rather unwillingly I walk up the hill to St Stephen's at 6.45.

It occurs to me that God has many houses in Rantersford. Apart from the RC church, there are three C of Es, a Methodist Chapel a Baptist Chapel, a Seventh Day Adventist Church, a Quaker Meeting-house and a Salvation Army Citadel. So as a newcomer, I have a lot of choice. However, I think I will stick with the dear old C of E, rubbish though I think some of its customs are. I sympathise with the little girl caught attacking the Bible with a pair of scissors. When asked what she thought she was doing, she said, "I am cutting out the bits I don't like." Wise child.

There is a light on in the church hall and several cars parked outside so I guess that most members of the choir, like the members of the WF, reside a journey away.

The only person I recognise is the vicar, but surely he can't be a singer as he needs to stand at the front and officiate at services. Perhaps he has come to give the traditional blessing and will disappear to his cold empty vicarage before we get going.

"Don't let the word 'audition' put you off," he says kindly. "You'll just need to stand at the back and sing the bits you feel most comfortable with. The organist has a very sensitive ear and will be able to make a judgement."

Oh dear, this is going to be a sort of trial, with me being proved guilty of singing the wrong notes.

A man with lots of nice fair hair and glasses seems to be the only other newcomer.

The clock strikes seven, and the organist hurries in wearing a coat with a fur collar. He casts an eagle eye over the assembled group, and they divide themselves expertly into a double semi-circle of male and female voices. There are more sopranos than altos, two tenors and one bass. The new fair-haired man is absorbed by the tenors, and I am manoeuvred into the soprano seconds.

"Open up your mouth," he commands, picking me out. "I want to hear you." Embarrassed I turn up my volume and miss a note. He observes but makes no remark.

I gather that there is to be an anthem at the Christmas Eve Midnight Mass and also that the choir is booked to sing carols at a posh hotel in a nearby village earlier the same day.

"I trust we can all be present at both?" he says threateningly.

Some timid souls plead family commitments but most nod with enthusiasm.

"What about our two newcomers?" He points with his baton. "I should have asked your names. Sorry about that."

The fair-haired man and I speak up and he welcomes us both.

"We have several weeks for practice before Christmas and I am confident that you will both fit in nicely by then. OK?".

Before either of us can reply, the vicar comes in with the keys and people put their coats on.

"How did you get on?" asks the vicar when we get outside. The fair-haired man is called Keith and he and I are a bit doubtful about the set-up.

"Do we have to come *every* Friday?" Keith wants to know, and I mumble that I fear I have bitten off more than I can chew.

"Don't worry, our Richard is a fine musician and has a knack of inspiring anyone with even a modicum of talent. Try it for a little while and then see how you feel."

Keith walks down the hill with me to catch his bus. He lives in a nearby village, which could be a problem in bad weather.

"See you next week," I say as I turn into Salvin Street. He grunts noncommittally.

Orlando is getting fussy about his food. The supermarket has a bewildering offer of tins and boxes and packets, and I have up till now been firm and only purchased the cheap but nourishing chunks of fish or meat.

Now I am landed with a big box of stuff which he refuses to eat so I have decided to take it to the address of a cat-loving lady given in the local newspaper. She has devoted her life to housing cats whose owners can no longer look after them. Every so often a gallery of photos of appealing felines appears in the paper, with notes on their temperaments and requirements, like an adoption agency. The house and garden must be unpopular with her immediate neighbours but I have heard that most people regard her as a saint.

"You don't know how the other half lives," I tell Orlando as I pack up his leavings. He blinks and turns his back.

The address is down by the river. Homes similar to those in Salvin Street are entered by a dark shared side-passage which makes them slightly superior but somehow sinister. I grope my way along and find a notice propped against the door. With difficulty I make it out.

'If no one is at home, please leave cat-food in the box." Not wanting to miss seeing the inmates, I knock on the door in the hope that someone will open it. Eventually someone does and light streams out.

"Please come in quick," says a quiet voice," I don't want any of them to get out."

I comply feeling like a character in a fairy story. The figure which presents itself is more witchlike than saintly, but not wicked. She accepts Orlando's offering gratefully and puts it in the kitchen.

"They are all good eaters," she tells me. "Would you like to meet them?"

She speaks as if the cats are guests at a respectable hotel.

Suddenly I am aware that a crowd has collected round my feet. All colours and sizes, they weave and rub around, some mewing as if in welcome. More appear on the stairs, confident, curious. There is a faint smell of flowering currant but nothing repulsive.

"How many do you have?" I ask.

"Twenty at the moment," the witch replies. "Plus two new ones in the outside cages waiting to be checked by the vet."

"Goodness me, how wonderful!"

She smiles. "They are my life's work," she explains, scooping up a black beauty and nursing it under one arm. "I do have some willing volunteers."

Fearing that I am in danger of getting too involved, I escape into the dark passage and hurry home to get on with writing my book.

Incidents for inclusion crowd into my mind thick and fast. Take that of the lost homing-pigeon.

One fine morning it walked into the library, bold as brass, and flew up on to the 'Easy Reading' shelf. There it stayed when the children came in at break-time.

"Miss, there's a pigeon," they kept telling me. "I know," I replied "I think it's lost its way."

"But it can't stay here, can it?" they reason. Raymond Bliss shood it out. It went, but was waiting on the step the next morning. I gave it some of my lunch sandwich and vowed I would put it in a box and take it with me at home-time. This I did, but when I put the box on my kitchen table and opened it up, the silly thing flew out of the window and away.

"Perhaps it's remembered where it lives," I thought relieved.

Would you believe it! There it was again on the library step next day. It allowed me to look at its leg and there was a ring with a number on it. I showed it to Mr Woollard, the art teacher, whose studio was next to the library.

"Should I send the number somewhere to let them know it's here?" I asked.

He looked gloomy. "They'll only wring its neck," he said. "When a homing pigeon goes astray, it's no good anymore."

I think a cat got it eventually, poor thing.

Chapter 6

The old milkman must have retired before I could wish him well, as a different one called for the money this Saturday. He is youngish with a red beard. Come to think of it, beards are unusual in Rantersford. Some male inhabitants are ill-shaved, but full-grown facial hair is rare. He seems rather shy and gets in a muddle with the change.

Terry has been keeping a low profile since the funeral. I do hope he isn't trying to make up his mind about training for the priesthood. Father Damian has visited him several times. Should I interfere? I may be wrong, and the Church may have no designs on him. But if it has, I must rescue him. There are too many unhappy homosexuals driving themselves into celibacy.

I go round next door after tea and find Terry watching snooker on the television. Not wanting to spoil his fun, or indeed my own, for I am a great admirer of the sport, I apologise and say I will come back later.

"Let's just see if Ronnie O'Sullivan wins," says Terry, sensing my interest. So we sit together and clap when the match ends.

The front room seems different from when his mother kept house. Fewer palm crosses and more cushions.

"How's Father Damian?" I ask, coming straight to the point.

"He has made a sensible suggestion."

Oh dear, is it what I feared?

"He thinks I should have a lodger."

"A lodger?" I repeat in amazement. How could I have so misjudged the good Father?

"What a good idea," I cry, "the house is too big for one person, and the rent will be useful. Has he got anyone in mind?"

"He says there is a Portuguese immigrant in the congregation who is unhappy where he is. He works at the supermarket. I was going to ask your opinion. You have always been so wise."

"Well, I certainly think it's worth considering," I say. "Have you met him yet?"

"Father Damian is bringing him round on Wednesday. His name is Fernando."

I am tempted to offer to be present, but stop myself in time. "Let me know how it goes," I say making my way to the street door.

"Of course," says Terry, seeing me out.

My head is in a whirl as I get ready for bed. I imagine various scenarios like plots for a tele-play. The one I end up with as I fall asleep is a perfect partnership for them both and a future free from pretence and guilt.

I wonder what Sid and Doris will make of it.

Another communication has come from the CND group. It is to remind me of the meeting about cancelling Trident at the Friends' Meeting House. They don't mean to let me escape, so I make a note of the date which coincidentally is next Wednesday.

I suspect that someone is pinching the milk off my step. Last Tuesday there was no bottle waiting so I mentioned it to the new man when he came for his money. He was very apologetic, and didn't charge, saying maybe he had forgotten to deliver it. I said perhaps it would be best if he rang the bell when he came so I could take it in straight away. He keeps his beard neatly trimmed and always has clean hands.

As I am walking down the hill to go to the CND meeting on Wednesday evening, I see Father Damian and a small dark-haired young man on their way up. They stop and the priest gives me his customary touch on the arm.

"Let me introduce Fernando," he says. "I was hoping we might see you."

The young man shyly gives me his hand.

"I live next door to Terry," I tell him, "I'll see you again soon."

They pass on and knock on the door of Number 17.

By the time I have got to the CND venue, I have paired Terry up with Fernando and am planning cultural outings for the three of us.

I take a deep breath to clear my mind and look round. The small lady in the bright skirt is pinning up a poster of a mushroom cloud. I can't be sure but I think it is the same skirt.

"Ah, so you've come," she remarks by way of welcome. Several people are sitting in little huddles having serious conversations. No-one seems to be in charge.

"Does it matter where I sit?" I ask.

"Suit yourself," shrugs Bright Skirt.

Suddenly a striking lady wearing a clerical collar breaks away from her clique and takes my hand. "Nice to see you," she smiles. This is better. "Are you a member of the national CND?"

When I reply that I have been that for many years she seems impressed.

"People in Rantersford aren't very keen on Peace Movements," she admits. "We try to organize protests but don't get very far."

Bright Skirt joins us. "They're all a set of half-wits. I prefer cats to people"

This last remark is met with a pitying look from the lady vicar, but it gives me a lead into a subject for conversation other than that of nuclear destruction.

"You must know the lady who fosters unwanted felines," I begin, "I met her recently when I took some cat-food to her home.

Bright Skirt livens up. "Good for you!" she cries, "I've got five. My neighbours treat their pets badly so they all come to me.

I guess she isn't popular with her neighbours but that would not worry her.

"Time to start," says the lady vicar loudly, and the little cliques break up into a neat row. I sit at the end near the door, but Bright Skirt puts herself next to me, blocking my possible quick exit.

"My name's Naomi," she whispers. I nod, but I think 'Bright Skirt' will be easier to remember.

The meeting, when it gets going, cannot be more different from the one at St Stephen's Women's' Fellowship. There, everyone was polite and eager to agree, all seeming to be of like mind. A common purpose to form and cement friendships came first, with volunteers willing to help when help was needed.

Here, argument and strong opinions surface to an alarming degree, the women automatically disagreeing with the men and each other. Naomi is particularly aggressive, even shouting down the lady vicar when order is called for.

Though suggestions are made, little seems to get done. Leafletting is judged unproductive; direct action rejected because it could lead to violence; soap-box oratory scorned as 'showing off'. So what can be done about the nuclear threat? The lady vicar is the only one with what I consider to be a sensible idea.

"Should we perhaps widen our scope and form a Peace Council?" she suggests.

There is a stunned silence. She bravely continues. "I mean there are several groups springing up which are sympathetic with each other, but with few members. If we all joined forces, we would be stronger."

Some mutterings go on, and a man with thick fair hair and glasses, whom I recognise as Keith from the choir, pipes up.

"You mean things like Amnesty International and the Peace Pledge Union and the Campaign Against the Arms Trade?" he asks.

"Exactly," responds the lady vicar. She smiles and looks at her watch. "Let's finish now and go away and think about it. We'll put it first on next meeting's agenda."

Everyone votes for this with a show of hands and, all passions spent, they disperse peacefully into the night.

Naomi tags on to me, as does Keith. He gets in first by telling me that he has decided not to join the choir as he was 'getting too much on his plate.'

"Do you want me to tell the organist?" I sense that he is in a funk about it.

"Please do," he says with relief. "See you somewhere I expect."

He hurries away for his bus, while Naomi and I agree to share a taxi. She lives on a council estate a couple of miles away, while I am quite near, but I give her half the full fare when I get out at Salvin Street She wears poverty on her sleeve in a rather embarrassing manner, and is more eager to accept charity gladly than to proudly reject it. Perhaps she spends all her pension on her five cats.

Sid and Doris are curious to know who the 'good-looking young man with the Father" is. They don't miss much. The fact that the windows at the front of the house here look straight on to the street means that passers-by can easily be observed.

"You'd better ask Terry," I say, not wanting to be a gossip but really keen to join in their speculations.

"He looks foreign," says Doris. "We don't want any immigrants living round here."

"Who says he's living here?" demands Sid. "You always imagine things." They set up an argument, as usual, quite unable to bury the hatchet. What a life!

The milkman has taken me at my word and now rings the bell when he delivers the milk. Usually he hops back on to his float without waiting to see me pick up the bottle, but today he is on the step when I open the door. I am still wearing my dressing-gown as I had overslept. The bottle is held in his grip so I put out my hand to take it and step back with the door wide open. To my surprise he comes forward, brushing past me, and places the bottle on the coffee table. As this manoeuvre is being made, I catch a strong whiff of a widely advertised after-shave.

My mind clicks into action. Why should a man with a beard wear after-shave? I wonder. He makes no move to leave the house and seems to be expecting a reaction from me. It is like a cinema scene in slow motion. Should I push him out and slam the door or ask him what he thinks he is playing at. Maybe I have got it wrong, and all he is doing is trying to help me with the bottle. Rude jokes about randy milkmen come into mind and I almost laugh. That does the trick. Men don't like being laughed at.

He lowers his eyes and sidles out.

"Thank you," I say coldly, and drop the latch. I consider reporting him to the Co-op dairy but give him the benefit of the doubt and decide against it.

There is a second ring on my bell later in the morning. Now fully clothed, I open the door to find Terry on the step. This is the first time he has called at Number 16.

"Come in," I say enthusiastically, eager to hear his news. We sit in the front, room, and he tells me that Fernando will be moving in next week.

"Have you got plenty of towels and sheets?" I ask, "I have more than I want if you need any."

He looks slightly affronted. Of course I should have known that his mother's cupboards would have been full.

"Well, I hope you get along with each other. I had a lodger when I lived in my previous house, and he was no trouble at all."

This was an exaggeration, to be honest. When money got short, the secretary of the school kindly suggested that I should be the landlady of a new Biology teacher. "Usually they want a flat," she had said, "but he comes from the North and they are old-fashioned there."

David was not old-fashioned in the stuffy sense but he was not a typical young teacher. Tall, with a slight hare-lip and hunched shoulders, he didn't eat meat or fish and liked a deep bath twice a week. His mother phoned regularly to see that he was all right. She kept up a relentless chatter, which he punctuated occasionally with a gruff grunt. I only charged him a modest rent so I expect she thought he wasn't getting enough to eat. Cauliflower-cheese was his favourite dish and he would eat a whole bunch of bananas at a time. One day he forgot his regular cheese-sandwich lunch and I took it in when I went later, at my accustomed hour.

This puzzled the children in the science lab.

"Miss, is Mr Hunter your son?" they wanted to know, sure that sandwiches must mean a domestic connection. At least they hadn't asked if he was my 'fancy man'.

"No," I said firmly, "I'm his landlady."

I overheard Kevin Dalby asking Aled Tomkins what a landlady was.

"Someone who cleans up and cooks meals when you go on holiday," Aled explained.

I suppose that's fair enough, though I like to think there was more to it than that.

"Does Fernando speak good English?" I ask, returning my wandering mind to the present.

"Yes, he learned it at school. His is a difficult language to learn, though it might be advisable for me to try."

Then I tell him how I had visited Portugal several times when a close friend lived there. Her husband worked for a car-manufacturing firm and the whole family moved abroad for four years. It is a beautiful country though there is a lot of unemployment, which is no doubt why Fernando is here, 'taking our jobs' as Doris would put it.

Terry is interested and says I must bring any photos I have to show him as he is homesick.

"You've got a lot of books," he remarks, looking round the room. "My mother didn't have much time for reading. She made lace."

"Please borrow any you fancy," I say. " I've read most of them in the past but now I'm afraid I treat them rather like wallpaper. The covers make a colourful background." I don't tell him I am writing one in case he thinks I am boasting.

He accepts a cup of coffee and then sets of for the Bank. I gather he doesn't start work until 10 a.m. on Fridays.

I concentrate on my writing, missing lunch and only stopping when my hand aches too much to hold the pen. It's strange how the book is taking shape, almost by itself. Incidents surface, some almost incredible, but I'm not needing to invent any. I change the names of the children and teachers just in case it does get published and someone recognizes themselves.

Because the pupils come and go, and I only intend to cover one academic year, readers will be left, as I am myself, wondering what eventually happens to certain children.

For example, take Thomas Pickard. He was a roly-poly boy with dark curls and big brown eyes. His appearance could best be described as 'cuddly' but his manner was eccentric enough to belie this. He had all the obsessive behaviour patterns of a young Doctor Johnson, touching the same bookshelf in the same spot each time he passed it, and his gait would rank highly in the Academy of Silly Walks. Whenever he left the library, he stood for a moment as if taking his bearings.

Then he pointed his finger in the direction he had decided to take, and followed it in a straight line, like a blind man holding a guide-dog's stiff harness. His voice, when he used it, was high-pitched and very 'posh' and his vocabulary was astoundingly sophisticated.

The other children regarded him with a certain amount of respect but I feared he would be the victim of bullies as he grew older. Sometimes he cried wetly and uncontrollably, and motherly fourth-year girls tried to comfort him, but he threshed his arms about and cowered away.

Choir practice again this evening. I will have to go, even if only to tell the organist that Keith won't be joining. I wonder if I am taking on too much, but I like music and Maureen would approve. So I set off in plenty of time. James the vicar is there with the key. He looks tired but musters a smile.

"Glad to see you back," he says in his nice Welsh voice. "Have you joined the Women's Fellowship yet?"

"I went to a talk about wildlife," I tell him, "but most of the members don't seem to live locally."

"No," he agrees. "The Victorian congregation lived in these streets and their children went to the church school, but times have changed. The vicarage is too big for a modern family and certainly too big for me."

There is an awkward pause while I wonder if I am supposed to know that his wife has left him. Then the other choir members begin to arrive, and he is taken up with talk about the next Parochial Church Council meeting. When Richard the organist hurries in, we all arrange ourselves in order.

"I see our new membership has been reduced to one," he remarks, looking accusingly at me

I bridle. "Keith has decided he wouldn't be able to come every week. He asked me to let you know."

I am on the point of adding that I wasn't sure that I would either, as I didn't like his manner, but he turns on the charm and says he is sure I will make an elegant addition to the throng.

We start on the anthem, and I soon feel a thrill to be part of what is undoubtedly a beautiful noise.

Chapter 7

Christmas approaches, and I must decide how to spend it. As it is the girls' turn to go to their father this year, I won't be seeing them, so perhaps I could invite myself to Maureen's. But what about Orlando? I suppose Terry or Sid could feed him, but he is scared of men and might run away and get lost. Then of course there are the choir commitments. Richard expects us all to reserve Christmas Eve for the Hotel Carols and the Midnight Mass. I would have to remain in Rantersford for those. There are still a few weeks to go before I must make a decision, but I cannot leave it for much longer.

The festive season has always been a problem for me. The spending and the eating and the stress conflict with the birth of Christ, making a nonsense of the whole event. Easter still holds its true significance, but even that is getting diluted with eggs and rabbits.

I wonder how Terry will spend his Bank Holiday.

The Women's Fellowship Christmas Fayre needs people to help on the day. As usual I can't remember the exact details, so I go round to Susan's to find out. After a long wait at her door, I hear dragging feet and she opens, revealing herself in a tight pink dressing-gown, showing the classic symptoms of a nasty cold.

"Don't come near me," she warns, holding a large hand-kerchief up to her face. "I don't want you to catch it."

I step back obediently and ask if there is anything I can do.

"No thanks. I've got plenty of stuff in the fridge, and I'm sucking throat pastilles. I'll be all right in a day or two." She makes as if to close the door, so I retreat, saying I will be in touch.

Sid and Doris are full of excitement.

"We've got another new milkman," they tell me in unison over the back fence.

"Oh, I say non-committally, "I hadn't noticed."

True, since the after-shave incident I have not been responding immediately to Red Beard's ring, and he has always driven away by the time I open the door.

"He made a pass at the woman in Number 51," says Sid. "She reported him to the Dairy, and now he's confined to the loading yard."

"Well I never," I say in mock astonishment. So I was right.

"The new man is very respectful, so you needn't worry."

I thank them for letting me know.

"Never trust a man with a beard," says Doris as if quoting a wise man's warning.

I still need details of the Christmas Fayre so phone Lorna Johnson. As usual her husband answers.

"Sorry to bother you," I begin, afraid he will be off-hand, "but could I speak to Lorna?"

He doesn't address me directly in reply but shouts loudly for his wife to take the call. She can be heard hurrying along a tiled passage and snatching the receiver.

"Hullo," she says sweetly. Equally sweetly I give my name and ask about the Fayre.

"It's next Saturday from 10 a.m. to 2 p.m. We need someone to help on the bric-a-brac stall. Can I write you in?"

I agree and she rings off.

I realize that Rantersford must be full of bickering couples finding it difficult to disguise their incompatibility.

I am well out of the unhappily-married state.

Today I take time off from writing to look through my many photo albums. The films of Portugal are scattered through several different years, and I pick out some to show Fernando. He is due to move in next door on Sunday after Mass. Sid and Doris are aware of this and don't approve. The word 'racism' is not in their vocabulary and I'm sure they wouldn't admit to it if it were. They get their views from the easy-to-read tabloid papers, and I suppose I should try to change their attitude in case it becomes a problem.

Sometimes I feel guilty about inhabiting a house big enough to hold a family. If Terry is willing enough to take a needy lodger, perhaps I should invite one of the homeless rough-sleepers who huddle in shop doorways to come in.

Then I remind myself that living alone has always been my ambition, so I can be a writer. Everyone knows that you have to be on your own to create succesfully; it is a selfish occupation. There is no real comparison with Terry, as he is lonely without his mother and needs company.

I sleep badly, imagining I have caught Susan's cold. What if I get ill on my own and nobody knows? Darkness holds terrors whatever age one is. As a chlld I cried for a night-light, afraid of nasty dreams, and now I dread sudden death. I repeat an appropriate prayer and drop off eventually.

Fernando has taken up residence next door, much to Doris' indignation.

"Foreigners are swarming in and taking our benefits," she chants. ""They should stay where they belong."

"But he's working in the supermarket and paying his taxes," I argue, "This country needs people from abroad."

Sid keeps quiet, not wanting to agree with her, but they both read the same daily newspaper. It's a good job I live between the two houses, so I can form a buffer.

A note on flowered notepaper has come through the door from Terry. He would like me to come for tea on Saturday to meet Fernando. That is the same day as the Church Fayre but it finishes at 2 p.m. so I can still accept. I will take the Portuguese photos and a packet of nice biscuits.

My days are getting filled up with choir practice, Women's Fellowship, CND, writing Xmas cards and, of course, writing my book.

St Stephen's church hall is looking very festive as I make my way to the bric-a brac stall. A lady who introduces herself as Debbie is already arranging a box of assorted ornaments, tea-sets, cut glass, necklaces and other unwanted articles on a table near the pulpit. I wonder how many of the things had been bought at last year's Fayre and are being recycled because the buyers had found no real use for them. A quick glance fails to reveal any valuable items to me, though Debbie picks out one or two and puts them on one side.

"When we first open at ten o'clock, a dealer will make a bee-line for us and bag anything she thinks she can sell at a profit," she explains. "She's been doing it for years, and we want to stop it.""

"What does she look like?" I ask, ready to watch out for this minor crook.

"Tall and fair," Debbie informs me, "and very pushy."

With ten minutes still to go, I stare round at the transformed church interior. Coloured paper chains and branches of holly deck the window-sills, and trestle tables are arranged strategically along the aisles, loaded with soft toys, games, pickles, tombola prizes, potted bulbs, home-made cakes, books and knitted garments, all clearly priced and presided over by people whose names I can't remember.

By the door sits a lady with a raffle-book, ready to sell tickets for a large basket full of food and drink.

Lorna and Pat and a fully-recovered Susan hurry to and fro, checking that all is ready, and as the clock strikes ten, a waiting queue surges forward, led by the tall fair crooked dealer. She makes straight for the bric-a-brac stall, but like a swooping bird, the vicar intercepts her, seizing her hand and engaging her in conversation.

Debbie and I exchange delighted grins. Somewhere in the background I am momentarily aware of Lorna. Are she and the vicar in league? Too busy dealing with genuine customers who are innocently foiling the dealer by taking their pick of any bargains, I dismiss a lurking suspicion that there is something more than a shared sense of fairness between Lorna and the vicar, but can't help wondering where Lorna's disagreeable husband and the vicar's absent wife come into this?

During a lull, Debbie and I take it in turns to go round the other stalls. I suppose I must buy something though I am trying to cut back on inessential spending. I end up with a small pottery bird and half-a-dozen fairy cakes.

I recognise members of the choir on duty behind various stalls but can't put a name to any of them. We smile politely. Will I ever make a friend of any? I hear Maureen's voice in my head. "Take your time. You are going to Terry's for tea this afternoon. See how that goes."

Ploughman's lunches and soup are available from noon, and I join the queue. A large lady in an apron presides, who I am told is a retired school dinner lady. She ladles soup into hot bowls with a brisk turn of the wrist. I must say everyone is working hard for the church, giving their time and talents with admirable generosity. I wonder how much money we are making. Probably the most dedicated will stay behind to count the takings after closing-time at 2 p.m. but I am due at Terry's for three, so must leave Debbie to clear up the unsold bric-a-brac on her own. Actually, we have got rid of most of it, so I shan't feel guilty.

I hurry home down the hill, bearing my pottery bird and fairy cakes, and change into a modest blue dress. I decide to put the packet of nice biscuits back in their tin and replace them with the fairy cakes. Not forgetting the Portuguese photographs, I lock my front door and knock on Number 17.

Terry opens the door at once, smiling a welcome and looking happier than I have ever seen him. He is wearing a thick dark-green woolly top and beige trousers which I don't think his mother would have approved of, but which suit him very well. I am ushered into the back room, where Fernando is waiting, hands outstretched.

Rather confused, I almost give him the bag of fairy cakes, but quickly transfer it to my left hand and offer him my right. For a moment I try to remember if the Portuguese employ the French greeting of lightly kissing each other on both cheeks, but he seems content with a firm shake. I put the cakes down on the sideboard, explaining where they have come from, and Terry thanks me and puts them in a tin with flowers on the lid.

Compared with Terry, Fernando is rather short in stature, as I found most Portuguese men are, and he has the usual dark hair, nice teeth and a charming smile. We sit on the three-seater settee with me in the middle, and I open my photo album.

Most of the pictures were taken in the town near Estoril where my friend lived. Fernando recognizes these but explains that he lived further inland in the north where the weather is hotter and the soil rather dry. He doesn't mention poverty, but I sense that he came to England in the hope of earning enough to send money back to his parents. This he *is* doing with advice from Father Damian.

To make conversation, I mention that when I was in Portugal on visits to my friend I was inspired to write a notebook of poems, illustrated with some of the photos. Terry asks if I can lend him a copy as he himself likes poetry. He puts the kettle on, and we sit round the dining table which has been laid with an embroidered cloth and paper serviettes - all very civilized and hospitable. There is a choice of neatly cut sandwiches and some tinned fruit salad and cream. I feel the ghost of Veronica hovering over the occasion, rejoicing in her boy's learned behaviour. I only hope her influence soon fades away and his true nature is able to blossom.

We are surprised by the advent of Father Damian while we are washing the cups and plates.

"Ah, I see you are entertaining," he booms. "Sorry to disturb you, but I was passing by and wondered how Fernando is settling in." Even he uses the phrase with which I was habitually welcomed when I first moved to Rantersford.

"I am very happy," Fernando assures him.

"Good. I won't stay as I must get ready for the six o'clock church service tonight. Shall I see you both at the Sunday Mass tomorrow?"

He doesn't include me, knowing that I am not of his persuasion, but smiles and pats my arm, pleased by my presence, and Terry sees him out.

"I must go too," I say in a little while, gathering up my coat. "Thank you for having me. You must both come round next door soon."

"That will be nice," they chorus, and they seem to mean it.

Chapter 8

I have decided to stay in Rantersford at Christmas and support the choir. Richard the organist is very keen for us all to go carol singing at the posh hotel and then attend Midnight Mass.

Sid has asked me what is my favourite tipple, and I said I like advocaat.

"You mean eggnog?" he sneered in disgust. "Well, I quite like sweet sherry too," I added, and that seemed to meet with more approval, so I guess I will be invited round for a drink on Boxing Day

I wonder if the CND group is giving a party. Maybe someone from there would be interesting to talk to when they aren't arguing about the state of the world.

Sure enough a note comes through the door announcing a New Year Get-together with shared food. I suppose that means we must all take sandwiches or sausage rolls or cakes and there will be lots left over.

My address book needs revising. When I come to write Christmas cards, I am surprised how many friends I still have. Some of them I haven't actually seen for years, but we exchange a few words besides the usual greetings, saying how we are and imparting family news. Postage is getting so expensive that I wonder if I can afford the stamps. It all adds up. However, I start on the As and when I have got as far as the Ms I stop, and write a poem which takes me till midnight.

Sending Christmas Cards

Now is the season when cards come
Falling like leaves upon the mat.
We have to match them with our own,
Posted hastily, tit-for-tat.

We must remember everyone,
Find a way to make quite sure
That no old friend has been left out
Check lists from last year and the year before.

Dare I ignore this spending spree?
Give to a charity instead?
Save money on the postage stamps?
Then distant friends might think I'm dead!

So I will sign and send my love
As always, since a child I've done.
Greetings, Peace, Goodwill henceforth,
Happy Christmas everyone!

The vicar takes me on one side after tonight's choir practice. Everyone else has gone, and he jangles the keys nervously as he speaks.

"Forgive me if I'm being presumptuous," he begins, "but I need a cleaning lady for the vicarage and I'm wondering if you would have time to do a couple of hours a week?"

I must admit I don't know how to react. Surely the Fellowship ladies must all have been falling over each other to 'do' for him now his wife has gone? But perhaps being a cleaner is a bit beneath most of them, with their cars and posh gardens.

"How much for?" I find myself asking. He names a generous figure, so I say I'll think about it.

I *am* thinking about it, and still don't know what to do. The money would certainly come in useful, and I would not have to 'declare' it, as it would be cash-in-hand and not enough to endanger the Enterprise Allowance.

I have never been inside the vicarage. It was built at the same time as the church, and no doubt has spidery corners. Does he only use some of the rooms to save fuel, and would my duties be confined to those? Or would he want me to go through the whole lot? I am fairly energetic and don't mind hard work, but I shouldn't lift heavy weights or scrub floors. Perhaps I ought to make a visit to clarify matters. I phone the vicarage number and get no reply. Would a letter through the door be best? Before resorting to this, I phone again, and he answers. His lovely Welsh voice beguiles me but I must be firm.

"Can I come and see exactly what you need done?" I ask.

"Certainly. Would Monday afternoon suit you? I must be at the hospital in the morning."

"Are you ill?" I am concerned.

He laughs. "No, I'm the C of E chaplain and have to visit patients."

I feel embarrassed and sympathetic at the same time.

"Sorry," I mutter, "I'll come about three o'clock on Monday." We ring off and I get on with my own housework

A cold wind is blowing on Monday afternoon so I put on my 1960s duffel coat and a scarf.

"You look sensibly dressed," he remarks, letting me in.

"I fear it dates me. I wore it on protest marches and don't like to throw it away."

"Don't you protest anymore? Surely there is still plenty to protest about."

He leads the way through a tiled passage to the kitchen, which is comfortably warm and puts the kettle on.

"I wouldn't want you to do upstairs," he begins when I question him about my duties. "I can manage the bedroom and bathroom, but the kitchen, sitting room and study are getting a bit much. My wife used to do it all."

I nearly ask him if that was why she left him, as surely it was a lot to expect.

"Perhaps you should have had a helper before," I say.

"You're right." He sighs. "She didn't have an outside job, and there are no children to look after, so I assumed she could be a housewife. A big mistake on my part. My mother never had any domestic help but people in Wales are used to hard work."

"But she can't have left you just because she doesn't like housework," I blurt out, full of feminist indignation.

He looks at me as if I have gone too far, and sighs again.

"No, there was more to it than that." He blows his nose and pours the tea.

"Perhaps she will come back," I say comfortingly.

"I pray that she will." With that, he shows me where the brushes and dusters are kept, and I look round the study and sitting room. It is agreed that I will come from ten till twelve on Wednesdays, starting after Christmas. He will give me a backdoor key in case he is called away but says he will try to be there part of the time.

Lorna Johnson is walking up the garden path with a full carrier bag as I leave. She looks surprised and a bit guilty, as if she shouldn't have been there.

"I'm just delivering some shopping for James," she confesses. I wonder if he will tell her that I am his new cleaning lady, and if she will mind.

Am I an idiot? Only an idiot would have been persuaded to clean for a deserted Welsh vicar. I ask myself why, and reluctantly come to the conclusion that I fancy him. I don't flatter myself that he fancies me, though he has in a way chosen me from a wide field. If Susan is to be believed, there is competition for his attention. Perhaps he doesn't see me as a sexual entity. After all, I am in my late forties so no threat.

I should confine my affections to Terry and Fernando, who do not pose complications. I find a picture post-card with a blank reverse and write a 'thank you' for having me to tea, inviting them both here next Saturday.

Nevertheless, I am becoming increasingly uneasy. I cannot imagine myself sweeping James' carpet and dusting his study. Will I have to answer the phone? Is the vicarage haunted?

My need for advice grows. Who can I approach? Maureen comes to the rescue. "Ask Susan."

Of course! She is not one of the posh ones and has a kind heart. So I go round to her house without further delay.

"Anything the matter?" she asks. I must be looking anxious.

"Not really, but I need advice."

She folds her hands across her tummy and leans back in her chair.

"Fire away," she commands.

So I tell her all, and her eyes open very wide.

"Well I never," she breathes. "I bet Lorna will be peeved."

"Do you think she fancies him?"

"I'm sure she does. Her horrid husband is furious about it. I don't know if James' wife packed off because of her, but there's more to it than meets the eye."

Oh dear, I am being led off track, so I bring the talk back to my role as cleaner of the vicarage.

"Why do you think he asked me to do it?" I want to know.

"Well, the place must be getting in a mess, for a start. You live nearby and are unlikely to gossip. Actually I nearly offered to do for him myself, but my back plays up if I lift anything heavy."

"So you think I should take it on?"

"Why not if you need the money. Give it a go and see how things turn out." She laughs. "Let me know what happens. I'll keep it under my hat of course."

I thank her and hurry home in the dark. This area gets a bit scary at night, and some people won't walk on their own, but I find that if one moves purposefully and has one's key at the ready, it's safe enough.

Chapter 9

I wonder whether or not to put up my Christmas decorations. Nobody except Terry and Fernando are expected to visit, and it's hardly worth putting up baubles just for them. I am sticking Christmas cards on to the doors with Blu Tac. They brighten up the rooms and don't blow about. Also, I have pinched some holly from a neglected garden and tucked it behind pictures. That will have to do. Next year my girls will be here, and we will get a tree then.

Arrangements have been made for the choir's Christmas activities. A mini-bus has been hired to take us to and from the posh village hotel on Christmas Eve. Our robes have been washed by Richard's wife, and tomorrow it is the final rehearsal for the Midnight Mass anthem. I'm enjoying the choir and feel honoured to be a member. Richard is well-known in the town for his dedication to music. He used to teach the subject at the local girls' grammar school, and originally built up the choir by persuading pupils with good voices to join. Once captured, most of them have been faithfully learning difficult classical pieces to a high standard.

As a newcomer, I am careful not to push my way in, for although pleasant, they are close, the chief thing which unites them being music. As it is only one of my interests, I can't see my way to making a real friend there. Come to think of it, Keith would have been a possibility, but he escaped.

Terry and Fernando come as expected at three o'clock, bearing gifts of flowers and chocolates. We stay in the front room as visitors would have done when the house was first built.

The boys sit side-by-side on my little two-seater settee, nice and friendly, so I bless Father Damian for his pastoral care, and wonder if James would have gone to as much trouble for one of his flock.

When I go into the kitchen to put the kettle on and arrange some cakes on the best plates, Orlando ventures into the room to inspect the guests. Usually he goes upstairs on my bed in the afternoon so I am pleased, imagining he will be a talking-point.

I return with a laden tray to find Terry standing anxiously over Fernando, who is gasping for breath.

I have never seen an asthma attack but have known parents of children who suffered from them, and this seems like a full-blown example. Either that, or a heart attack!

I bundle Orlando out of the room and open the window. We prop poor Fernando up on a chair with cushions, and not wanting to cause more panic by dialling 999, I run next door to ask Sid for Dr Flynn's phone number. Probably Terry has got it written down somewhere, as Veronica had been his patient, but in the heat of the moment we need immediate help. Sid is at home, and when he grasps the situation, rises to the occasion very well. He comes back with me carrying his diary which has the doctor's number written in the appropriate section at the front, gives Fernando a sympathetic glance, and uses my phone.

Dr Flynn is 'between patients' at his surgery and comes at top speed.

"Cat fur," is his diagnosis. "It's a real curse." He puffs with a magic machine and looks accusingly at me.

"Troublesome creatures, cats," he says. "Cause a lot of worry for me. If it's not fur, it's septic scratches and bites." He closes his bag with a snap and tells Terry to take his friend to the pharmacy to get an inhaler.

He and Sid stay for a cup of tea and a cake, and then they all depart.

I go to look for Orlando and speak sharply to him when I find him hiding under my bed. The poor animal cannot understand why he is in disgrace.

I blame him for the failure of my tea-party, at which I had hopes of forming a happy threesome, with visits to galleries and theatres This now seems doomed, as Fernando will be afraid to come here again, and Terry will feel unwilling to come on his own. I can only hope that they might invite me to Number 17 occasionally but my search for a close congenial friendship will have to continue.

People keep asking me if I will be 'alone at Christmas'. Some of them even seem on the verge of inviting me to spend the day with them, as if I am a lonely old person in need of being cheered up. Very kind, to be sure, but I hope I am succeeding in convincing them that I don't fall into that category. The fact that I have two daughters who are coming to stay *next* year but are going to their father's *this* year, means that I have to explain about my divorced state. In Rantersford this is still generally regarded as one of either misfortune or disgrace. One of the male members of the choir called Bernard gave me a lift home recently, so I asked him in for a cup of coffee.

Putting on a sympathetic expression, he asked, "Are you a widow?"

The very word sounded old fashioned, almost insulting, so I laughed.

"No, I'm divorced."

He jerked as if he'd been stung and spilt his coffee down his trousers. Since then he has avoided me. Susan says his wife died two years ago, and he is looking for a respectable replacement.

Christmas Eve has come at last. In spite of this year's unseasonably warm weather, there is a nip in the air today. Not, I think, cold enough for snow, so there shouldn't be a hitch in the choir's plans. The hired mini-bus is due at St Stephen's at 6 p.m. and Richard has impressed upon us that we mustn't be late. His wife will bring the clean robes, into which we must change when we arrive at the hotel.

I am unfamiliar with the nearby villages, but I gather that the place which has booked us used to be a minor Stately Home with Scottish connections. The guests will be wearing kilts and tartans, and we must include 'Auld Lang Syne' in our repertoire.

I wonder if the vicar will come too? He is not in the mini-bus when I climb aboard, so I guess he is conserving his strength for Midnight Mass later. I suppress a pang of disappointment and look round for someone to sit next to.

Bernard avoids my eye as if afraid I might take the liberty of seating myself beside him. I smile and ask a quiet girl called Alison if she is saving a seat for anyone.

"No, please sit by me," she says, hitching herself nearer the window to make room. She doesn't look much older than my daughter Elizabeth, so I feel at ease and we chat about her favourite composers. Music is such a consuming passion with this lot. Do they have any other interests?

We pass through several small villages in the gathering dark. Some would be better described as hamlets, with no street lights. Fortunately, our driver is a professional heavy-goods man, so we can relax. After about an hour of which I can only describe as a Mystery Tour, we draw up outside our stone-built, brightly lit destination.

A man in some kind of uniform comes out to welcome us, and we troop in, laden with robes and music sheets. Richard is wearing his fur-collared coat, looking suitably artistic. The host seems to know him well, and they chat and laugh.

"Coffee now to warm you up, and sherry and mince-pies after the carols?" he suggests. We agree with enthusiasm and are led into a private room beyond an impressive staircase. After coffee in elegant china cups, we don our robes and stand awaiting orders. Richard lines us up and ushers us on to the staircase. The custom is to arrange ourselves decoratively on the ascending steps, small people at the bottom and taller ones further up. Luckily the stairs are wide and shallow, so we balance safely.

Guests gather in the hall, sitting on comfy chairs, the men dressed in the regulation tartan kilts and the women in bright red and green long dresses. Latecomers have to squeeze past us on the stairs, very apologetic.

At last everyone is ready, and Richard introduces us, promising an informal evening of popular songs and carols. Requests will be invited. Let's hope we can all manage those. I had imagined a more religious programme, but this audience has evidently come here to get away from a family Christmas and have a jolly time.

St Stephen's choir must save the serious stuff for Midnight Mass later.

We launch into 'Hark the herald angels sing,' followed by 'O little town of Bethlehem'" and go on to 'Rudolf the red-nosed reindeer' and 'The Twelve Days of Christmas'. 'Away in a Manger' comes next.

Someone wants 'The Holly and the Ivy', which we can't quite manage, but our two tenors and one bass make a good job of 'We Three Kings of Orient Are'.

Applause is saved for the end, after 'Auld Lang Syne'. When it comes, it is loud and sustained and includes Scottish shouts of approval. Richard generously joins in, and we clap back. To my surprise, I find myself starting to cry and have to blow my nose on a tissue. We mingle for the promised sherry and mince pies. Everyone is very friendly. Even Bernard relaxes and compliments me on my hair. I hope he doesn't overcome his objection to divorce, as I don't fancy him.

When we go outside for the return journey, a fine dusting of snow is falling, so I was wrong about it not being cold enough for that. Our driver assures us that it won't come to much and won't delay us. It had better not or we will be late for Midnight Mass. Richard leads us through a final mobile rehearsal of the Anthem, after which some of us nod off.

We get back to Rantersford about nine o'clock. This gives us two clear hours before we need to reassemble. Some of us go home while others have a snack at a café. I hurry home to Orlando who is anxiously waiting for his evening saucer of expensive fish flakes. I need a quiet time to rest my voice.

There is a note on my door mat from Sid and Doris inviting me round for a drink on Boxing Day at noon. I wonder if I will get advocaat or sweet sherry? Will it be in a clean glass?

The snow hasn't settled but I wrap up warm in my old duffel coat. I think of James getting ready to conduct the service and wanting his wife back. I'm starting my cleaning job at the vicarage on Wednesday. Have I done the right thing by agreeing to it? Maureen tells me not to worry so I clear my mind for God.

The pews are nearly all full when I slip through to the choir vestry. My robe is hanging neatly on its hook. Richard's devoted wife can't sing but accompanies us everywhere, in charge of our uniforms and keeping an eye on our behaviour, rather like the matron of a boarding school.

The service has a strong tradition in Rantersford, people travelling in from local villages possibly for the only time in the Anglican church year. There is incense and the ringing of bells and genuine reverence.

Victorian England is conjured up in the candle-light under 19th century arches and pillars. One almost expects to hear the prayers in Latin but St Stephen's does not go that far, even at Christmas. The anthem from the Messiah sounds near-perfect and applause is permitted. Richard bows and returns to the organ loft. The vicar's clear Welsh voice rings out for the Christmas blessing, and the choir processes down the aisle behind the crucifer and the acolytes to the vestry. There is a contented shuffling from the congregation as they put on their outdoor clothes and overflow into the churchyard.

"Happy Christmas," we cry to one another as we disperse to our homes.

Susan did not attend, as she says it is too late for her to venture out, so I walk down the hill alone, door-key at the ready but with steady steps. The street lamps are still on and I find myself humming "Lead kindly light amid the encircling gloom, lead Thou me on".

Chapter 10

I am woken at half-past eleven by the sound of the phone. It is my daughters ringing from their father's.

"Are you all right? We rang you earlier but you didn't answer."

"I'm fine," I assure them. "Looking forward to seeing you next Christmas."

They laugh. "We'll be over to see you before then."

We talk affectionately and I realize that I am no longer lonely without them and am thankful that they are mature enough to fall in with the sharing arrangement which has evolved since their parents split up. I am even able to ask after their father with genuine goodwill.

"He's OK. He's just putting a chicken in the oven."

They don't ask what I am having for my Christmas dinner, which is fortunate, as my reply would perhaps shock them. Free from the fluster of conventional preparations, I have decided to down-grade this year, and purchased some fresh salmon and a tub of top quality ice-cream. I squint at the bedside clock. It says noon.

"You'd better go and help him with the sprouts," I say", "I'll write soon."

We ring off and I get dressed.

This is the most relaxed Christmas Day I think I have ever spent. My mind goes back to early childhood when my brother and I struggled to stay awake to see Father Christmas fill our stockings. Once I did catch a glimpse of him and was pleased to note that his red robe was very similar to my father's dressing gown. Do children believe in him these days? We certainly did.

Then there were the years of war and shortages, and my father's ill-health. I recall the awful time when our anxious mother dropped the chicken with its trimmings on to the kitchen floor as she took it out of the oven and we all cried.

Later there came arguments over which in-laws should be invited to stay, and the strain of trying to hide our increasing marital discord.

Now all that is over, and we have come through.

I phone Maureen and tell her I am following her good advice but although I am making new friends, I haven't found a special one yet. "Keep looking," she says, "You've got a lot of old friends to fall back on, including me."

The salmon and ice-cream go down well, and I am drinking a glass of sherry when there is a knock at the door. It is Susan with a box of chocolate biscuits.

I invite her in and we have a nice chat about the carols and Midnight Mass. She went to the 'Family Service' which James feels he must offer for parishioners who have children or are too old to stay up late. She is cheerful but I suspect she feels a bit alone. I don't know if she was ever married but she doesn't mention grandchildren or mix with her immediate neighbours who talk of nothing else.

Boxing Day dawns miserably wet. The light snowfall on Christmas Eve melted straight way, and a dreary drizzle has taken over. Sid and Doris are expecting me at twelve o'clock, so I have a bath and dress in a bright jersey and skirt, and wrap Susan's chocolate biscuits in Christmas paper. Is this ungrateful and mean of me? I decide it is not. It is simply that I feel I must not arrive empty handed and I have already been given a superfluity of sweet food which I will never be able to eat. Also, I am short of money and must economise.

As it happens, I should have waited to take my bath till I got home again. I don't want to be critical, but I can truthfully say that I have never been inside such a dirty house as Number 15 Salvin Street. Up till now I have only glimpsed the back kitchen when Doris goes in and out or Sid flings the door wide open to disperse the smell of burnt toast. The front door is on the side of the house because our section of terraced houses ends with Number 15. A wide alleyway leads to a path behind the row, along which, according to the 100-year-old lease, the owners have the right to drive their cattle from an ancient field now built over.

The front door is rarely used, people preferring to use the back gate, which is never locked. Sid's friends like to come and sit on his bench and chat, out of Doris' way. Today, as an invited guest I ring the front door bell and wait. There is a commotion on the other side and a fumbling with keys. At last the door opens to reveal a dishevelled Sid.

"Why didn't you come round the back?" he demands. "We never use the front."

I apologise and hand over the biscuits. He lets me into a dark hallway with stairs leading up at the end. I can't actually see the condition of the floor and woodwork, but the smell indicates damp and decay.

Doris bustles out from the dining-room and almost drags me through. Here the light from a low watt bulb with no shade reveals a muddle of chairs on a carpet so stained and greasy that my shoes seem to stick to its surface as I walk across. In the centre of the room is a large table on which stand several bottles and three glasses. So I am to be the only guest.

"Sit down," Doris commands. "Have a good Christmas?"

"Yes thanks," I reply perching on the edge of an upright dining chair. "Did you?"

"No," snaps Sid before she can answer. "The chicken was burnt and the sink got stopped up."

Ignoring him, Doris waves an arm at the bottles.

"What will you have?"

I squint at the labels. One says 'Snowball."

"That's your eggnog," Sid tells me, "You said you like it."

So I did, but not adulterated with fizzy lemonade.

"Thank you," I murmur weakly.

The glass, as I feared, is unclean.

"So Terry has got a foreign lodger," Doris remarks.

"Yes," I say. "He is Portuguese and very pleasant."

I sip my Snowball and pray that she doesn't start her tirade against immigrants, but the Lord isn't listening and she holds forth.

Sid's face is a picture. He is trying not to agree with her, as that would be crossing the battle-line, and knowing my view he does not want to offend a guest but he has been influenced by the easy-to-read tabloid newspapers delivered regularly to his door. He pours himself a large glass of beer and tells her to shut up.

Her attention is diverted by Susan's biscuits.

"These look nice," she says, unwrapping them. "No one gave us anything this year."

At first I fear that she has realized that the biscuits are a second-hand gift, but then realize how few close friends they really have. There are only three Christmas cards on the mantelpiece, and one of those is from a charity.

Dolly the cat wanders in from the kitchen, tail erect. "She got most of the chicken" says Sid, stroking her fondly. "She came off best with her Christmas dinner."

"I just had salmon and ice-cream," I confess. They look at me with genuine concern.

"You should have come round here," cries Doris. "No one should be alone on Christmas Day."

I feel a sudden warmth for these simple-hearted neighbours, and accept another Snowball . We drink a toast to the future. They let me out by the front door, and as I gain the street, I encounter Terry and Fernando returning from a walk.

It is the first time I have seen them since Orlando laid Fernando low. They shake my hand and say I must go round one day soon as long as I leave the cat at home! So that means they still want to be friends.

It's the Wednesday after the Christmas holiday and I am due at the vicarage to start my cleaning job. James has given me a key in case he's not in when I arrive at ten o'clock. I am wearing loose trousers and a long-sleeved sweat shirt.

There is no one in, and the place is a mess. No wonder James' wife cleared off if she was expected to keep this example of Victorian domestic architecture in order. When I came for my 'interview' if it can be called that, the kitchen was warm and there were some cheery

8 0

decorations up, but now all that is over, and the word desolate comes to mind.

I go to the cupboard where the brushes and dusters are kept but change my mind and turn to the sink which is full of dirty cups and plates. The water in the tap is hot. This is encouraging so I find the washing-up liquid and set to work.

James comes in as I am emptying the bowl and seizes a tea-towel.

"Sorry not to be here on your first morning," he says briskly. "I'll help you get started."

While he dries up, I collect a dustpan and brush and sweep the floor. I wonder if he helped his wife with the chores or left her to do them all.

"Perhaps you could just do the sitting-room today, and I will tidy the study in time for you to sweep and dust it next week. I must write next Sunday's sermon now if I can find paper and pen."

He goes along the tiled passage and shuts the study door behind him.

"Is he having a nervous breakdown?" I ask myself. My ex-husband was 'bi-polar', or however that condition is now defined. He was up one moment and down the next, and it became very difficult to deal with. The sitting room is chilly but I warm myself up with vigorous sweeping. Some of the furniture is good quality and the curtains are tasteful, but the three-piece is battered and needs recovering. No ornaments are to be seen except for a big mantel clock which has stopped at three forty-five.

I wind it up and it starts to tick. Maybe his wife took her pretty things with her when she went.

At eleven o'clock I make a pot of tea and put it on a tray. Should I shout "tea-break", or knock on the study door? He comes out before I can decide, rubbing his hands enthusiastically. We sit on the battered sofa and drink from mugs which I suspect come from a jumble sale.

"How's the sermon going?" I ask, not wanting to bore him with personal chat. He looks surprised and then pleased at my interest.

"Quite well, I think," he says, "It's about the martyr-dom of St Stephen." It is my turn to look surprised until I recall the carol which goes: 'Welcome be ye Stephen and John, Welcome innocents everyone, Welcome 'ere the year be done.' Saints' days are usually ignored these days except for St Valentine's.

In the manner of a Sunday School teacher, James goes on to inform me that he was the first Christian Martyr, stoned to death. Also the patron saint of this church.

"I know," I say shortly, picking up the tray.

"Sorry," he smiles, "I'd better get on with it."

While I am washing the mugs, I look out of the kitchen window and see Lorna Johnson walking up the path. She isn't carrying a plastic bag so I wonder what her excuse is for calling this time.

I open the door before she can knock, as something tells me that James shouldn't be disturbed. To say she looked startled would have been an understatement.

"What are you doing here?" she asks.

"Cleaning," I reply. "I'm the vicar's new cleaning lady. He's writing his sermon for Sunday."

"Oh. Well, I only wondered if he wants anything from the shop." she explains unconvincingly.

I don't offer to call him, but he must have heard our voices for he comes along the passage.

"Hullo Lorna," he says in a neutral kind of voice. "I don't think I want anything today, thanks."

"I'll just check the fridge," she says, not to be so lightly dismissed.

I set about dusting the living room, but keep my ears open, trying to size up the situation. Perhaps there's nothing in it. After all, they might have an arrangement whereby she picks up things he needs when she does her own shopping in the car, so he doesn't have to spend valuable time trailing round with a bag. On the other hand, they could be talking in a kind of code to put me off the scent.

Anyway, it's none of my business.

The back door closes and he returns to the study. At twelve o'clock I put the brushes and dusters away and wash my hands. Should I knock on the study door? Money hasn't been mentioned today, though a sum was agreed originally. As I am dithering in the tiled passage, he comes out with an envelope in his hand.

"Thank you very much Clare," he says, handing it over. Then he scratches his head in an embarrassed way. "I wonder if next time you come you could bring me a small brown loaf from the corner shop. I usually run out of bread by Wednesday."

Certainly," I say. It is all I can do not to wink. So he doesn't want Lorna to do his shopping, even though she is more than willing.

On the way home I call at Susan's.

"How did you get on?" she asks, putting on the kettle. So I tell her and she chuckles. "The poor man. Lorna's husband won't put up with it much longer. Did she have a black eye?"

"I didn't notice. But surely things haven't got that bad. I think he wants his wife back. Does anyone know where she's gone?"

"Swansea, to her mother's. She hasn't gone off with anyone else."

I wonder if I can do anything to re-unite them. Maureen tells me not to interfere, so I try to forget about it.

Chapter 11

Another note from CND has been put through the letterbox, saying that the New Year party will be on Monday at 7.30 in the Friends' Meeting House. Will Keith be there? The buses from and to his village might not run late enough to make it worth his while. And what about Bright Skirt? I have already forgotten her name. I suppose I'll have to buy a quiche or something similar for the 'food share'. Drink isn't mentioned. Will there be games and music? What shall I wear?

Suddenly overcome by guilt, I take myself up to the spare bedroom with my writing materials and clear my mind. After all, I am being paid by the government to be enterprising, not to socialize and speculate about drink and dress.

I re-read what I have written so far and ask myself if it is any good. This is the first doubt I have felt. Maybe it is a complete waste of time. But no, it is original, amusing, and will interest anyone who cares about a child's development from the age of eleven to seventeen. I take a deep breath and get on with it.

Richard the organist and his wife are away for a short holiday, so there is no choir practice this Friday. I wonder if the other members will find something else to do. Personally, I will be relieved not to have to walk up the hill in the dark for once. Then on Sunday I will sit with the congregation and pray as well as sing the hymns. Sometimes one gets drawn into giving a performance up there in the choir stalls.

Rantersford is well-known for its large number of charity shops as well as its wide choice of places of worship. Nearly every organisation is represented along the High Street, from Oxfam to the PDSA. These, plus every variety of 'eateries,' make up most of the occupied shops. Several businesses have disappeared since my arrival in the town, and when I remarked on this to Susan, she said it's the same everywhere. Supermarkets are taking over.

As I won't have time to go to the nearest big town which has a good department store before the CND party, I do a round of Cancer Research, Red Cross and the RSPCA and come across a dress to rival Bright Skirt's get-up. If fits nicely and takes the usual decade off my true age.

Armed with a Quiche Lorraine I set off for the Friends' Meeting House. The New Year isn't really new anymore, but I try to put myself in festive mood by thinking of Scottish bagpipes. A long table has been moved into the middle of the meeting room, and chairs arranged round small folding card tables. Plates bearing the regulation sausage rolls and assorted sandwiches mount up as people come in and deposit their offerings. I add my quiche, cut up into portions for easy consumption. There are several bottles at one end of the table, some already opened, but no one is actually drinking yet as there are no glasses. The lady vicar hurries in with a box of large wine glasses. I offer to help her put them out, and she accepts with a smile.

"Thank goodness we don't have to wash them afterwards," she says. "I hired them from a pub and they just want us to note any breakages."

"Let's hope there aren't many of those," I say, envisaging a drunken orgy. She has left off her dog-collar tonight, which I guess could be the equivalent of a lady 'letting her hair down.'

"My name's Clare," I tell her. We shake hands.

"Mine's Ruth. I'm the curate at St Michael's."

She puts the empty box under the table and goes to hang up her coat. St Michael's is a new church on a council estate where there are lot of 'problem families'. The vicar there is reputed to favour happy-clappy hymns and a pop-group type choir.

I don't recognize some of the people crowding in. Did it say 'partners welcome' in the newsletter? Maybe I could have brought someone with me, but who? I'm still on my own, aren't I?

"Perk up," says Maureen. "Look out for someone here." I pour myself a glass of white wine and cast a glance round the assembly. A man with glasses and lot of fair hair catches my eye.

"Keith," I cry rather too loudly, but he comes over without hesitation.

"Hullo Clare, I thought you might be here."

I don't say I had wondered the same of him, but I am glad.

He pours himself a beer and we sit at a little card-table, careful not to spill our drinks.

"How's the choir?" he wants to know. I tell him about the Christmas trip to the posh hotel, and he snorts in a derogatory kind of way. I guess he has left-wing learnings which I sympathise with in moderation.

"I'm thinking of moving into Rantersford," he informs me, "the village buses are being cut, and I don't like cadging lifts."

I stop myself asking the questions which spring to mind, such as "Are you intending to buy a house or rent one? Where do you work? Can't you afford a car? Are you married?"

It doesn't do to seem inquisitive, though I must admit I am interested. Actually, he answers all these queries without me having to voice them. He explains that he used to be his mother's carer. She had multiple sclerosis, but died recently, so he got a job at the Argos warehouse.

"It's too far to cycle, and I can't drive because my sight isn't good enough."

"I'm sorry," I say, imagining the poor fellow with his bad eyes looking after his ill mother, stuck in a cut-off village.

"It's time I sorted things out," he says briskly taking a pull at his beer. "I shall look for a flat to rent."

"Well, there are plenty of those," I tell him. "I bought a terraced house when I moved here last year, but there are lots for rent."

Ruth returns and begins to organize a Quiz. "I've got some brain-teasers, she announces, "let's have two sides and take them in turn."

There are one or two muted groans, but most people obligingly divide themselves into two groups and put on alert expressions. I see Bright Skirt across the room. She is eating a slice of my quiche and ignoring Ruth's instructions. I rather hope she hasn't seen me. I bet she was a spoil-sport at school.

The questions are based on what used to be called General Knowledge. I can answer the ones on books and music and natural history while Keith's interests lie nearer science, sport and history. Between us, we do quite well for our side, and help it to win.

"Well done," sneers Bright Skirt, still clutching a full plate. "I avoid silly games at parties and concentrate on the food."

Keith looks at her plate. "So I see," he remarks. Then he turns to me and suggests that we choose something before it's all gone. This we do, refilling our glasses, and sit down with Ruth.

"Any decisions about becoming a Peace Group?" he wants to know. She is pleased that he is interested in her suggestion and says it will be discussed at the next ordinary monthly meeting.

"Will you both be there?" she asks hopefully. She seems to see us as a couple. Keith looks at me and we both assure her that we will.

"I'd better go now to catch my last bus," he says, putting on his duffel coat. Afraid of being left to the mercies of Bright Skirt, I say I must go too, and we set off together. Salvin Street is on the way to the bus station, so he takes note of my house number and says he will be in touch. The he runs down the hill. I hope he doesn't miss his bus and have to walk home.

Orlando is waiting for his supper. "Have I met my kindred spirit?" I ask him. Then a horrid thought strikes me. What if Keith is allergic to cat-fur like Fernando! Too tired to work out a strategy to cope with this possible snag, I go to bed but sleep badly.

It is Wednesday again and I must clean the vicar's study. He lets me in this time and eagerly takes the small brown loaf which I have remembered to buy on my way.

"I ran out of bread," he confesses, cutting a slice and putting it under the grill. "Can't start the day without toast and marmalade."

So Lorna Johnson has not been round with a plastic bag. It's the Women's Fellowship meeting tomorrow so I will see how she treats me.

"I've got to be at the hospital to visit patients at eleven," James informs me. "I've tidied the study so you can dust it and sweep the floor. I'll make my bed and sort the washing."

"Right," I say, and collect dusters and brushes from the kitchen cupboard. I picture his poor wife doing the chores and getting fed up. How can I find out more about the real reason for her going?

The study is dark, so I switch the light on and try not to read any of the papers on his desk. I'm surprised at him letting a member of his congregation into his private place, as it will surely contain information which is confidential, such as certificates and letters from the Bishop. He must trust me not to pry. Feeling flattered, I flick at the dust and straighten the books. I come across a framed photograph of a sweet-faced lady with wavy hair and a frilly blouse. This must be his missing wife. Dare I use this photo to re-introduce the subject of his solitude? Not yet. I'll wait and see how Lorna behaves towards me tomorrow evening.

At mid-day I put the brushes away and lock up. This energetic cleaning gives me an appetite, so rather than go home for a sandwich, I take myself to the supermarket for a treat. Fish and chips and mushy peas is one of my favourite meals, and as they do small portions, I don't feel guilty or extravagant. While I am queuing up with my tray, I catch sight of Fernando filling up the bread shelves. He moves as gracefully as a ballet dancer stacking loaves and checking expiry dates. Surely he deserves a more interesting job, though he looks happy enough. Terry must be taking good care of him.

The mushy peas are rather dry and don't taste as nice as usual but the fish is delicious, and I eat up all the chips. Then I buy a few food items and walk home. My book is progressing, but it is getting a bit difficult to recall events in enough detail to make them convincing and interesting to what I hope will be the ordinary reader.

Tired and depressed I go to bed early. Orlando Jumps up to snuggle against my back, but I am not comforted. At precisely 1.15 a.m. I wake up with a tummy-ache. Those cursed mushy peas are in revolt. Or is it appendicitis? Where illness is concerned, I have always been a pessimist. My mother was the same, so perhaps I get it from her.

"Don't be silly," says Maureen, "get up and fill a hot water bottle. The pain will go off."

I do her bidding and eventually she is proved right, though I don't fancy any breakfast, and decide not to go to the Women's Fellowship this evening. This means that my plan of observing Lorna Johnson's behaviour will be thwarted. Serve me right for being unchristian. The poor woman is probably very miserable.

By tea-time I am feeling better, so when Terry calls in on his way home from the bank and invites me round for coffee I am tempted to accept.

"Are you celebrating something?"

"No, we just thought it would be nice to chat. Fernando says he saw you at the supermarket yesterday but you didn't see him."

I can't very well admit that I had seen him but didn't want to risk losing my place in the dinner queue. We have a very pleasant evening, and I sleep well.

Richard is back from his holiday, full of plans for an Easter concert. Stainer's 'Crucifixion' is his choice. There are some lovely tuneful bits, and it's not so difficult as the 'Messiah'. I stick to the second sopranos and always open my mouth wide, though following this score is sometimes beyond me.

I wish Keith hadn't given up, as I am still the only new member. Maybe he will rejoin when he has found a place to live in town.

Susan telephones me to ask why I didn't attend the Women's Fellowship meeting. To my ears, people's phone-voices take some getting used to, so as I've only ever spoken to Susan face to face, I don't at first know who she is. This seems to upset her, but when I tell her about the mushy peas she is full of sympathy.

"You didn't miss much. It was a talk about flower-arranging. A lady brought lots of bits and pieces and stuck them in vases and then we had to do some ourselves. I'm no good at that sort of thing."

Actually, I think the subject would have helped St Stephen's flower-ladies, whoever they are, as their efforts on display behind the altar usually leave something to be desired.

"How was Lorna/" I ask.

"Very quiet. Seemed to have something or someone on her mind."

I say I'll see her at church on Sunday and ring off.

Chapter 12

Sid and Doris seem to be keeping themselves to themselves since Christmas but I see Sid in his yard this morning.

"Everything OK? I ask.

"Doris has taken to her bed," he informs me in a neutral tone.

"Oh dear, what seems to be the trouble?"

"She doesn't say. Just won't get up."

"Perhaps you should get Dr Flynn to look at her."

He snorts unsympathetically. "I think she's putting it on."

"Well, if she is, he'll know, and if she's really ill, he can make her better. Would you like me to phone him?"

"You can if you want," he says grudgingly. So rather than penetrate the probable squalor of Doris' bedroom, I dial the number noted when Fernando had his asthma attack. The doctor himself answers. I gather his practice has neither a partner nor a receptionist. Surely even Rantersford can't be so old fashioned? It's almost as if the NHS doesn't exist here. Anyway, he says he'll call 'after lunch', which of course could be any time before tea.

Sid thanks me but there follows a loud disagreement through the bedroom wall.

I notice that the flowers behind the altar at St Stephen's are more tastefully arranged than usual on

Sunday, so the speaker at the WF must have had an influence on someone. Could it have been Lorna?

I am becoming obsessed with the business of the vicar's wife in Swansea. I have to work out who is to blame, if blame is in fact part of it. Was there anything between Lorna and James in the first place? Is Lorna's husband so nasty because he is jealous, or is he nasty anyway and driving Lorna away? Did James' wife have her suspicions and act upon them without a fight? Or did she just get fed up with having no children and being expected to stay at home and clean the vicarage? How can I find out?

Then I ask myself why am I so curious? Do I fancy James myself? This last is a difficult question, as at one time I must confess I did, but now I feel more sisterly towards him and want to cheer him up and put things right. Next Wednesday I will pluck up courage and speak to him about it.

Dr Flynn came as promised to see Doris. It seems that her liver is out of order. Sid complains that he is getting no thanks for carrying trays of food upstairs which she refuses to eat. "She won't be hungry if it's her liver," I tell him. "Has he given her a prescription for some medicine?"

"Yes, I went to Boots but she won't take it."

My mind boggles at the picture of the interior of Number 15 Salvin Street. While she was up and about Doris did at least wash clothes and do the shopping, but what must things be like now?

"Can you manage?" I ask, fearing I might have to offer practical help.

"Of course," Sid snaps, "It's her who makes the mess. While she's in bed I can tidy up."

I am relieved but still anxious. "Did Dr Flynn say he would come again?" I ask.

"Yes. He's coming this afternoon."

"Good. Give her my love and let me know what he says."

"She doesn't know what love is, so that won't help but I'll tell her you asked after her." He goes inside and shuts the door.

I will not allow myself to take sides and, anyway, I don't know where my sympathies lie. I am only so thankful that I got away from my own unhappy relationship before it became as toxic as this. I seem surrounded by miserable couples in need of help. Perhaps I should take up Marriage Guidance Counselling.

It is Wednesday again, and I must try to sort out the vicar. I walk past the corner shop without buying his small brown loaf, my mind on other things, and only remember it as I'm nearing the vicarage. Should I go back? Maybe he has got enough bread left, or possibly Lorna has run the gauntlet and been before me. I let myself in with my key and call "Hullo," but no answer, so he must be out on a mission. Inside the breadbin I find a rather stale crust and feel guilty. Has he had his morning toast?

He doesn't come home until coffee-time and seems pleased to see me. I apologise about the bread and offer to nip out for it before I finish.

"Oh, don't bother," he says, "I can get it myself this afternoon."

"Lorna hasn't been then?" I begin, determined to broach the subject.

He looks at me in a doubtful kind of way as if trying to guess what I mean by such a question. Have I gone too far? I put the broom on one side and risk a rebuff.

"I know I'm being presumptuous, "I begin," but I saw a picture of your wife in the study last week and I recall that you did once say that you miss her."

At first I fear he is going to tell me to mind my own business, but he shuffles his feet and rubs his head in a hopeless manner and says, "So I do, but I can't think of a way to put things right."

"How about sending her a letter," I suggest, "I find I can usually communicate best by writing words on paper. You do a good sermon, so I'm sure you could make her respond."

"I think she got fed up with my sermons," he mutters. "She said I used to preach at her."

"Well, tell her you're sorry and that you won't do it anymore."

"Oh, there's more to it than that," he admits. "Other people are involved, all due to misunderstandings."

I wait for him to continue. The coffee gets cold.

"Lorna's husband strikes me as being a very unpleasant person," I prompt.

He picks up the hint. "Yes, but he is jealous. Lorna is very active in the parish, and she likes to help. He thinks we have been carrying on but I don't see her that way."

"I think she sees you that way," I tell him. "Maybe your wife got the impression that Lorna's husband had a reason to be jealous, and she's gone home to mother because she didn't know what else to do."

"It's all the most awful muddle," poor James cries. "Vicars aren't supposed to have marital problems."

I am tempted to laugh. "Everyone gets them," I say. "I speak from personal experience."

The clock in the sitting-room strikes twelve.

Time for me to go and I haven't finished the cleaning. "I'll get the bread and bring it back," I say. "I haven't earned my pay today"

I put my coat on an let myself out. He doesn't try to stop me so I call at the corner shop and return with a small brown loaf.

"You are very kind," he says, giving me the usual white envelope. "I'll spend the afternoon trying to write to Gwen."

"Good," I say. "See you next week."

When I get home, I pour myself a glass of sherry. I feel I deserve it.

Sid puts his head over the fence. "Dr Flynn says Doris has got jaundice. She's gone yellow all over, not just her face." He seems astonished rather than alarmed. "She's got to have a blood test. Could be serious."

"Is she still in bed?" I ask, taken aback at the news. "How can she get to hospital for a blood test?"

"They'll fetch her in the big vehicle that takes people for day appointments. It's coming sometime today."

"Do you want me to go with her?" I ask.

He shakes his head. "I'll go. They might have to keep her in."

A querulous voice from upstairs calls, "Sid, I'm going to be sick."

"Well, you've got the pot," he shouts, "I'll come as quick as I can." He stumps away, and I retreat inside Number 16. I feel quite sick myself to think of poor Doris. One of my aunts went yellow all over, and she died of pancreatic cancer.

The hospital mini-bus comes at lunch time but the medics have a job to get her in. In my opinion, she should have gone in a proper ambulance, like Terry's mother. It is early evening before Sid returns.

"They've put her in the observation ward, said they didn't like the look of her. Can't say I did, either."

At first I thought he was indulging in black humour, but he was just thinking aloud. "It'll seem quiet without her tonight," he adds in a puzzled manner.

As far as I am aware, they have never been away for a holiday in all the years they have lived together, stuck in their unhealthy symbiotic relationship like characters in a Greek tragedy.

There is a knock at my front door later, and half-expecting it to be Sid, I open to find Keith on the step. This is a pleasant surprise. "Nice to see you" I say. "Come in."

He steps over the threshold and looks round appreciatively. "These houses look nice when the furniture is in," he remarks, "I've just been visiting some empty ones that are for rent."

"Have you found one?" I ask eagerly.

"I think so, but I need a second opinion. Could you possibly come and have a look at it? It's just up the hill and round the corner from here."

"Of course," I say, grabbing my coat and scarf. I leave the light on and lock the door. It's cold outside, with a moon. We pass Terry and Fernando's front window. The curtains are not yet drawn and they can be observed sitting companionably together reading a newspaper.

I tell Keith about Doris' jaundice and he is concerned. "I suppose the neighbours round her are a friendly lot, not like in a village where there is lots of gossip."

St Stephen's tower looms up in the darkness. "

"Quite near for choir practice. Do you still go?"

I assure him that I do, and that we are doing Stainer's 'Crucifixion' at Easter.

He stops outside a large corner house.

"Is this it? Isn't it a bit big?" I am surprised.

He laughs. "It's divided up into flats. The bosses of the local industries used to live near their workers to keep an eye on them, and their own homes were large and well-built. This is one of them."

I should have known this as it is local history. Keith rings the bell and the door is opened by an efficient looking lady in a long skirt.

"I came earlier about the flat. Can I have another look at it?"

"Sure!" The lady steps aside. She glances at me as we enter. "I thought you said it was for one."

"I'm just a friend," I say hastily. This is the second time we have been mistaken for a couple. Ruth at CND made the same assumption at the party. Keith jokingly takes my elbow as we follow up a wide flight of stairs. It is gratifying to pretend to be as one.

In electric light it is difficult to imagine the flat full of furniture and personal belongings, but it is clean with high ceilings, and the kitchen and bathroom are adequate. There is one bedroom with plenty of storage space.

"This is nice," I say. "How much is the rent?"

He clears his throat. "It's reasonable."

"Sorry," I whisper, conscious of being inquisitive. The tall skirted lady hovers. "There is someone else after this flat," she warns, "If you want it, you will be wise to pay a deposit now, and move in when convenient."

Keith looks at me with raised eyebrows. I nod and move respectfully away so he can pay in private.

On the way back down the hill he thanks me for my help and admits that his mother always took the big decisions as he has difficulty making up his mind. My spirits take a dip as I realize that I am yet again having to assume the role of mother or sister or just a friend. Or, in this case, am I?

"I'll have to run to catch the last bus," he says, "so I won't come in, but may I see you again soon?"

I breathe a quiet sigh of relief.

"Anytime at all." I say, quoting from the Beatles. This is more like it.

Chapter 13

At the next choir practice I tell Richard that Keith might be joining again as he is moving house.

"Good, we need more tenors," is the response. "Friend of yours, is he?"

Bernard is listening to our conversation and looks disappointed when I answer in the affirmative. I fear that he has overcome his aversion to divorce, so I always slip away quickly after practices before he can offer me a lift. I certainly don't want to be his dead wife's replacement. Surely there are lots of ladies in the congregation eager to marry him.

A lady who writes religious poetry has been invited to come and read it to us at the next W.F. meeting. I had better attend even if only to check up on Lorna. I wonder if James has heard from his Gwen in Swansea yet. I seem overburdened by other people's problems. It's time to retire to the spare bedroom and get on with my own writing.

Poor Doris is still in hospital, and I fear she is going with same way as Veronica. Sid doesn't seem to want me to visit her but I feel I should.

"It's a waste of time," he says. "They've given her some pills and she sleeps all the time. When I go I just sit there."

"Well, she might wake up and be pleased to see you. I could come too, with some flowers."

"She hasn't been pleased to see me for twenty years but come if you want."

So I go with him as I did with Terry. The curtains are drawn round Doris's bed when we get there, which is not a good sign, but they are only giving her a wash and soon we are sitting one each side of her.

To Sid's surprise she opens her eyes and smiles at the bunch of assorted chrysanthemums which I have placed on her locker.

"How's Dolly?" she asks in a weak voice.

"She's fine," I say. "Sid is remembering to feed her and she comes over the fence to see my Orlando."

"Good." Then she is asleep again like a switched off light.

"How weird," says Sid, using an unexpected word. "All she's worried about is the cat."

"At least she doesn't sleep quite all the time. Are you going to have a word with the nurse?"

He wanders over to the desk and a plump girl in a tight uniform consults a chart. They speak in quiet tones. Then a young man in a white coat joins them.

Oh dear. I am sure Doris is dying. Without her to do battle, Sid will fade away like an old soldier. He rejoins me and pats her unresponsive yellow hand.

"She's on the way out," he whispers. "Poor old girl."

He sniffs and sadly we set off back to Salvin Street.

The local CND seems to have changed its name officially to the Rantersford Peace Group. A notice has come thus headed, inviting me to a meeting. I wonder if Keith will be there? I have heard nothing from him since our flat search, so perhaps he is busy moving in. I suppress the desire to offer help with arranging his furniture as that would be taking things for granted. After all, we are not really a 'couple', even though I wish we were. I don't even know his village address.

Maureen's opinion on the matter hasn't come through yet. I half expect her to tell me to be my age and remind me that I am better on my own. Usually she is right.

As if conjured up, a letter from Keith has come in the post. He has hired a van and a driver to transport his stuff on Saturday and will see me at the Peace Group on Monday.

Wonderful! I suppose he must have a driver as he can't see well enough to drive himself. I hope whoever it is will help him carry heavy things upstairs.

I approach the vicarage for my cleaning stint in cheerful mood but James tells me that although he wrote a long letter to Gwen, she hasn't answered yet. He doesn't seem too disappointed, as she will have to think about it and her mother might interfere. It's his usual hospital duty and he hurries off straight away, leaving my pay on the hall table. I put a small brown loaf in the bread bin and start to dust the study. Gwen's photo seems to be looking at me as if she is sizing me up.

"I'm not after your James," I tell her, "and he's not after anyone else. He wants you back." She appears to smile, but it could be a trick of the light.

By eleven o'clock I am ready for a cup of coffee. It seems lonely without James but I am entitled to a break, so I put the kettle on and take a mug out of the cupboard. Almost on cue, Lorna Johnson walks up the path. I reach for another mug and open the door.

"The vicar is visiting the sick," I tell her. "would you like a coffee?"

She evidently hasn't given up on James even though he made it obvious that he doesn't want her to do his shopping.

"I was just passing," she says brightly. "Sometimes he has nothing in the fridge." Simultaneously we both reach for the fridge door, and I win.

"It seems fairly well stocked," I remark. She has to agree. My offer of coffee has been neither refused nor accepted so I pour two mugs and hand her one.

"Sit down," I say, and like an obedient schoolgirl, she perches on a stool.

I must take this God-given opportunity to sort her out but how on earth am I going to do it? Then to my surprise, she bursts into tears. I hastily relieve her of the hot mug and put an arm round her shaking shoulders.

"There, there," I say, "What's the matter?"

"I can't stop loving James," she sobs. "I know he doesn't want me and I've made such a mess of everything."

Now we are getting somewhere.

"Well, James is very attractive," I begin, "but I think your husband is jealous, and that makes him angry with everybody. Does he hit you?"

The question slips out before I can prevent it. She pulls the sleeve of her coat lower over her arm.

"Sometimes," she admits miserably.

I have a vision of her ending up in a women's refuge and the whole parish taking sides.

"We must think what is to be done," I say firmly. "James says he wants his wife to come back from her mother's in Swansea and, if she does, that would make things look better, wouldn't it?"

"Yes, but will that help my husband to forgive me? He thinks people are laughing at him behind his back."

"Well, you'll just have to say you're very sorry and risk getting a black eye." I know this is a cruel thing to say but she has got to be made to take action. "I'll let you know if Gwen decides to return. Let's hope things get sorted out with no real harm done."

She nods and gulps her coffee down.

"Thank you for being so understanding," she says.

I let her out of the front door, secure in the knowledge that as James has left my pay envelope ready for me, he does not intend to be back before noon. I wash both the cups and put them away in the cupboard like a character in a crime novel destroying evidence.

On the way home, Maureen tells me not to get too pleased with myself. "You're on tricky ground," she warns. True.

Terry calls round after supper and asks if Doris is ill, as he hasn't seen her recently. I don't like to remind him of his mother's death but can't avoid it. "She's very ill in hospital," I say.

He looks a bit shocked but asks me to convey his sympathy to Sid. "Maybe she will recover," he says. "I hope so."

Knowing how Doris never had a good word to say about him or his friend Fernando, I am glad to have been an effective buffer to the end.

I wonder how Sid will cope with living on his own. Maybe he'll be happier than he's ever been, as I am myself in similar circumstances, but on the other hand he might suffer a mental collapse, lost without the stimulation of argument and conflict. Dolly the cat can't be a sufficient substitute, just as my Orlando isn't really enough for me.

There has never been mention of any grown-up children or other relatives. Can a man so 'Rantersford born and bred' have no family members living locally?

The hospital keeps Doris alive for two days longer than expected but she dies on Sunday. I come home from Evensong to find Sid sitting on his bench beside Dolly.

"She's gone," he announces. "Your vicar is a good bloke. He came to see her on Wednesday and again yesterday. He says he'll take care of the funeral."

Of course! James was visiting the hospital while I was cleaning the vicarage and dealing with Lorna. Doris must have been on his sick-list but I don't expect he would connect her with me, as she was not a churchgoer.

Then comes another surprise. Sid has a daughter living in Bridlington. Apparently he was married before to a lady called Joyce, and they had a baby girl called Eliza. Joyce died when Eliza was a teenager, and Sid married Doris hoping she would be a new mother. Needless to say, that was a mistake, and Eliza left home at the earliest opportunity. Sid kept in touch with her, thus adding to the many bones of contention between him and Doris. What a sad story.

Anyway, Eliza plans to come down for a few days to stay with her Dad, now her stepmother is no more.

I wonder what to wear for the Peace Group meeting. I want to look attractive but not bizarre like some of the other members do. Bright Skirt seems to have a collection of colourful garments which I don't think Keith likes. He said he'd see me there, but I hope he intends to walk me home afterwards. As the weather has turned cold again, I decide on a green jersey, black trousers and my old duffel. Perhaps he will be wearing his duffel. If so, we will look even more like a couple.

The usual people are assembled when I arrive but no Keith so far. Ruth waves from across the hall. She is holding a pile of leaflets. I gather that the point of the meeting is to discuss the best way of distributing them to the public. They contain details of British arms sales to countries which have a shocking disregard for human rights.

Keith hurries in just before the meeting starts. He looks round the room and, remembering his poor eyesight, I go over to him. He is pleased to see me, and we sit on adjoining seats.

Bright Skirt flops down on my other side. She is wearing a multicoloured waterproof jacket and shiny boots.

"Leafletting does no good," she whispers. "We've done it before and the idiots don't read them."

Ruth stands at the front and makes a sensible speech about healthy plants growing even on stony ground. Surveys suggest that out of every 100 leaflets distributed, five are read and followed up. That doesn't sound much but even five new members in our group would make a difference.

Some people clap and she goes on to suggest a plan of campaign. She holds up a street-map with certain streets marked. "We could have a blitz on this area," she says.

At the word 'blitz', Keith and I exchange glances. It seems inappropriate to use a word which indicates mass destruction rather than peaceful action but, as most of the members are too young to have experienced an air-raid, to them the word is mere jargon. Copies of the leaflet are given out and time allowed for reading them. They are based on an article in a Campaign magazine and are well-written and neatly put together.

"Any comments?" asks Ruth.

Keith puts up his hand. "If you need volunteers to deliver a leaflet to every house on the chosen streets, do we all do it at the same time, or when we can get round to it? And do we work in pairs or singly?"

Everybody pricks up their ears.

"It won't work, whatever we do," grumbles Bright Skirt.

Ruth frowns. "We must be optimistic," she says. "Keith is making some important points. How many people think we should try to cover the whole area in one fell swoop?"

A majority of hands go up. "And I think we should go in pairs," says a nervous -looking girl with long blonde hair. "It gets dark so early at this time of year."

Again Bright Skirt sneers. "It will be a waste of shoe-leather. Writing a letter to the local paper would do more good."

"Not everyone takes the local paper," a shabbily-dressed lad observes.

There's more argument and things are getting out of hand until Ruth calls for order and opens a big planning calendar. "Let's choose a convenient date and make a list," she says firmly. "It's the least we can do." So everyone gathers round and at last things get sorted. Keith and I agree to be a pair but Bright Skirt wants to work on her own.

"Right," says Ruth, "we'll all meet here in three weeks at 7.30 and set off together. I'll bring the leaflets."

"Are you getting a taxi?" Bright Skirt asks me as we leave the building.

"No," says Keith firmly, "we're walking." He takes my elbow in a masterly fashion and guides me away.

"I can't stand her," he mutters in my ear.

Conscience stricken I turn and wave. "See you in three weeks," I call, but she is marching off.

I turn to Keith. "Has everything fitted into the flat?" I ask, giving him my full attention.

"It's looking more or less O.K. You'll have to come and give me your opinion. It's too late tonight, so we'll fix a convenient time."

"Pin him down," says Maureen.

"Are you joining the choir?" I ask. "You're very near the church. If so, I could go back with you after the practice on Friday. Richard doesn't like keeping us after nine o'clock as most of us live away."

Number 16 Salvin Street is reached and I get out my key. Number 15 is in darkness.

"The lady next-door has died," I say, suddenly sad. Poor Sid must miss her in a way.

"Oh dear, I'm sorry, though I never met her. I've not seen my new neighbours yet. I hope we'll get on."

"They'll be fine," I tell him. "See you on Friday."

He pats my hand. "Take care," and he's off up the hill.

"I think he'll do," says Maureen, "but don't rush things."

Chapter 14

If Gwen hasn't written by Wednesday, I will have to think of another strategy. But she has!

James is waiting for my arrival with the bread, as he has run out again.

"I don't know what I would do without you," he says gaily crunching his toast. "Gwen is coming home on Saturday She says she misunderstood how things were and wants to make up for it."

"Jolly good." I say with schoolgirl enthusiasm. "Do you want me to Hoover the bedroom?"

Too late I realize that this could be taken the wrong way. He pauses before replying. "No, I'll do it. You stick to the downstairs."

"Right." I get on with it and he goes into his study humming a hymn.

I wonder if Gwen will appear in church on Sunday as if nothing has happened, and how Lorna will react. From the choir stalls I won't get a clear view so I will have to ask Susan to keep an eye out. I can trust her not to gossip to anyone before then. I call at her house on the way home.

"You have done well," she says when I tell her the news. "It'll be nice to have Gwen back. She is a lovely lady."

Now all I have to worry about is Lorna and her potentially violent husband.

"Leave that to them," says Maureen, "you've done enough."

I get to choir-practice early to find Keith having a word with Richard. They shake hands so I presume that means Keith is now a member. Good. No time for a chat as we take our places.

Before we start, Richard announces that the vicar's wife is on her way home after a spell in Swansea helping her mother and will be in church on Sunday. There is an appreciative murmur. So that's all right.

Stainer's Crucifixion is coming along nicely. I think I can hear Keith's voice among the tenors so he must be able to read music. I wonder what his hobbies are, if any. Actually I don't really know much about him so far but feel we have some things in common.

Bernard makes as if to offer me a lift after we finish but Keith rescues me and we set off for his flat. "Does he fancy you?" he asks when we are out of earshot.

"I fear so," I say. "He is a lonely widower. At first he retreated when I told him I am divorced but now he seems to have overcome that objection."

For a moment I fear that Keith might share Bernard's attitude as he keeps silent. Then he laughs.

"Well, he would probably disapprove of me because I'm divorced too."

At this we both laugh together, so loudly that a passer-by gives us a wide berth.

The light is on in the shared hall, so we mount the stairs and Keith unlocks his flat. The place is what is usually called 'sparsely furnished.'

"I don't seem to have quite enough of everything," he explains. "When Mum died, my sister and I divided up the stuff between us. She took most because she's like that. But there are plenty of second-hand furniture shops in Rantersford so I'll soon get sorted."

I take off my coat and sit down on the only comfy chair. He lights the gas fire.

"Coffee or etchings?" he asks.

I don't know what to make of this. Surely he isn't suggesting that we embark on an immediate affair?

"Ignore it," advises Maureen. "Say you'd like to look at his books."

"Coffee please," I say firmly. I get up and inspect a rather battered G-plan unit which carries books and gramophone records. He goes into the kitchen and soon returns with a tray on which are the two mugs and a milk bottle. One of the mugs says, 'I hate Thatcher' and the other "Keep Calm and Carry On'. I select the Thatcher mug and add milk.

"She snatched the kids' milk," I remark, "and she sold council houses, but I don't actually hate anyone these days."

He sighs. "That's because you go to church for the right reasons. Maybe some of it will rub off on me if I'm in the choir for long enough."

Desperate to lighten the conversation, I indicate the gramophone records and say that I see he likes orchestral music as well as vocal.

"Ah yes. I met my wife at a music club but the subject turned out to be the only thing we had in common."

Maureen groans. I look directly into his beautiful blue short-sighted eyes and say, "I'm too tired to go into the details of either of our failed marriages at the moment, though I am interested. Suppose you come round to my place for a meal one evening when we are more relaxed."

He rubs his head in the same way as James does when he's agitated. "I'm so sorry," he says, "I'm tired too, and I did so want your visit to be enjoyable. I don't always think before I speak."

"That's all right," I say, patting his arm. "How about supper on Tuesday, at 7.30?"

"Yes please." He helps me on with my coat. "I'll take you down the hill."

We descend the imposing staircase and go out into the cold night. He offers me his arm and I take it companionably.

It is strange to think that today, Saturday, Gwen is travelling from Swansea and Eliza from Bridlington, converging on Rantersford. They do not know about each other but I know about both of them.

Eliza makes my acquaintance first. Sid brings her round to talk about the funeral. She is a large friendly young woman with dyed blonde hair. I don't offer her words of sympathy about Doris, as I know she didn't get on with her stepmother, but I say I am glad she has come to be with her Dad.

"The house is in the most awful state," she says. "We can't ask anyone back there for a cup of tea after the funeral. Do you know anywhere nearby which does that sort of thing?"

"I don't, but surely the vicar will. James is a very helpful man. He visited her in hospital and says he will do the funeral at St Stephen's up the hill."

"Oh good. Maybe we could use the church hall if they have one."

"Not many people will come," says Sid mournfully. "She didn't make friends easily."

"I'm sure some neighbours will," I say. "We could put an announcement in the local paper."

So sensible arrangements are made and they go back next door. I hope Eliza finds some clean sheets in the airing cupboard.

Gwen's return to church on Sunday is quite an occasion. The idea that she has been away 'helping her mother' must have been put about by Richard, who is surely aware that there was more to it than that. But there are no sly asides in the congregation and everyone welcomes her back. The only person who must have been upset is Lorna and she manages to hide her feelings well enough. She shows no visible signs of abuse from her husband, so let's hope he has forgiven her.

I wonder if James will want me to continue to clean the vicarage. If he has learnt anything from Gwen's absence, he mustn't expect her to do all the chores herself.

For some reason, I am assuming that Keith doesn't eat meat. I myself prefer fish, so I buy two fillets of plaice and frozen peas from the supermarket for our supper on Tuesday. I have heard nothing from him since our unsatisfactory get-together in his flat, but I will be ready to welcome him at 7.30.

I look out for Fernando but he isn't evident. I suppose he does most of his work in the back. I wonder if he and Terry would get on well with Keith. I'll introduce them if I get the chance.

Doris' funeral is to be next Friday at 10 o'clock at St Stephen's with tea and cakes in the church hall after- wards. Eliza gets on well with James who asked her to tell him about Doris so he can 'celebrate her life' with a few words during the service. She admitted that she couldn't think of anything nice to say about her step-mother, so Sid pulled himself together and managed to summon up one or two virtues in the woman he had hated for so long.

What a dreadful situation! I hope someone cries when I die.

Keith arrives promptly looking very smart. His hair has been recently trimmed and I rather think he is wearing some new glasses. He is bearing a bottle of wine.

The only inconvenience I have found inside 16 Salvin Street so far is the lack of space to hang coats and hats. I suppose I could buy an antique hat-stand or put up a row of hooks but they would take up valuable room. Perhaps the people who lived here when the house was built kept their coats on indoors and wore scarves round their heads.

I take his duffel and hang it on the back of an upright chair in the front room.

"We're eating through here," I say, leading him into the dining room at the back.

"Something smells nice," he says, rubbing his hands."

"I hope you like fish," I say.

"It's a bit too late if he doesn't," quips Maureen. But he does, so I guessed right.

I take two glasses from a box of six which was given to me as a leaving present when I moved home.

"You pour," I tell him. "I'll dish up."

I go into the kitchen which is in disorder due to my agitation over various heated vegetable-dishes. It's a long time since I cooked for two, but I have enough equipment to cater for half a dozen. Should I offer him some of my stuff?

"No," advises Maureen. "That will look as if you are planning to adopt him."

Certainly I must avoid becoming his mother or sister or aunty. 'Lady-friend' is what I would like to be, though that sounds a bit old-fashioned.

"It's nice and cosy here," he says, sitting down at my oak dining table. "I rather rattle about in my flat."

"How many of you were there when you were growing up?" I ask.

"Just me, my sister and our parents. We lived in a rural council house. Dad worked on the land. He died in a tractor accident when I was twelve."

I help him to a large portion of peas and potatoes. "And now your Mum has died too, so you are an orphan."

He laughs. "I expect you are too by now."

Has he worked out how old I am?

"Yes, but they both died of old age, not from accident or illness."

More questions crowd into my mind. How long was he caring for his mother? Why did his marriage fail? Did they have any children?

"You can't ask everything at once without seeming pushy," Maureen warns. "Be patient and it will all come out in conversation."

When I go to fetch the pudding, Orlando wanders in. "Are you allergic to cats? I ask urgently.

"No, Why?"

"Well, last time I did some entertaining it ended in disaster, because one of the guests had an asthma attack and we had to call the doctor."

"How awful for you." He sounds genuinely sympathetic, so I tell him about Terry and Fernando.

"They sound interesting neighbours. What are they like the other side?"

As we drink coffee from my best cups, I outline the saga of Sid and Doris, ending with Doris' death.

Over the evening the conversation progresses naturally, and we exchange information about ourselves in equal measure.

His marriage to a local girl only lasted five years and they had no children. I don't like to ask for details but I gather she went off with someone else, so he went back to his mother who, by that time, needed looking after. His sister had moved away and wasn't much help.

"I had trained as a male nurse," he tells me, "so that came in useful, but it went on for so long."

I wanted to hug him for being such a good son but controlled myself, and suddenly it was eleven o'clock.

"I must go, I'm on the early shift at Argos tomorrow."

I fetch his coat and he thanks me for a very pleasant evening. "Would you come to me next Tuesday? I was one of the four boys who took cookery at school."

Interesting.

"I'd love to," I say.

Maureen approves.

I lead him to the front door, where he presses my hand.

"See you at choir of Friday," he says, and runs up the hill. Strange how he seems to impelled to run, even when he doesn't have a bus to catch.

—⁓—

Gwen opens the door of the vicarage when I get there today. It sees to be a sign that she is now in charge. Should I hand over the key which James gave me? Is she going to tell me that my services are no longer required? She is wearing a flowered pinafore as if ready for domestic work.

"Hello," she says, smiling pleasantly. "I'm glad you've come. James says you have been invaluable. This place so easily gets out of order and it was too much for me on my own."

Good. He must have apologised to her for his old-fashioned ideas about wifely duties.

"He's at the hospital this morning, so I can do the study while you do the living-room, if that's all right by you."

"Of course." I hang my coat up on the convenient Victorian hat-stand. "I'm glad you want me to continue."

She speaks with a lilting Welsh accent, very musical.

"Are you in the choir?" I ask.

"Yes, if Richard will have me back."

"We're doing Stainer's Crucifixion for Easter," I tell her, just so she'll know I am a member myself. We share out the brushes and dusters and get to work.

James comes home at coffee time, eager to give her a kiss. He smiles at me and says he is glad to see me as usual.

"So that's sorted," says Maureen. "No need to worry about them anymore."

I feel a rush of pride at having done a good deed, like the Girl Guide I once was.

I attend the Thursday WF meeting chiefly because I am anxious to observe Lorna's behaviour with Gwen. I was even prepared to shield one from the other if necessary, but I needn't have worried as neither of them were present.

Pat the secretary introduced the speaker, who proved to be an excellent choice. She writes a wide variety of poems, some of which have won prizes in competitions. For us she had chosen to read what she called her 'Biblical Re-thinks'.

At first I imagine that they will be humorous versions of well-known stories, but no, they are profound and original without being too controversial.

They all concern well-known Biblical events, told from the point of view of a minor character. Sometimes the teller is indignant and puzzled or desperate and doomed, but each poem leaves the listeners with food for thought. Poor Lazarus hadn't wanted to be raised from the dead and the Gadarene swineherds were very cross about their loss of livelihood. King Herod could see no alternative to the slaughter of the innocents, the third servant protested about his unjust treatment, while the paralytic couldn't cope with being cured. Animated conversation follows.

If he could have been present, James might have gleaned material for his sermons. I ask the poet if she has any publications and she produces a few pamphlets from her bag. I buy one to lend to James and even Keith if they are interested.

I walk home with Susan who confesses that she doesn't read poetry but had liked the speaker's voice. She is pleased by the vicar's wife's return from Swansea but disappointed that she and Lorna hadn't come face to face.

"I was looking forward to a scrap," she admits rather shamefacedly, "but that isn't very Christian of me, is it?"

"No," I agree. "I think we'll just have to accept that it's all been sorted out and try to forget about it."

"Real life isn't like the television, where exciting things happen all the time." Susan muses sadly.

I wish we had more in common so I could be a closer friend.

Chapter 15

Eliza is still with her father in the squalid house he has inhabited for the past twenty years. I gather she has been trying to clean it, as quantities of soapy water have been sloshing around in the yard but little headway seems to have been made. I catch loud cries of incredulity coming from the open back door.

"How have you put up with it? It's a wonder you haven't died of food-poisoning. Look at the inside of this breadbin. It's black!"

Doris's funeral is at 10 o'clock today. A notice has appeared in the Deaths column of the local paper and several neighbours have said they will come. Terry and Fernando would have been among them but neither the Bank nor the supermarket allows time off for funerals of neighbours, only close relatives. Flowers have arrived at the undertakers and Susan will be in charge of tea and cakes in the church hall for those able to stay afterwards.

Sid has acquired a black suit from a charity shop and Eliza is wearing a navy-blue jacket and skirt. The only suitable garment I can find in my wardrobe is a long grey coat.

James is standing in the porch shaking hands with mourners. He gives Sid a comforting pat on the shoulder. I recall Veronica's RC funeral with its contingent of

Irish relatives and Father Damian's formal mass. This is a much simpler occasion but respectful nevertheless.

We sing 'Oh God our Help in Ages Past' and 'Abide with Me', with prayers in-between and James says nice things about Doris. Eliza stares ahead but Sid fumbles with a white handkerchief.

The undertakers drive the coffin and James, Sid and Eliza to the crematorium where a short ceremony is held. Soon they are back to join everyone in the church hall to be waited on by Susan. The cakes are eagerly eaten up and the giant teapot refilled. Rantersford people always do justice to food and drink, whatever the occasion. James waits while the ladies help Susan with the washing up.

"How is Gwen?" I ask.

He smiles. "Fine, thanks to you. You must come over for coffee one evening soon. She needs friends."

We all say goodbye and disperse.

Death, it can be said, has been properly dealt with.

How quickly Fridays come round. It's choir again already. I'm feeing rather tired but smarten myself up and walk up the hill to St. Stephen's for the second time today.

Gwen is there, looking a bit shy. Richard welcomes her back. Evidently she is one of his leading sopranos and her return will add tone to Stainer's Crucifixion.

I can't help noticing that on Sundays some of the members don't always take their place in the choir stalls. Richard insists on full attendance at practices but at services when the worshippers need leading, he doesn't record absentees.

Susan is critical. "Treats the church like his private concert hall," she has been heard to mutter, but most people are proud of St Stephen's musical reputation.

Keith is a few minutes late. My heart sinks. What if he doesn't come? To my intense relief he sidles in and gives me a nice smile.

"How did the funeral go?" he asks as we walk together down the hill after the practice. Pleased that he remembers my activities and is interested, I give him an account of Doris's send off.

"You must be tired," he says.

I wish I could interpret some of his comments. Lurking at the back of my mind is always the fear that he has guessed my age, and sees me as an older sister or, horror of horrors, a mother replacement. Why else would he presume I must be tired after a busy day?

"He's just concerned," says Maureen. "But if it worries you, why not ask him how old he is?"

We arrive at 16 Salvin Street. "Do you want to come in for a cup of something?" I ask tentatively. Maybe he's tired too and wants an early night.

"Yes please. We need to fix a day when you can come to me for a meal."

Good. I take out my key and we enter. Orlando wants his supper but I make him wait while I put the kettle on.

"How about next Tuesday, if that's convenient?" suggests Keith, stroking Orlando who responds politely. I make decaffeinated coffee on the assumption that the usual stuff will keep us awake.

Taking the bull by the horns, I say "There's something I'd like to ask you, Keith."

He looks alarmed. "Oh, what?"

"How old are you?"

Maureen cheers.

"Forty-eight," he answers. "I have always looked younger than I really am."

123

I laugh with relief. "So am I. I mean I'm also forty-eight and I've always looked younger than I am, too."

"Fancy that!" He suddenly seizes me in a bear-like hug, only releasing me when I show signs of breathlessness.

"Not that age would have made any difference," he adds. "I fancied you from the first.

The first? I try to recall the now-distant evening when a fair-haired man with glasses had come to join the choir and then thought better of it. I can't say I actually fancied him then, but I found him attractive. Why have I been so unsure of his feelings for me all this time?

"Your mother has a lot to answer for," observes know-all Maureen. "she damaged your self-confidence when you were a child."

We spend the rest of the evening sitting on my little settee, having what I can only describe as a heavy necking session. I surface at one point to ask, "Am I your little bit of fluff?"

"Certainly not," he replies, "You are my lady friend."

"How lovely," I murmur, "I'd like to be that."

Eventually Orlando jumps up beside me in a jealous rage. I look at my watch. "It's ten past twelve!"

Keith gropes for his glasses. "So it is. I must go. Are you OK?"

"Yes of course. Very OK." I fetch his coat and help him into it. At the front door he turns and gives me a last bear-hug before running off up the hill.

Eliza has done her best to persuade her father to return with her to Bridlington but he has refused.

"I was born and bred in Rantersford and I want to die here," he keeps repeating.

"If you stay in this house on your own, you'll die before your time," she argues. "It needs fumigating and selling to the council for a homeless family."

I'm not sure that I want to live next door to a homeless family but I can understand Eliza's concern. Without Doris to fight, he could degenerate into an aimless and dispirited old man. Dolly's company will not be enough.

"Why don't you just go for a little holiday," I say. "I can feed Dolly while you are away."

"Bridlington's full of holiday-makers," he snorts. "There's none born and bred there. They've all moved out." Strange logic but I understand how he sees it.

Terry and Fernando have invited me for tea on Sunday. I say I would like to come but must leave in time for Evensong at 6.30.

I am boiling an egg for my tea on Saturday after a long day of writing, when the phone rings. My hand is stiff and my eyes ache so I answer in a rather brusque manner.

"It's me," says Keith's voice. Are you all right?"

My heart leaps up. "Yes. Nice to hear from you. I've been earning my Enterprise Grant all day."

"Just thought you might like to have a little chat."

"Chat? What about?"

"Well, anything really."

How stupid of me to have forgotten that 'couples' keep in touch by exchanging light-hearted banter between face-to-face meetings. I try to picture him all alone in his sparely furnished room and ask if he is warm enough.

"No, not really. The heat from the gas-fire goes up and gets lost in the high ceiling."

Eager to help, I offer to let him have my spare electric radiator.

"That would make a difference if you're sure you can spare it. Not as nice as having you here to cuddle, of course."

I remember our session on the settee and let out a shameless giggle. He growls like a bear.

I tell him I'm going for tea with Terry and Fernando on Sunday but will be at Evensong.

"See you there then." He rings off.

By now my egg is very hard-boiled so I peel it and eat it with lettuce and salad cream.

I look forward to tea with Terry and Fernando. Should I suggest that Keith and I make up a foursome and go to a play or concert some time? Orlando makes it impossible for them to have a meet at Number 16, so hospitality can't be returned here. When the time comes, I go round with a bottle of Ribena. Men sometimes neglect their diet, and I know that blackcurrant juice is rich in vitamin C. I hand it over and Terry is pleased, as his mother always had some in the house.

"She set great store by it," he says, putting it in the pantry.

Fernando looks well and happy. He shows me a photo of his family in Portugal to whom he regularly sends a proportion of his wages. I don't expect Terry charges him much rent and Father Damian is no doubt keeping an eye on things.

With a possible outing in mind, I ask if they like music. Terry looks furtive, as if his mother might be listening, and confesses to being a Jazz fan.

Fernando asks what is Jazz and says he would like to hear some.

"They sometimes have Jazz concerts at the local Town Hall," I tell them. "I'll find out the date of the next one and we could get tickets. I have a friend who I am sure would like to come too."

Actually I don't know what Keith thinks of Jazz but hope he likes it, as I do myself. I had a brother who played the trumpet in a Trad Band, much to our mother's disapproval.

A dainty tea has been set out in the dining room, consisting of cucumber sandwiches, cheese scones and butter, apricot Swiss roll, and ice-cream and fruit salad. Veronica's approval is palpable. I wonder if Fernando gets cheap food from work. If so, his choice is excellent. The time goes pleasantly by till 6.15, when I tell them I must go to church as I sing in the choir. They are impressed.

"We go to the Roman Church on Sunday mornings," says Fernando, "but there is no fancy singing."

Terry smiles indulgently. "We do have music on the organ but no choir."

As I put on my coat I ask after Father Damian.

"He's fine," says Terry. "I have a lot to thank him for."

"I'm sure you have," I agree with a smile, and shake them both by the hand.

"See you again soon," they say in unison.

I hurry up the hill without needing to go back home first, and meet up with Keith as he approaches from his flat. We enter St Stephen's together and put on our robes in the vestry. Richard is pleased to see us as there is a rather small contingent at the ready. He hurries up into the organ loft and we pace to the stalls.

James preaches a good sermon about the wedding at Cana but I find my mind wandering. Should we go back to Keith's flat after the service or are we seeing too much of each other? The answer comes as we leave the church.

"I'll walk you back home," he says," but I won't come in tonight. I've got some letters to write."

"OK." I take his arm and tell him about my tea at Terry and Fernando's and ask him if he likes Jazz.

"I like Trad and Dixieland but not the very modern sort."

"Good, so do I."

We arrive outside Number 16. "See you on Tuesday, about 7.30."

"Fine. I'll bring the little electric fire."

"You mustn't carry it all that way. I'll hang on while you go inside and fetch it and I'll take it home now."

How considerate he is, or is he just feeling the cold and doesn't want to wait till Tuesday? I unplug the fire from my spare bedroom and hand it over. We exchange a rather clumsy embrace, with the fire getting in the way.

"Is it too hot not to cool down?" I ask, quoting Cole Porter.

He laughs. "No, I've got you under my skin."

Then he trots off up the hill.

Sid is so far making a good job of living on his own. He has confined most of his activities to the back part of the house. When the sun shines, he sits on his bench beside Dolly, drinking coffee or tinkering with bits of bicycle. Friends of his own age often join him in the yard but never go inside the house. I guess their wives have forbidden them to enter Doris' notorious kitchen in case they catch something. Presumably Sid has built up a resistance to most germs or he would have suc-cumbed by now. He occasionally takes a bag of clothes to the High Street launderette, which Doris never did. At last he has escaped being dripped on. Most days he puts his head over the fence and shouts "Are you all right?"

If he forgets to do this, I put my head over and shout the same question. Thus we are keeping an eye on each other.

As I pass the Town Hall on a shopping expedition, I pick up a leaflet about coming events. A well-known Jazz band is playing soon. I will show it to Keith and suggest that we get tickets for us and Terry and Fernando.

Chapter 16

On Tuesday evening there is a cold wind blowing and before I arrive at the flat it has rain in it.

"Come in quick," says Keith. "You must be all wet." He runs his hands down my back as if he is checking a farm animal. This I find stimulating rather than shocking, and I turn to give him a kiss.

He laughs. "Food first," he prompts. "It's all ready to put on the table. Come up."

We mount the staircase together and he takes my coat. The gas fire is on full and this, together with my little electric fire, makes the room lovely and warm. There seems to be more furniture than before – two comfy chairs instead of one, and a dining table with barley-sugar legs which expands when needed. This is now laid with matching cutlery on a William Morris cloth.

"This all looks very nice," I say enthusiastically. "Shall I sit up?" He draws one of the two dining chairs back with a flourish and pushes it forward as I lower myself.

"I have worked as a waiter as well as a nurse," he explains when he returns from the kitchen bearing a laden tray. Baked fish and mashed potatoes are neatly doled out on to heated plates, with broccoli in a separate dish. Parsley sauce steams from an antique jug and wine glasses glint beside a full bottle.

"This is better than a Rantersford eatery," Maureen remarks. It certainly is. There is even a folded serviette beside my plate.

The glasses are filled and we start to eat.

"Never marry a man with a weak stomach," was one of my mother's constant refrains. My poor father had contracted an obscure germ in Galipoli during World War One and was on a strict diet of milky solids. Thanks to my mother's meticulous care, he lived to be ninety-one. Keith shows no sign of stomach trouble as he works his way through the meal so I add a point in his favour, even though I would not necessarily have taken my mother's advice.

"So you've been a waiter, a male nurse and now you're working for Argos," I remark as he spoons out a fruit trifle.

"Yes. I'll have to find a better job. But it seemed to be the only thing available at the time."

"I couldn't find anything suitable when I moved here. I'm still on an Enterprise Grant."

"I presume your ex-husband pays you something? I had to give my wife a proportion of my income but she soon married again and then it stopped."

"Lucky you. My ex-husband doesn't believe in marriage so unless I get married again, he'll have to go on forking out."

"Are you considering remarriage," he asks bluntly.

"Careful!" whispers Maureen.

"Well, I like being on my own so far," I parry, "but if the right person came along, I might consider it."

"I find myself in the same position," he admits. "So much has happened lately, with my Mum dying and me moving here."

A wave of sympathy overcomes me and I get up from the table and lean over the back of his chair, stroking his hair and shoulders.

"That's nice," he says. "You have a kind of electric touch. Did you know that?"

I recall early boyfriends, one of whom had made the same observation. "I must be careful not to give you a lethal shock," I joke, returning to my trifle. Over coffee, I show him the publicity about the Jazz concert.

"That looks good. Shall we go?"

"I'd like to, and I think Terry and Fernando would like it too. Could we all go together and then you could meet them?"

"Yes. Shall I get four tickets?"

"If you let me pay half," I insist. "I've got enough for that."

"O.K." We clear the table and he stacks the washing up. "I'll do that before I go to bed."

With a kind of jolt, I snap out of the dream I had fallen into. I remind myself that soon we will have to go out into the cold windy darkness to 16 Salvin Street. Then he will come back to do the washing up while I feed Orlando.

"I see from my diary that it's the Peace Council leaflet blitz next Monday," I say briskly. "Let's hope the weather isn't too bad."

He groans. "Do we have to do it?"

"Yes," I say firmly. "It's something we both believe in."

"You're right. We'll wear our duffels."

"Like a proper couple," I add.

"Is that what you want?"

"Do you?"

For answer he gives me his warm bear-hug, and we collapse on to one of the armchairs.

Time passes pleasantly until Salvin Street calls and we rise up. The rain has stopped but the wind is stronger. We hold hands and battle down the hill.

"Anyone would think we both have mothers who would disapprove," he laughs, as I take out my key. I laugh too and give him a push. "Thanks for a lovely evening. See you at choir practice on Friday."

"And at the Peace Council on Monday," he responds. "Sleep well.

He turns and runs up the hill.

———

It's vicarage cleaning day again already. James is there when I arrive but he is due at the hospital soon.

"Gwen and I would like you to come for coffee one evening," he says. She smiles and nods.

"I'd like that," I say, trying to work out a free time in my head. Friday – choir, Sunday – church, Monday – Peace Council. I assume Saturday will be no good for James as he will be preparing his Sunday sermon.

"How about next Tuesday?" I suggest, hoping Keith hasn't decided that Tuesdays belong to us.

James flicks through his wall-diary.

"Fine. Is there someone you would like to bring?"

This is a happy surprise but I hesitate.

"Could I let you know on Sunday?" I feel I should consult Keith before committing him.

I realize that I haven't crossed paths with Lorna Johnson for quite a long while. I hope she isn't nursing a black-eye and having to keep a low profile.

I get on with my writing after lunch. The money from the grant is coming in regularly so I must keep my side of the bargain.

Before bed I phone Elizabeth, my elder daughter, who is studying Geography at Leeds University. She keeps in contact with me by letter, as does her sister Katherine, but I feel the need to hear a voice sometimes. One of the students who shares the flat answers, and I have to speak up above the sound of a party going on.

"Who? Liz? I'll get her."

I don't like the shortened Liz, and always insist on using the full beautiful-sounding Elizabeth. But she has every right to be called whatever she pleases.

"Hullo Mum. You O.K?" She sounds fine.

"Just wondering how things are going," I assure her. "Are you entertaining?"

"Yes, it's Tony's birthday."

I recall that Tony is the boyfriend of one of the sharers. "I won't keep you then. Any chance of you coming here soon?" I suddenly want to see her and maybe introduce her to Keith. What will she think of him?

"It's exams next week but after those I'll fix a weekend. Love you." And she rings off.

Should I phone Katherine? She might be in bed by now, or out with friends in Hull. I expect she goes under the name of Kate or Katy when she's not with me. Her father and I took such care with their names, though he wouldn't have them christened. He has no time for God.

I go to bed feeling depressed but wake up better. It's Friday tomorrow and I'll be seeing Keith at choir-practice.

Sid doesn't put his face over the fence to enquire after me, so I take my turn. There is no response which is unusual. I go down the garden path and peer over.

"Are you all right?" I shout. Dolly is on the doorstep waiting to be let in. After an interval Sid opens the door, much to Dolly's and my relief.

"What time is it?" he asks, rubbing his eyes.

"Eight o'clock," I tell him. "Did you have a late night?"

"Yes, I watched a programme about space travel on the tele. Very interesting."

I am glad he is able to please himself. Doris would never have let him watch that.

"Good. How's Eliza?"

"She's nagging me to go to Bridlington. I suppose I'll have to go just for a few days when it suits me." He shuts the door and I return to my kitchen.

Since I moved to Rantersford all those months ago, I have woven a kind of net spreading out over the Mill Hill area in which I have caught various people. I imagine a social gathering to which I invite them all - James and Gwen, Terry and Fernando, Father Damian, Sid, Doctor Flynn, Susan, Bright Skirt, Ruth the curate, The Peace Council, Richard the organist, the choir, the Women's Fellowship, Lorna Johnson, the cat lady.

Such a mixed bunch! Veronica and Doris are dead and gone and now Keith dominates the scene.

Is this what I want? I sigh and get out my exercise book. I seem to be living in two worlds, past and present. Where is the future?

Stainer's Crucifixion is nearly good enough for Richard but not quite. Now Gwen is back, the sopranos are stronger, but the tenors and basses lack power.

James has a lovely voice but presumably he will be too busy preparing the Easter services to come to rehearsals.

Richard has a suggestion. Could Gwen coach her husband in the evenings? She knows it all by heart, having sung it before in Wales. I imagine them sitting side by side in the vicarage, sharing a borrowed copy of the vocal score, maybe picking out the tunes on the piano.

When James comes to lock up after the rehearsal, Richard takes him on one side and puts the idea to him. At first he looks a bit doubtful, but when Gwen takes his arm and says, "Go on, we can do it," he agrees.

So that's sorted.

On the way home I tell Keith I'm worried about Lorna Johnson. She hasn't been to church for two weeks and she wasn't at the last Women's Fellowship meeting.

"Do you know her address?" Keith asks. "You could go round and see if she's ill."

"I'll ask Susan. She knows where everyone lives."

Then I dismiss the matter from my mind and concentrate on making us a quick cup of hot chocolate. Before we part, I remember to ask him if he would like to go with me for coffee at the vicarage on Tuesday. I do hope he will but don't want him to feel we are doing too much together.

"James and Gwen have invited me for coffee on Tuesday. They said if I would like to bring a friend, he would be very welcome."

There is a pause. "What did you say then?"

"I said I'd let them know on Sunday."

"Let them know if you want to take a friend, or if you can go then at all?"

I hadn't seen it this way. True, I had hesitated to suggest a Tuesday, but felt I shouldn't assume that Keith has reserved Tuesdays for our get-togethers.

"I accepted for me, but I didn't know whether or not you'd want to go with me."

There is another pause. He seems to be doing some quick thinking. "Can I let you know later? I'm not sure what I'll be doing then."

My heart sinks. It really does. I can feel it deep down somewhere near my guts. I have somehow annoyed him and he is getting his own back. But is he cross because I have used up a Tuesday for something other then him, or because I have presumed he would want to accompany me to a social occasion?

"Yes, of course," I say in a small voice. "Do you want any more cocoa?"

"No thanks, I must be off."

"See you on Sunday, then."

He grunts, and for the first time walks instead of runs up the hill. Orlando jumps up beside me and I stroke him in an absent-minded fashion.

Is this our first tiff? In books, lovers always have a quarrel and then make it up. But I've only got tomorrow, Saturday, to mend matters.

"Why should you do the mending?" Maureen asks. "Let him stew. He's being unreasonable. Go to James and Gwen's by yourself if he doesn't apologise."

I give the faithful Orlando some extra cat-food and get ready for bed, still puzzling over Keith's behaviour. I thought we understood each other so well. Why should he suddenly find fault with me? My ex-husband's moods used to switch without warning, but Keith seemed so steady till now. Perhaps he doesn't love me at all and has just been making use of me because he's lonely. Then I realize that in spite of my wide circle of friends, I am lonely myself. Without Keith I will have to start all over again trying to find my soul-mate. Tears of self-pity trickle down unchecked.

"Pull yourself together," snaps Maureen. "Men are all the same. Go to sleep and sort him out tomorrow."

I try to do her bidding but find it impossible. How can I get him back when I don't know why he has gone? Maybe he was just feeling fed up and will get in touch before the Sunday deadline. What if I hear nothing? Should I go to James and Gwen's on my own on Tuesday regardless, or write a letter and put it through his door. What do I say in the letter?

I twist and turn all night, much to Orlando's discomfort. Usually he sleeps on my feet, keeping us both warm, but tonight he jumps down in favour of the airing cupboard.

I get up at 6 o'clock and make a cup of tea. My face in the glass is awful. I certainly look my age today. I half hope Keith doesn't see me like this or he would go off me anyway.

The newspaper comes at six-thirty and I try to read the headlines. Disaster seems to be striking the world over but what does that matter to me? Keith is all that matters.

At seven-thirty the phone rings. What personal disaster is on its way? One of my girls must be ill. No one else would phone so early in the morning. I pick up the receiver, eyes tight shut. "

"Yes?"

"It's me, Keith." He sounds contrite. "Sorry to disturb you so early."

"That's O.K. I've been up for quite a while. I couldn't sleep."

"Neither could I."

"I hope you're not ill."

"No, are you?"

What a stupid conversation! Then we both start to speak at the same time, trying to apologise for an unspecified iniquity.

I win. "What did I do to annoy you last night?"

"Nothing. It was all my fault. I was suddenly incapable of thinking straight."

"Is everything getting too much," I ask, trying to understand. After all, he must have been under stress for some time, what with his mother dying and him moving house and getting a new job.

"Am I the last straw?"

"No indeed, you have lessened my load, not broken my back, but I do feel like a camel with the hump."

"Can you come round now and talk about it, or do you have to work on a Saturday?"

"Not till nine-thirty. I'll be with you in five minutes." He rings off.

Well, what does Maureen think of that? She makes no comment.

I wash my face and unlock the front door. He arrives out of breath, having run down the hill.

It seems he felt I was pushing him into a corner when I suggested we should both go to the vicarage. He likes being with me in a group or on our own, but the thought of us presenting ourselves as a couple makes him nervous. Almost as if we are going to see the vicar 'on business'.

I laugh. "I'm sure he wouldn't think that. He and his wife just want to do some entertaining now they are back together. I don't mind going on my own."

He glances at the table. "Have you had any break-fast?" I ask.

"I don't think I have," he admits. "I came here straight away."

I lay another place, and we both eat cornflakes and toast. I pretend we are a couple. I don't know what he thinks we are.

At nine-fifteen he sets of for the Argos warehouse and I do the washing up.

Chapter 17

While the choir is waiting for the service to begin on Sunday, I am able to let Gwen know that I will be coming on my own on Tuesday evening. She smiles and nods.

On Monday most members of the Peace Council turn up dutifully for instructions from Ruth. Bright Skirt has gone on strike in protest at the idea of a blitz, so we don't have to deal with her. A list has been made, covering most of the streets on the edge of the council estate where the housing is densest.

"I've given you Danethorpe Crescent," Ruth tells me and Keith. "It's rather rough but if you keep each other in sight you should be all right. "

"What does she mean by a bit rough?" I whisper to Keith as we clutch our bundles of leaflets. I know how to deal with rowdy teenagers but not their parents.

"Play it by ear," Keith advises. "If anyone gets awkward, shout and I'll come. You start on this side of the road and I'll do the other."

The street-lights are frequent so we don't have to grope and, if they are folded, the leaflets go into letter-boxes easily enough.

Occasionally someone will snatch from the inside, or a dog will fling itself at the door, barking wildly, but generally we keep up well. Danethorpe Crescent curves round in a wide semi-circle and ends up near where it starts, so we don't have to walk back on our tracks.

Ruth is standing on the corner. "Well done," she says. "The others are in the pub. All the leaflets have gone, so we can't do anything else until we get feedback."

Evidently most of the inhabitants of the area spend their evenings in the Vale Hotel, for we have job to squeeze inside. The others are struggling to get served at the bar, so I perch on a stool while Keith joins the scrum. He makes his way back in my direction bearing two full glasses of shandy, but I can tell that his eyes can't pick me out accurately so I stand up and wave, losing my stool to a crafty lady in a headscarf.

We are reunited and I gratefully take my drink. It's a long time since I've been in a pub with a man, or indeed without one.

Ruth circulates skilfully through the crowd, having a word here and there. She seems to know more people than just the Peace Council members but, as she is the local curate, I expect they are part of her flock. "Next meeting in two weeks," she shouts above the general hubbub. We nod and make our way out into the chilly night.

"That wasn't too bad, was it?" says Keith, taking my arm. "Can you walk home or shall we take a taxi?"

"I can walk if you continue to take my arm."

I can hardly believe that we have been through the trauma of Friday night and come out as if nothing has changed. But our relationship *has* changed, for better or worse. I'm not sure which.

While we are walking through the nearly deserted streets, he asks me if I have found out if Lorna Johnson is ill.

How awful of me! I had forgotten all about her.

"I'll ask Susan to come with me tomorrow afternoon. I don't like to go to the house on my own. Lorna's husband is an unknown quantity."

"I wouldn't have thought of you as being scared of anyone." He was really surprised.

"I'm not usually, but there's something scary about him. I've only spoken to him on the phone and he sounded nasty."

"Do you want me to come too?"

I laugh and squeeze his arm. "No thanks. Susan will protect me. I'll tell you what happens next time I see you."

"When will that be?"

"Well, I'll be cleaning the vicarage on Wednesday and it's choir practice on Friday. Quite a full week."

"How about Thursday?"

I can't resist playing his game. "I'm not sure what I'll be doing then. Can I let you know later?"

He stops suddenly by a street-light and drags me into a bear-hug. "No, I want to know now. We mustn't start that again, not ever."

I stroke his lovely thick hair, not caring if anyone sees. "No, we mustn't," I say. "Phone me on Thursday."

We continue to walk with our arms round each other and soon we are outside 16 Salvin Street.

"I won't come in now," he says, letting me go. "It's nearly eleven o'clock and you must be tired." He is his old considerate self again.

I give him a gentle kiss and let myself in. Orlando is pleased to see me and I relax with him on the settee before bed.

Susan is at home when I call. She is making marmalade, wearing the usual pinafore and curlers.

"Come in," she says enthusiastically. "I'll have to keep stirring but you can sit here."

I take the proffered stool and ask if she's seen Lorna lately.

"No, she wasn't at church on Sunday and I did wonder if she is ashamed to show herself now Gwen is back."

"I don't think shame would stop her going to church. She is a religious person and does a lot of work for the parish. More likely she is ill, and we should go round and ask after her."

"Maybe her husband has beaten her up and she's hiding the bruises."

Oh dear! Susan has been watching too much soap opera. But truth can be stranger than fiction, as they say.

"Do you know where the Johnsons live?" I ask. "I do think I ought to call round."

A fancy address book is unearthed from a cupboard under the telephone.

"Don't burn the marmalade," I warn in alarm.

She hands the book to me. "Look it up under J." she commands, violently stirring the preserving pan.

I find the address. "Twenty-nine Woodlea Close. Where's that?"

"It's on the posh estate. Quite a long walk. They've got a car, of course."

"We could go on a bus."

"O.K. I've got a bus-pass so it won't cost me anything. When should we go?"

"How about this afternoon, if you've finished the marmalade by then. We could meet at the bus station at two o'clock."

"Yes. I'll bring you a jar if it's cool enough."

I refuse a cup of tea as I don't want to interrupt her any further, and take my leave.

One sometimes has to burrow quite deep to find the kind hearts Rantersford people are renowned for.

There is a bus due at 2.15, so we don't have to wait long. Susan is wearing the tight red coat. A generous still-warm jar is handed over.

The ride is along a pleasant main road, with several diversions past detached residences. We get off at Woodlea Close and find Number 29. It is painted green, with a neat garden gate. I notice that the upstairs front room has curtains drawn across.

"There you are. I said she might be ill."

"It could be him who is ill", Susan suggests not wanting to be outdone.

We press the bell and wait. No-one comes so Susan presses it again. At last the door opens to reveal a large dark-haired man in a boiler-suit.

"Mr Johnson?" I ask uncertainly, for he looks more like a plumber than a householder.

He glares and nods.

"We have come to see Lorna," says Susan firmly. "She hasn't been to church lately and we are concerned about her."

A fleeting look of alarm crosses his face. "She's away," he snaps. "Gone to see her sister in Liverpool."

"Oh. Thank you," I say. "sorry to have bothered you."

He shuts the door.

As we close the garden gate, I look up at the bedroom window. The curtains twitch.

"She hasn't got a sister in Liverpool," says Susan excitedly. "He's locked her up in there."

It certainly seems suspicious. I feel suddenly cold. "We must tell someone," I say.

"Who?" Susan wants to know.

"I'm seeing the vicar this evening. He'll know what to do."

"Gwen won't like that," Susan objects. "You know how she feels."

"That's all been sorted out," I assure her. "They are quite friendly now."

Susan grunts. A bus going back to town draws up and we hurry to catch it.

I invite Susan in for a cup of tea when we reach Salvin Street, and she admires Orlando.

"I had a cat once," she says," but it got run over."

"He doesn't go out in the front," I say anxiously. "Just into the back garden."

We munch biscuits and wonder about Lorna.

"Do you think he's killed her and she's in the bedroom?"

"The curtains moved when we were leaving."

"He could have nipped upstairs quick and was checking we'd gone."

I clear my mind. "We'd better not say anything to anyone till I've seen the vicar this evening. If he thinks it necessary, he will call the police."

Susan wriggles excitedly in her chair. "It's like an Agatha Christie murder mystery," she breathes.

"No, they are fiction," I insist. "We mustn't let our imaginations carry us away."

She gets up and brushes crumbs from her coat. "I must be off but let me know what the vicar decides to do."

I promise and she bustles away.

Sid shouts over the fence while I am getting ready for the vicarage. "I'm going to Bridlington tomorrow. Can you feed Dolly?"

"How long for?"

"Only about a week. I'm not stopping there long." He hands over a stack of cat-food tins and a spare back-door key.

I don't know how Orlando will take this but I want to help. "Give Eliza my love and take care." I say.

"Bless you," he says unexpectedly. He at least did not beat his wife or lock her in the bedroom, even though he must have been sorely provoked.

I decide to wear my blue wool dress which suits my colouring and is nice and warm. The weather is still chilly in the evenings and the vicarage heating is inadequate.

Gwen had said 'about eight' so I set off at ten to. I don't mind that Keith is not going with me, as he has explained that he would feel uncomfortable, and I do understand why.

The light is on in the porch as I approach, and James opens the door before I quite reach it.

"We saw you coming," he says. "Come in."

He takes my coat and we go through to the sitting room where Gwen is waiting. They have gone to the trouble to make me welcome, with a bright fire in the grate and the standard lamp casting a soft glow.

"Sorry your friend couldn't come," Gwen says," but I'm sure we'll find plenty to talk about."

Actually I had been hoping to ask her about Dylan Thomas, who was born in Swansea, but I feel I ought to tackle the Lorna Johnson mystery first. Hoping that it won't upset either of them to be reminded of the recent trouble, I launch into an account of Susan and my visit to 29 Woodlea Close.

"Susan says Lorna doesn't have a sister in Liverpool, and we were sure she was somewhere in the house. We haven't seen her in church lately and, if she was ill or away, surely she would have let someone know."

Gwen is visibly concerned.

"I said to James only yesterday that I hadn't seen her for a while and wondered if she was all right."

"I should have phoned," admits James, "but I must confess that I didn't want to risk having to speak to her husband. He can be very disagreeable."

"He certainly can," I agree. "But is he capable of actually harming her?"

"The statistics show that seven women a month are killed by their partners in England and Wales," James announces. His job no doubt involves such matters.

"Goodness me," cries Gwen," We must do something."

James gets out of his chair and starts to walk up and down. I feel guilty for spoiling their sociable evening but am relieved that they are taking me seriously.

I take a deep breath. "It did occur to me that someone should contact Social Services or even the police."

"Yes," says Gwen firmly. "Someone should. How about it, James?"

"What? Now?"

"Perhaps tomorrow would be soon enough," I say. "The authorities will need to check up on his record, if he has one."

I already see Mr Johnson as a criminal of some kind, maybe a murderer or at least a bigamist. Susan's fantasies are infectious.

"Right. I'll do what needs to be done first thing tomorrow," says James briskly. "I don't need to go to the hospital this week, so I'll have time to spare. You'll be here to help Gwen, won't you Clare, as it's Wednesday."

"Yes of course."

"Maybe you'll need to be interviewed about your side of the story."

Gwen hurries into the kitchen to make the coffee, soon returning with a tray of sandwiches and wafer biscuits.

"This was supposed to be a pleasant social evening" she remarks sadly.

"Yes, let's try to forget about Lorna till tomorrow," says James, rubbing his hands.

I take a sandwich and start on about Dylan Thomas. Soon the conversation takes a more interesting turn. Gwen shares my love of literature, which pleases me, as no-one else in Rantersford I have met so far has been bookish. Should I tell them I am writing a School Librarian's diary?

"Yes, why not?" says Maureen. So I do. They are both intrigued and we talk on till ten o'clock.

"I'll take you home in the car," says James, fetching my coat. "It's very dark out there."

"I'll be all right," I protest, but he insists and I am glad.

Chapter 18

I sleep badly, my imagination working overtime. I shut my eyes and see Lorna tied to her bed, denied food and subjected to indescribable torture. Or she has been strangled and dismembered by her husband wearing a boiler suit.

By morning I am a nervous wreck and can't wait to get to the vicarage to check that James has taken action. I know I suggested Social Services or the police, but I've no idea how one contacts either. Would anyone take us seriously? Domestic violence is difficult to deal with, according to the newspapers, and not until a shocking case occurs, do details reach the public.

James is on the phone when I get there for my usual domestic duties but I don't expect much dusting and sweeping will be done this Wednesday.

A casual call to Pat of the Women's Fellowship, asking if she has heard from Lorna recently, is answered in the negative, but the hospital has given the contact number of a Social worker who specializes in domestic violence. She is called Gladys Grantley and is on her way.

"We'd better rehearse what we are going to say," advises Gwen. "She's got to understand that it's urgent."

Maureen suddenly comes on my wavelength.

"Maybe she has left him because he's so awful, and he doesn't want people to know."

No one has thought of that, but it could be the real explanation. Think how foolish we'd feel if it's true! I pretend I've thought of it and put the idea forward.

Both James and Gwen stop in their tracks. Then Gwen says that if Lorna is found safe and well, everyone will be thankful, but we must still check. Sensible lady, the vicar's wife.

Gladys Grantley is tall and grey-haired with a lined face, evidence I suppose of having been affected by her job, but is outwardly calm and business-like. She reveals that Colin Johnson of 29 Woodlea Close was reported to the police by his wife two years ago for attempting to strangle her. However, as is often the case, she withdrew the complaint before he could be arrested and nothing further has been heard from her.

"Oh dear," cries Gwen, "Poor Lorna. We knew he was unpleasant, but not that bad."

"How can we find out if she's there or not?" I ask.

"I can call and demand to be let in to talk to him, but I can't search the house," she explains. "If he refuses to co-operate, I will inform the police and they can take over."

"Do you need me to come with you?" asks James. "My collar might have a calming effect on him."

"It might enrage him," objects Gwen. "He doesn't approve of the Church."

"I'll be all right, thank you," Gladys assures us. "I'm used to this kind of thing. I'll go there now and let you know how he reacts."

She drives away in a red Ford car. James goes into his study and Gwen and I start on the housework.

"How utterly awful! To think we had no idea," murmurs Gwen.

I don't like to tell her that I knew he sometimes hit her, but I thought it was because he was jealous of James.

Maybe there is a simple explanation after all. She could be in Liverpool with a sister. Susan might have got it wrong about thinking one doesn't exist.

We finish the chores and have a cup of coffee but Gladys hasn't either reappeared or phoned, so I go home via Susan's house. She is eagerly awaiting news and seems disappointed that none is forthcoming, apart from the attempted strangling two years ago.

"He'll have bumped her off and buried her in the garden," she says. "You mark my words."

"What makes you so sure she hasn't a sister?" I ask.

"Well, she might have a sister, but not in Liverpool."

"She could have moved to Liverpool."

"No, everyone here knows everything about people's extended families, and no one ever moves to Liverpool. It's too far."

"What about Bridlington?" I ask, thinking of Sid's Eliza.

"Yes, I know of several people who have moved there."

Rantersford is certainly a strange place. I was just beginning to feel part of it, but now I'm having my doubts.

"I'll let you know when I hear anything but keep it all under your hat."

"Of course. I'm not a gossip. I just like solving mysteries."

I give her a kiss on the cheek and go home.

Gladys Grantley is back at the vicarage when I phone later. Colin Johnson had let her in and stuck firmly to the sister in Liverpool story. He said Lorna had packed a bag of clothes and toiletries and been gone when he got back from work a fortnight ago. There had been a quarrel and he had hit her. Her nose had bled, which explained some dried blood stains on the staircase. The curtains were drawn in the bedroom because he had told the next-door neighbour that she was ill in bed. He doesn't want people to know she has left him.

"Does Gladys believe him?" I ask.

The phone is handed to her by James, so she can speak to me directly. "His story seems plausible," she says "except for the sister in Liverpool. He couldn't or wouldn't give me her address. To me she doesn't sound like the sort of person who would simply go away without telling any of her friends."

"So what do you advise?" I ask.

"I'll get the police to follow it up as a missing person case, but they only search urgently for missing children, so we can't expect a big reaction."

"How about finding out if a single rail ticket for Liverpool was bought at the station on the date he says she left?" I ask, surprised at my own perception.

There is a pause and a dry chuckle.

"You should have been a detective. I'm only a social worker. See you again, maybe."

She hands the receiver back to James. He sounds calmer and tells me to try and dismiss pictures of violence form my mind.

"Lorna is probably safe and sound, staying with her sister and, when she feels able, will get in touch with someone at St Stephen's. We must all say a prayer for her."

Of course. Why didn't I think of doing that before? After all, we are supposed to believe in Guardian Angels who are ready to give protection to those who need it, when asked.

I make a very late lunch of scrambled egg and phone Keith. He has just got home from work.

"I thought I was supposed to be phoning you on Thursday," he says, "and it's still only Wednesday and you are phoning me. That makes me feel good."

"A lot has happened since Monday," I say, suddenly exhausted. "I'll tell you tomorrow. Come for supper. We don't have to wait till next Tuesday."

"O.K. Thanks. By the way, I got four tickets for the Jazz concert you mentioned. I'll bring them with me and we can ask your next-door Gays if they'd like to go with us."

For a moment I am indignant that he had referred to Terry and Fernando as Gays, and then I see no harm in it, as that is now the accepted term for homosexuals. I am glad he hasn't wanted details of Lorna's disappearance. I couldn't have gone over all that again. I say a heartfelt prayer for her and go early to bed.

I wake up at midnight, trying to remember something I have left undone. It suddenly comes to me. I haven't fed Sid's Dolly! He would have gone to Eliza's while I was preoccupied with Lorna, thinking I was looking after his pet. All those tins of cat food and his spare key are on a shelf in my pantry.

I struggle out of bed disturbing Orlando, who was happily snoozing on my feet, and grope my way downstairs. It is pitch dark outside, and I can hear the occasional motor going down the hill. Is she shut in the house or waiting on her doorstep? I open a tin and put a generous portion on a saucer. Will she come if I call?

To my relief, she jumps over the fence into my garden when I call her name, and follows me back inside the kitchen. She is no fool. I put the saucer down some distance from Orlando's feeding-place in case he gets jealous. Usually they are friendly with each other but this is different. He stalks in while I am pouring milk and stares at the intruder. She glances back at him over her shoulder and continues to eat.

"It's all right," I tell him, "she's only visiting."

They make a beautiful pair, he with his brilliant ginger fur and green eyes and she with her long tabby coat and eyes like burning amber.

"Be good," I say gently, and drag myself back upstairs.

In the morning they are both waiting to go out and return together to breakfast later.

I spend the day worrying about Lorna and trying to decide what to buy for Keith's supper. He must be told about the excitements of yesterday and maybe he will have a sensible opinion to offer, but for the life of me, I can't see beyond the facts.

An unhappily married middle-aged woman has disappeared. She may have gone to visit a relative in a distant town, or she may be lying murdered at an unknown location. Sooner or later, the answer will surface, but what can be done in the meantime?

I walk down to the supermarket for fish and see Fernando stocking up on the bread counter. This reminds me of the proposed visit to the Jazz concert, and I tell him I will call round this evening with tickets if he and Terry are interested. He is eager but, in the circumstances, I can't feel much enthusiasm.

Even buying fish seems inappropriate.

"Cheer up," says Maureen. "She's probably enjoying a holiday in Liverpool. It's a fine city. You've done all you can."

So I choose trout fillets and try to look forward to seeing Keith eat them. He always has a good appetite, but is nice and slim, not like some of the Rantersford men who slouch round the town. I wonder what, if anything, he sees in me.

As soon as he arrives, I suggest that we go next door to ask if Terry and Fernando want to go with us to the Jazz concert.

"Perhaps we ought to treat them," Keith says. "I could pay for myself and Fernando and you could pay for yourself and Terry."

This sounds a generous idea, but I don't know how it will be received. I think Terry assumed we would pay for ourselves but sit together.

We knock on the door of Number 17 and Fernando answers. I introduce Keith and they shake hands. Terry appears wearing an apron so I guess supper is being prepared.

"We won't come in," I say. "It's about the Jazz Concert on Saturday. Would you like to come with us?"

"Yes please," they both say. They seem to have developed a habit of answering questions in unison. That surely indicates true 'togetherness.'

"Good," says Keith, "I'll bring the tickets."

"Thank you," they chime. "See you later."

We return to Number 16.

"A nice pair," says Keith. "As we suggested going out together, I expect they think we will pay and then they will treat us next time."

"If there is a next time," I say to myself. I'm getting unsure of everything again.

"How's Lorna?" Keith asks.

The subject of Lorna Johnson's disappearance has taken over too much of my attention, and I must leave it to God and Gladys Grantley or it will obsess me.

"I'll tell you after supper," I say firmly. "How are things with you?"

"The job's getting a bit of a bore. I think I should go back to something more worthwhile, like nursing or social work."

"Not social work," I say hurriedly, reminded of Gladys's grey hair and lined face. "It's too stressful. Even being a waiter would be better."

"Oh no, that was worse than nursing."

"Best stay with Argos for a bit, then." I help him to more trout.

"This is delicious," he says appreciatively. "You are a good cook."

I think of my poor mother confined to preparing milky dishes for my Dad.

"Do you get indigestion?" I can't help asking, prompted by her advice about not marrying a man with a weak stomach.

"Never. Why do you ask?"

"Don't tell him," warns Maureen. "He'll think you want to marry him."

"But I do."

Maureen cuts out.

"No reason," I reply, getting up to fetch the pudding. I'm desperate to change the subject.

"I wonder if our Peace Council blitz has had any effect," I say.

"Not according to that Naomi. I bumped into her in town and she was very sneery about it."

"Naomi? Oh, I call her Bright Skirt because I can never remember her real name."

"Did you invent a name for me when we first met?" he wants to know.

"No, I didn't need to. Keith is easy. It suits you."

"I used to think of you as the lady with the nice legs," he confesses. And then he blushes.

I laugh in delight. At school I was 'the one with fair hair and glasses' but I don't tell him that.

"At school I was 'the one with fair hair and glasses,'" he says.

I am astonished. It is as if he had heard my thoughts and repeated them aloud. Of course, we do both still have fair hair, though I no longer need glasses, but nevertheless I find it strange.

"You were going to tell me about Lorna," he reminds me when we are washing up. I clear my throat.

"Well, it's a long story," I begin.

"Then let's wait until we're sitting down with a cup of coffee. I like a nice story, but not if it's *too* long."

"It isn't *nice* at all," I say miserably. "And it hasn't got an end yet."

"You mean it's a mystery?"

So I start at the beginning and go on till I get to the bit where James hands over to God.

"Heavens above!" he exclaims appropriately. "What a carry-on. You must be worried silly."

"I am that. It's driving me to distraction."

He puts his arms round me and strokes me like I stroke Orlando. It has a soothing effect.

"Did you ever work with animals?" I ask dreamily.

"I used to help my Dad when I was a boy. He taught me how to settle nervous horses."

"Well, if you can't face working as a nurse again, you would make an ideal hospital porter," I tell him. "They need to calm people down while they are being wheeled into the operating theatre. When I had my tonsils out, there was a lovely man who told me a story as he pushed me along through white corridors. I was only eight years old and he made me feel safe"

"I'll bear that in mind," he promises. "But what can we do about Lorna?"

"Nothing. As far as I can see, we must just wait until she surfaces, dead or alive. James says seven women a month are killed by their partners in England and Wales."

Keith shudders. "I don't understand how anyone could murder their partner. They are supposed to love each other."

"Perhaps her husband hasn't murdered her," I say. "Maybe he's telling the truth and she *has* gone to see her sister in Liverpool."

We stop thinking of her and concentrate on each other.

At eleven-thirty Keith scowls at his watch and says he must go.

"I wonder if there'll ever be no need for either of us to leave the warmth for a cold walk home," he says jokingly.

"I'm only just beginning to get used to living alone," I say. "And you have had even less time to yourself. We mustn't give up freedom before we are ready."

"Yes, you're right. Sometimes I'm lonely, and then I change and appreciate my own company."

I fetch his coat and help him on with it but he turns suddenly and traps me inside the lining.

"I love your bear-hugs," I murmur. "I know you won't eat me up."

He laughs and lets me go.

"Choir practice tomorrow," he reminds me. "I'll be glad when Easter comes and we can finish with Stainer's Crucifixion."

He goes out into the cold and sets off up the hill.

Chapter 19

Afraid she might not get her fair share, I try to feed Dolly and Orlando together. Sid hasn't contacted me since he went to Bridlington, and I am beginning to wonder if Eliza has persuaded him to desert his beloved Rantersford. But no, after exactly a week away, he is back, looking well but pleased to be home.

Dolly takes some time to forgive him for leaving her but, when I hand over the remaining tins, she returns to Number 15. Orlando misses her and jumps over the fence more often than he used to. Even cats need friends.

James is unlocking the choir vestry when I arrive for choir practice. No -one else is there yet so I ask if any news has come from Gladys. He shakes his head and tells me not to worry as no news is good news. I'm not so sure.

"What do we say when people start to ask why she isn't at church?" I want to know.

"We'll have to use the Liverpool story," he sighs. "It might be true."

Bernard stumps in, followed by Keith. They exchange glares. James pretends not to notice and goes back to the vicarage to relieve Gwen from phone-duty. Friday is a busy evening with parishioners ringing up to speak to the vicar, so he can't attend practices, but they are continuing their private duets.

"We are just about perfect," says Richard happily as we go through the music for Easter yet again. Devout Christians like him still regard Easter as more important than Christmas, so we do our best to please.

Easter is early this year. I recall how one childhood year, my March birthday fell on Good Friday. I felt guilty getting presents at such a sad time. My mother explained that Easter is a 'moveable feast', but if Jesus was born on December 25th, why couldn't he have died on, say, April 10th? Then we would know when to take our holidays.

The walk back down the hill is less chilly than usual, so spring must be on its way.

"Jazz concert tomorrow," says Keith as we approach Salvin Street.

"So it is. We've had a lot on lately, haven't we?"

"Too much?"

His tone is considerate, so I say "No, I'm looking forward to an outing with the boys. It starts at 7.30 so could you call for us about seven? Then we'll have plenty of time to find our seats. You've got the tickets, haven't you?"

He takes out his wallet. "Yes. Row F – 5,6,7,8." I give him my half of the money as agreed. Number 17 is in darkness so we have a quiet hug and part on the step.

The audience at the Rantersford theatre is mostly composed of grey-haired jazz enthusiasts left over from the fifties. Some have walking-sticks which get in the way, but all are eager to welcome a well-known band from long ago. The players also have grey hair, and some balance their instruments on their paunches. Only the drummer looks in good physical order and he is sitting down.

However, when they begin to play, their energy is amazing. The trumpet player is particularly good. As usual, he is the leader at whom the others glance for guidance. His name heads the group, which in this case consists of trumpet, clarinet, double bass, trombone, piano and drums. They take it in turns to do solos and the favourites get a short round of applause.

Terry and Fernando seem to be enjoying it, tapping their feet rhythmically. As I look along Row F, I notice they are holding hands, as indeed are Keith and I.

During the interval we cool down with ice creams paid for by Terry. No St Stephen's members are to be seen in the audience, as I suppose Jazz isn't their kind of music. My mother hated it and did her utmost to persuade my brother to 'give it up' as a bad habit like biting his nails. Both he and I suffered as a result of her disapproval, but that was a long time ago and we came through.

After the Jazzmen have played their last number to rapturous applause, we pick our way past slower members of the audience, who seem in no hurry to leave. They greet acquaintances only met up with on rare occasions such as this and stay to chat. Some approach members of the band to congratulate them on their performance. All very matey.

"Shall we go somewhere for a drink?" suggests Keith, but Terry looks at his watch and says Fernando must get up tomorrow for the early shift so they had better say no. I'm tired too, so am glad, and we set off for Salvin Street. When the terrace houses in Mill Hill are advertised for sale, it often says 'conveniently close to Town Centre' which is true. There is no need to catch a late bus to get home.

"Thank you very much," chorus the boys. "We like Jazz."

Then we all laugh and say goodnight. Keith comes in for what I think will be a quick hot drink.

"What would you like?" I ask, flourishing a teaspoon.

"Only you," he answers cryptically.

"What does that mean?"

"Can I stay the night?"

Is he too tired to run up the hill to his chilly flat and might as well sleep here, or does he want to make love to me? I can't tell.

He takes both my hands in his.

"Please."

"Say yes," commands Maureen. So I do, and we do, and it is wonderful.

Finding someone next to you in bed when you wake up can come as a shock if you have become unused to it. At first I freeze, and then relax in a delicious state of contentment. Keith's glasses are on the bedside table. I reach over and gently put them on his nose, so he will be able to see me clearly when he opens his eyes.

It is Sunday! I look at my watch and turn over in alarm. "Wake up," I say, giving Keith a shake. "We'll be late for church."

"Good God," he mumbles, "Surely we can miss it just for once."

"Of course you can," agrees Maureen. "You are in a state of mortal sin anyway."

I clutch my knees in distress. "What about the choir? Richard depends on us."

"It's our morning off," Keith says with conviction. "Come here."

He pulls me back down beneath the warm duvet and gives me a kiss.

"You look very detailed."

"You've got your glasses on," I tell him, giving in.

"So I have."

He takes them off again and puts them under the pillow. We snooze contentedly for another hour, and then I get up to make a pot of tea. Orlando is waiting crossly beside his empty saucer.

"Sorry," I say. "You don't come first this morning."

We have a lovely day together as a real couple, thinking only of ourselves. I even forget about Lorna Johnson, though she comes back into my mind as evening creeps on.

"Maybe she's surfaced in Liverpool, all safe and sound," says Keith when I mention her.

But I am not convinced.

"I suppose James would have let us know if the social worker has contacted him."

"James will have been too busy on a Sunday talking to God to do anything about it. You can phone first thing in the morning. Now I must be off to my lonely pad."

When he has gone, I tidy up the house and say a prayer for Lorna.

As if by a miracle, and I believe in miracles, the phone rings.

It is Gwen.

"Hope you and Keith are all right," she begins. "You weren't at church today."

I mumble an excuse, but she isn't scolding.

"Good news. Pat, the Women's Fellowship secretary, has had a picture postcard of Liverpool from Lorna. It says she has gone there to stay with a 'friend', not a sister, so part of his story could be true."

Relief floods over me.

"Thank you, God," I whisper. Then I switch to detective mode.

"Is it post-marked Liverpool and is it in her handwriting? He could be trying to put us off the scent."

Gwen laughs. "I don't think so. James has told Gladys Grantley and she is satisfied."

"Is there a Liverpool address on the card?"

"No. James thinks we will have to wait for her to make contact again. Then we can go on from there."

"Go on in what way?"

"Well, if he hits her again when she is living with him, she will have to be persuaded to divorce him or at least get him our of the house. Gladys can see to the ramifications of all that."

I must admit I am somewhat surprised at the ease with which Gwen is able to talk about other people's marital problems. Her own recent absence from the vicarage can be compared with Lorna's from 29 Woodlea Close. In Gwen's case there has been a happy uncomplicated return to normality, while poor Lorna faces possible rejection and distress. There are no children to worry about so I suppose things could be worse.

I wonder if the friend in Liverpool is wise and supportive. I don't think I could have managed my 'amicable' divorce without the help of Maureen.

As soon as Gwen rings off, I use the phone to contact Susan. She must be told about the postcard before she conjures up any more vivid scenarios. As expected, she is deflated by the news.

"So it won't be in the papers after all. Nothing exciting ever happens here."

Then she brightens up. "What if the friend is a he, not a she? Maybe she was having an affair and has run away to him."

"But she was in love with James," I protest. "I'm sure she wouldn't have been carrying on with someone in Liverpool at the same time."

Really! Susan sometimes goes too far.

She realizes she is being uncharitable and back-pedals.

"You're right. I should be glad she is safe. Do we say anything about it to anyone at St Stephen's or just keep quiet?"

"Keep quiet," I say firmly. "I'll tell you as soon as I know more."

We wish each other good night and I get ready for bed.

As I lie trying to relax, my mind goes up and down from joy when I think of Keith to misery when I think of poor Lorna.

Sleep eludes me completely. I can truthfully say that I do not sleep a wink. I get up at six, exhausted.

At eight Keith phones to say he must talk to me after work today. He sounds strangely cold and distant. I agree to come to his flat after tea and he rings off.

What can be wrong? We parted so happy on Sunday evening. Can he be regretting everything and wants us to part?

I hear my mother's voice warning me about 'going to the bad'. She has been dead for ten years, but I shall never be free of her. Maureen understands but cannot help.

The sherry bottle in the sideboard is nearly empty. I haven't needed to resort to it recently but now my willpower is weak and I tip the dregs into a glass and gulp them down. Then I embark on a thorough house clean. The vicarage has benefitted from my efforts lately, leaving me little energy for my own abode. I must distract my mind by physical activity.

On my third visit to the dustbin, Sid leans over the fence. He stares at me.

"Have you been ratting?" he asks.

"Ratting? What's that?"

"Doris would have said you look as if you've been through a hedge backwards," he translates.

I smooth my hair, which does feel rather untidy.

"No, just doing housework. How are you?"

I don't ask if he's been doing his housework as I'm sure he rarely sweeps or dusts.

"I'm fine but Dolly isn't well. She won't eat anything."

"Oh dear. Should you take her to the vet?"

"I haven't got anything to put her in. Does Orlando have a carrier I can borrow?"

"Yes, I'll find it. You'll need to phone the vet to make an appointment."

"I expect they charge a lot."

"Yes, but she's worth it, isn't she?"

"She's my best mate," he admits.

I go to look for Orlando's carrier. It's a posh affair with a complicated opening and closing mechanism. He hates it.

"It's all right," I assure him. "It's not for you, it's for your friend."

But he doesn't trust me and hides under the bed.

"They'll see her at three o'clock today. I'll book a taxi," Sid reports as I hand the carrier over. He's always sensible in an emergency.

I hope Dolly doesn't have to be bumped off. Now I've got something more to worry about. What with Lorna and Keith, I could do without a sick cat.

I take a quick bath, wash my air and feel better. A picture of a young Sid with a small terrier dog comes into my mind. He gets in a mess setting it on to rats in a barn. This explains the term 'ratting'. I live and learn.

I wonder if I should offer to go with Sid to the vet in case the worst is diagnosed but decide against it.

At 3.30 he is back with an empty carrier!

But no, the vet is keeping her in while she is treated for a hair ball.

"Her innards are stopped up with fur," he explains. "I should have been brushing her. I'll use Doris's old hairbrush on her when I get her back."

So that's a relief.

Now I must pluck up courage to go round to Keith's flat. As the sherry bottle is empty, I pray for strength.

Chapter 20

Somehow I get up the hill and then up the grand staircase.

Keith opens the door as soon as I knock.

"Clare, you look awful," he exclaims. "What's the matter?"

God's strength deserts me and I burst into tears. Full of alarm, he puts his arms round me and pulls me inside.

"Tell me, has someone died?"

I cling like the proverbial limpet so he has to half-carry me to a chair.

"Don't leave me," I beg, like a forsaken maiden. "I couldn't bear it."

"I'm not leaving you," he says soothingly, using his horse-calming technique. "It's all right. I love you."

Have I heard him right? He says it again, sensing my incredulity. "And I want you to love me more."

"I do," I whisper. "I thought you were fed up with me."

He pats my bottom. "Silly girl." He's still giving me the hysterical horse treatment so I sit up and blow my nose.

"You said you wanted to talk to me," I explain," and you sounded cross."

"I was trying to sound serious. I didn't want you to think I was taking advantage."

"I never think that, but sometimes I don't know what you have on your mind."

"I have you on my mind when we are apart, and you on the rest of me when we are together."

It's like trying to solve a riddle. Do I have an answer?

"Does that mean we are a couple?" I ask, hoping that I have got it right at last.

"A couple of what?"

"There you go," I say, "you're doing it again."

"Well, I've always thought it's an odd word to use about people. 'Lover is a bit strong, though that's what we are, aren't we?"

I nod. "But I can't introduce you to anyone by saying, "This is Keith, my lover, can I?"

"You could but they might be shocked. 'Fiancé' is old-fashioned, and 'intended' is even more so. It's all very difficult."

He runs his hand through his lovely thick hair.

"I seem to remember that I was 'engaged' before I got married," I say tentatively.

"That sounds like a toilet on a train."

We laugh together.

"I was 'going out' with my wife."

"That sounds like a dud firework."

"It was!"

We laugh again.

"Never mind. As long as we know what we are, that's all that matters."

But do we? The word marriage hasn't been uttered. I sigh and stand up.

"It's supper time. Have you got anything in the house?"

"Not anything special. Let's go out for a meal. Let's celebrate."

Another questionable word. What exactly would we be celebrating? But I say, "Yes, that would be nice." and we put on out coats and go down to the Spotted Dog.

There we see Bernard from the choir sitting at a table with Angela, the leading Alto. We smile and find a seat as far away as possible.

"So he's found someone decent at last," Keith remarks in an undertone.

"That's a relief," I say. "I'm glad. I wonder how he describes her when introduced."

We jokingly make up a list of possible epithets over salmon and cucumber sandwiches and white wine.

I want to ask him if he's done anything about finding a more interesting job, but Maureen says "Better not. He'll think you are investing in him."

As it happens, I don't have to risk it as he comes up with the subject himself.

"The Argos job is badly paid and very dull. I think I'll try the NHS, like you suggested."

I squeeze his hand in approval but make no comment.

"The flat costs more than I can really afford," he admits. "It's convenient, and I like it, and of course I have no travel expenses, but the rent is more than we paid for the village council house."

"My in-laws rented a council house," I recall. "When they wanted to move, they managed to swap with another authority tenant."

"Sounds a sensible rule, but I don't think anyone in Rantersford would have wanted to swap with someone in a village with no regular public transport."

"Probably not," I agree.

"I'd better go back now," He sighs. "I've left some washing in the shared machine."

I long to do his washing and cook his meals. Then I remember how certain I had been about being better on my own, and confusion sets in again.

Bernard and Angela have disappeared, but I feel sure their behaviour is beyond reproach. How bored I would have been with him.

"Sid's cat is spending the night at the vet's," I say as we walk towards Salvin Street. "She's got a hair-ball."

"A what?"

"Cats swallow a lot of fur when they wash themselves. Sometimes it gets stuck in their guts."

"How disgusting," shudders Keith. "Humans are so fortunate to have discovered soap and water."

Then we laugh uncontrollably at the picture of us licking ourselves clean.

"I could lick you and you could lick me," gasps Keith. "That would make it a bit more acceptable."

Numbers 15 and 17 are both in darkness.

"I won't come in tonight," he says quietly. "I wonder if Terry and Fernando will ask us both round sometime."

"I'm sure they will. They want to be our friends."

"See you at choir on Friday," we say in unison.

He gives me a bear-hug and runs up the hill while I let myself into Number 16.

I hurry round to the vicarage on Wednesday, hoping to catch James before he goes on duty at the hospital, anxious to hear news of Lorna. He and Gwen have just finished their breakfast and the postman comes while I am washing up.

"Ah," cries Gwen, waving a white envelope. "Postmark Liverpool."

I turn from the sink, and James looks over his wife's shoulder as she rips it open.

"Dear Gwen," she reads aloud, "I'm very sorry that it has taken me so long to contact you and James, but I had to escape from Rantersford and lie low. Everything got too much, so I packed a bag while Colin was at work and came to stay with my good friend Margaret in Liverpool. She looked after me until I felt well enough to sort things out, though I fear my unexplained absence might have worried my friends at home."

"I should say it did," interrupts James indignantly.

"Anyway, Margaret and I plan to come to Rantersford this Saturday, staying at the Queen's Hotel. We will phone you when we arrive. Very best wishes, Lorna."

"Well, the mystery is solved," says James, putting on his coat. "She seems to have forgotten that preparations for Easter will be occupying us next week, not to mention Stainer's Crucifixion on Palm Sunday. Gladys Grantley will have to sort her out."

Gwen looks at the letter again. "She doesn't say if Colin knows she is coming."

"If she's staying at the Queen's Hotel, it looks as if she doesn't want to go back to Woodlea Close while he's there," I observe.

Gwen's face takes on an anxious expression.

"She and her friend Margaret won't want to stay at the hotel for long. It's very expensive."

We all realize that the situation, although now no longer crucial, is still full of problems.

"I must be off to comfort the sick," says James, and away he goes.

"Gladys will know what to do," says Gwen.

I am not so sure. A homeless child can be taken into temporary care, but adults are a different matter.

"I don't think Lorna would like living in a Women's Refuge. There's one near the railway station but it is heavily disguised in case angry partners attack it."

"How awful. I wonder if anyone in the Women's Fellowship would put them up for a few days."

"What about Pat? "I say. "She works with Lorna on the committee and she was the one to get the postcard."

"That was just to sort out an item on the next agenda. It didn't explain her absence. I'll phone Gladys now."

Mindful of my job, I collect the vacuum cleaner and start on the living room floor.

Gladys is of the opinion that we should wait till Saturday when she will interview Lorna and find out how she feels about returning to Colin. Last time the subject of domestic violence arose she decided to give things another go and, if she reacts the same way again, Colin will be contacted about an anger-management course and told he must stick to the rules. She would then return to Woodlea Close under the protection of Social Services.

If, on the other hand, she has had enough of him, she will have to fight to get an exclusion order on him so she can return to the house. He must find somewhere else to live. Then divorce would follow.

Gwen and I stare at each other in horror.

My mind flashes back to my own divorce which, although distressing, had never involved physical abuse, and been amicably completed after two years separation. Poor Lorna is in a far worse position.

"Let's hope this friend Margaret is a tower of strength," I remark. "Is there an address in Liverpool on the letter?"

"No, just the date."

"So nothing can be done till she phones from the Queen's Hotel on Saturday."

Gwen frowns.

"James will be very busy with Holy Week services leading to Easter Day, and of course, there's Stainer's Crucifixion on Palm Sunday."

We both sigh deeply and get on with the chores.

I report to Susan on my way home. She promises to keep quiet but is full of sympathy for the once scorned Lorna.

"Where will she live if she can't go back to that awful man? I could have her here. I've got a spare bedroom but I don't expect she'd like that. It's not posh."

No indeed, but it is a kind thought.

"Don't worry," I say. "She could always go back to Liverpool with her friend Margaret until everything is sorted."

A letter from my daughter Elizabeth is lying on the mat. She suggests that she and Katherine come to visit me after Easter. Normally this would be a cause for rejoicing but at the moment it is one more stumbling block.

What will they think of Keith? How much about the relationship shall I tell them?

At least they won't be here during the Easter holiday itself. I won't be so busy with church events later and will be able to take them on trips to stately homes in the area. Even to the seaside. Maybe the boys next door could come too, as long as they don't see them as romantic possibilities. My mind flutters like a moth in a net.

Dolly is home from the vet. The cat-carrier is returned to its place in the loft, much to Orlando's relief. Sid reports that the bill is a disgrace.

"People spend more on their pets than on their children," he complains.

"There should be an Animals' Health Service," I agree. "Have they made her better?"

"She's eating again, and I'm brushing her like they said."

"That's all right then. Are you doing anything at Easter? My girls are coming here the week after."

"Eliza wants me to go up there again, but I'd rather not. It's too much fuss."

"There's a lot going on at church," I tell him. "The choir is doing a concert on Palm Sunday. Do you want to go to that?"

"I'll think about it," he says doubtfully.

Tomorrow I must spend all day on my book. If I can concentrate my mind on it, that is.

There is no Women's Fellowship meeting this month, which means that Lorna's absence won't be so obvious as it might have been, but rumours will no doubt start to circulate soon.

After the final choir rehearsal, I go back with Keith to his flat. He is genuinely worried about me, which is gratifying.

"I hope you're not getting het up about Lorna phoning the vicarage tomorrow," he says anxiously. "The Social Services should take over."

"Yes, but I want to know what she says. James and Gwen will let me know just in case we need to help in any way."

"You are too kind." He gives me a nice hug.

"By the way, both my daughters want to visit after Easter." I tell him.

There is a pause, during which I hold my breath.

"That will be nice for you," he says eventually.

"I want it to be nice for you as well."

"I'm not sure what they will think of me. Maybe they'll suspect me of exploiting you."

"Exploiting me? How do you mean?"

"Well, you've bought your own house and I'm only renting."

"But I haven't got a proper job and you are working. I could be exploiting you."

It comes to me that someone, maybe his ex-wife or even his mother, belittled him as my own mother did me, and it has affected him deeply.

Risking rejection, I put my arms round him and hold him tight.

I feel him relax.

"I don't care what anyone else thinks. I think you are wonderful. I find you overwhelmingly attractive and I miss you when you aren't there. So too bad if my daughters don't approve. They will have to lump it."

"Then I'll do my best to charm them," he promises. "If they resemble you, I'll have nothing to worry about."

We have a nice cuddle and he makes a cup of tea.

"It's Peace Council on Monday, isn't it," I remind him.

He groans. "I suppose we'll have to go. Such a lot of gadding about."

"It's not gadding. We're putting the world right. I've written a poem about it."

"Really? You'll have to read it to me."

"I will, but not now. I must be off." I put on my coat.

"Do you have to go?"

"Yes, but you needn't see me home. It's not very late and you must be tired."

"Rubbish. A nasty man might jump out on you. When I've got clean sheets on the bed, I hope you'll stay."

"Yes, of course." I am tempted to take my coat off again but exercise control as I don't want our love-making to become automatic.

We pass Keith's landlady on the stairs and she wishes us goodnight.

"I'll lock the door when I get back," Keith tells her. "I won't be long."

"Right. Thanks." She smiles at me approvingly and I smile virtuously back. I'm glad I'm not staying the night.

Chapter 21

All things considered, I think it would be best if pressure could be put on Colin to agree to attend marriage guidance sessions and for Lorna to give him one more chance. I know domestic violence is on the increase but the powers that be are dealing with it. I remember Sid's battle with Doris in the yard and their continual disharmony. Could Keith and myself ever find ourselves reduced to such behaviour?

The phone rings at eleven o'clock on Saturday. Gwen says Lorna and Margaret have arrived at the Queen's Hotel and she will call for me in the vicarage car. We won't contact Gladys Grantley until we've spoken to Lorna.

The car park at the hotel is filling up but we find a place and enter the imposing door.

Lorna and Margaret are seated on a settee in the foyer drinking coffee. Two more cups are ordered but this isn't the place for a private conversation, so we transfer to their room on the first floor where the décor is, by my standards, luxurious, with bedside lamps and a drinks-fridge. I wonder if Keith and I will ever stay in a room like this.

Margaret seems quite at home here and suggests that we sit on the sides of the twin beds. This we do. Lorna takes a deep breath and apologises for putting us to any trouble on her account.

"That's all right," Gwen assures her. "We understand that you and Colin have been going through a bad patch."

At this Margaret snorts indignantly. "It's been a very big bad patch. Colin has always been a bully."

I join in. "What does Lorna want?" I ask. "A social worker has interviewed Colin and she thinks that if he agrees to being supervised and takes an anger-management course, Lorna might feel able to give him another chance. He seems genuinely sorry for his abusive behaviour but has difficulty controlling himself."

"Who involved a social worker?" Margaret wants to know. She is very protective of Lorna.

"My husband was worried about her unexplained disappearance," says Gwen," so we got in touch with Social Services. The police have also been involved."

"Oh dear," gasps Lorna, "I didn't want all this to happen."

"Surely you must have realized that people would speculate," I say sharply. "You were classed as a missing person. The social worker on the case is due here expecting you to discuss with her how you view the matter, so she can act on your behalf."

I can hear myself talking like a bossy official but Lorna must be made to co-operate. I suspect that her friend Margaret has a strong influence and will not easily relinquish her hold.

"You mean *now*?" asks Lorna.

"Yes, it really is essential."

Gwen phones Gladys who comes at once. She sizes up the situation, silences Margaret with a single look and concentrates on Lorna.

"It's up to you," she says. "If you decide you can't return to your home while your husband is there, you will have to prove that he is physically abusive and get an exclusion order on him. This usually leads to divorce. On the other hand, you could return to the house and I will arrange to have him supervised. If he hits you again, you must call the police, who will remove him."

Poor Lorna is very upset. Margaret puts an arm round her.

"You could always come back to Liverpool with me," she says, defying Gladys.

We all wait while Lorna battles with her innermost thoughts. She shuts her eyes to cut off outside influences. It's like a still from a silent film. Then she opens up.

"I'll go back. I must have someone to love."

At this Margaret is highly indignant.

"I love you. We all love you. He's not worth loving."

"But he says he loves me, even if he can't show it."

Gladys sighs.

"They nearly all say that, but maybe it will work if he knows you are protected, which you will be. I'll be off now. Don't go home till tomorrow as I have to interview him again."

She shuts her briefcase and hurries away. What a life!

Margaret silently opens the drinks-cupboard and takes out four glasses. "I'm having a whisky. Help yourselves."

Gwen chooses a bitter-lemon, Lorna has a vodka and I take a brandy. Then we all feel better.

"We'll stay here tonight," says Margaret. "I'll drive her to Woodlea Close tomorrow."

"I'll phone Colin before then," adds Lorna. "Thank you all for helping me. I wouldn't have managed on my own."

She insists on giving us all an affectionate hug, and Gwen and I depart.

"Well I never," breathes Gwen when we reach the car park. "Who would have thought it?"

I myself am not surprised but I fear for Lorna.

"Please God, deliver her from evil," I plead silently. Surely He will listen.

James takes our news philosophically. "We must keep an eye on her. Friends could arrange to call at the house regularly. Perhaps the W F committee should be made aware of the position."

It pleases me that Gwen shows no jealousy when her husband speaks of Lorna. She is secure in his love for her, which is the ideal for a happy marriage.

I wonder if my own basic insecurity drove my husband away. Am I better on my own? Keith is very different from my girls' father, so hopefully we are more suited. Then I remind myself that marriage has not yet been discussed, and might never be.

"We'd better have fish and chips for lunch," says Gwen. "It's nearly one o'clock and a proper meal will take too long to cook."

James is so lucky to have his practical domestic wife back. He chooses a clean carrier bag.

"Shall I get three portions?" he asks. "You're very welcome to join us."

"No thanks. I'm having a tin of soup," I say, as I don't fancy a big meal. He seems reluctant to let me go.

"Are you ready for Stainer's Crucifixion tomorrow evening?" he asks as we draw up outside 16 Salvin Street.

I can hardly believe it's so close. "Richard seems to think we all are," I reply.

After my tinned soup, I remember that I had asked Sid if he might like to go to the concert.

I call over the fence. "Do you want to go to church tomorrow to hear the choir?"

It seems that he does. "People on their own should get out once in a while," he says, as if repeating what someone has told him. I wonder if he and Doris used to go to the cinema or to a dance in their early days.

"It starts at half-past six, but I have to get there early to put on my robe. I'll look out for you."

"Robe? It sounds like a coronation."

"No it's just so we all look alike. A sort of uniform."

He grunts and looks puzzled. Doris's funeral was probably one of the few occasions when he has been inside a church.

"I'm sure you'll like it. You don't have to pay."

Then I wonder if Terry and Fernando should be told about it, so I write a message on a fancy notelet, informing them of the details.

Perhaps we could all go for a drink together afterwards. My mind skids around, overtired by recent events.

I phone Keith. His number is engaged but no sooner have I put my receiver down again than it rings, making me jump.

"Hullo" says his voice. "The phone seems to be behaving strangely. I just rang you and you were engaged."

I laugh. "Better on the phone than a train toilet."

Quick on the uptake, he laughs as well, reminded of our previous conversation.

"I'm wondering what happened at the Queen's Hotel."

I recount the whole episode, and he isn't sure that Lorna is doing the right thing by returning to Colin.

"He sounds a nasty piece of work, and that sort like beating people up. They can't help it."

"We'll have to keep an eye on her and say a prayer."

"Talking of prayer, it's Stainer's Crucifixion tomorrow, isn't it? What time do we have to be there?"

"About six o'clock. It starts at half-past. Sid will be coming, and I've mentioned it to Terry and Fernando."

To my surprise he suggests that we could all go round to his flat for a cup of coffee afterwards.

I smile to myself. "Then you wouldn't have to walk me home down the hill because I'd have three strong men for protection."

"It seems a long time since I had you to myself," he complains.

"If Peace Council finishes early on Monday night, you could have me afterwards."

"You make yourself sound like a dose of indigestion mixture, which is what I'll need after wrangling with Naomi."

I feel guilty at having brushed aside Bright Skirt's efforts at friendship.

"You need every side in an argument. She has her place."

"O.K. As long as her place isn't too close to me."

"Who is paying for this phone call?" I ask. "It's been going on rather a long time."

"I think it's me. But I don't mind. I got my pay packet today."

"Have you decided to stay at Argos after all?"

"For the time being. I can't seem to get round to applying to the NHS."

"O.K. There will be less on after Easter."

"Will that include you?"

"How do you mean?"

"Having less on."

I am not as quick on the uptake as he is, but I get it eventually.

"I dress according to the weather," I say primly. Then, relenting, I add "and that will be getting warmer as time goes on."

"Good. Meet me at the church."

I ring off. What a silly conversation. Is he teasing me?

Orlando wants his supper and so do I.

"You don't seem to have a hair-ball," I say to him as I give him a larger than usual helping of Topcat. After scrambled egg on toast I go to bed early, hoping I'll sleep well and thus rest my voice for Richard tomorrow.

During choir rehearsals, we have been guided hypnotically by Richard's hands. His power comes from a passionate love of music, and he has the ability to transfer this with remarkable effect. He has got us to the point where we will make no mistake, hit no wrong note. He has confidence in us and we in him.

So by six-thirty we are all in our places, facing a full church. People have come from far and wide, sure of an uplifting experience. Many of them are not regular members of the congregation. Indeed, I can pick out only a few familiar faces. To my pleasant surprise,

Lorna Johnson's is one of those. Beside her sits a big man who I had last seen in a boiler-suit. Now he wears a smart jacket and tie and a calm expression.

The organ starts its introduction and we all stand up.

Stainer's Crucifixion is not comparable to Handel's Messiah. It was written for ordinary people to sing, less demanding but with some dramatic tunes. It concentrates on the Good Friday story, and as it progresses it becomes deeply affecting.

There is no interval, and at the end the applause starts quietly and increases in volume as people show their appreciation. Some are wiping their eyes and blowing their noses. Richard comes down from the organ loft and we file out solemnly and hang up our robes in the vestry.

"Well done," he says, very pleased.

I know we should have been singing for God but we were really doing it for our choir-master.

Keith and I go to look for Sid and Terry and Fernando, all of whom are lingering in the porch.

"Please come back for a hot drink to my place," says Keith. "It's not far."

Terry and Fernando are pleased to accept the invitation but Sid says "No thank you. I must get home."

No special reason given but I think he feels out of place. Nevertheless he enjoyed the music and thanked me for telling him about it.

"See you later then," I say, patting his arm. He sets off down the hill, and the rest of us walk along to Keith's flat.

"Did I spy Lorna and her abusive husband in the audience?" Keith mutters as we remove our coats.

"You did," I reply. "That's surely a good sign."

"It's probably only a gesture for public consumption. You'll have to keep an eye on him."

Fernando is staring round at the high ceiling.

"This is a big house," he says.

"Keith only lives in part of it," Terry explains. "It's called a flat."

"A flat what?"

We laugh kindly. English must be fiendishly difficult to learn, with all its double meanings.

The kettle boils and I make a big pot of coffee. By now I know where things are, which drops a hint to the boys that I have been here before. They will surely view us as a 'couple', whatever the Portuguese word is for that.

The conversation dwells on jobs, which subject men seem to be obsessed with. When introduced, I often find that men break the ice by telling each other what work they do. The unemployed must have an embarrassing social life.

Fernando seems happy at the supermarket, unlike Keith who complains about Argos and speaks of the desire for a change. Terry is moderately faithful to the Bank, saying that the pay is good. I pour more coffee and open a packet of biscuits. We munch away and I start to nod off.

"We must go," says Terry, sensing my fatigue.

"You don't need to take me home," I tell Keith, as previously planned. "I'll be safe with my next-door neighbours."

"Right," Keith agrees. "I'll call for you tomorrow for the Peace Council meeting."

We all wish him goodnight and spill on to the street. It feels strange not to be giving him a hug, but hands are shaken and we set off.

"What is the Peace Council?" Fernando wants to know. "Are we at war?"

Terry reassures him. "No, it's a group which meets to prevent wars."

"Good. I don't like the idea of a war."

Stories of the Spanish civil war must have affected neighbouring Portugal's school children.

They wait outside until I have unlocked my front door, and then we wish one another goodnight, and I go inside.

Orlando is waiting in the front room.

"It's a good job they didn't come inside with you here," I tell him, remembering the asthma catastrophe. Suddenly exhausted, I grope my way upstairs and fall into bed.

Chapter 22

Too much seems to be happening in quick succession. Never a day goes by without an activity or appointment. Today it's Peace Council. I tick it off on my wall-calendar. I am tempted to blame Maureen for advising me to join things and make new friends.

"Ungrateful creature," she flashes. "Where would you be without me?"

Now I must write to Elizabeth and Katherine to fix their visit after Easter. They'll have to share the spare bedroom or I could sleep downstairs with Orlando.

I open a packet of Easter cards and add "Let me know when you are coming to see me," under an affectionate greeting. This saves time and puts the ball in their court.

On the way to the main Post Office, I buy four Easter eggs – one for Keith, one for Susan and one for each of the girls. I'll have to save theirs as they would get squashed in the post.

The shops are full of chocolate novelties and hot-cross buns. Religion doesn't get much of a mention. I hum one of Stainer's tuneful bits and say a prayer for Lorna. Then I find my exercise book and get on with the school librarian's diary.

—⁓—

The usual people, plus a few new ones, have assembled at the Friends' Meeting House for the Peace Council meeting. I get the chance to have a few words with Bright Skirt before Keith arrives. One of her five cats has gone blind or she thinks it has.

"He keeps bumping into things and can't find his saucer of food," she tells me. "But his eyes don't look cloudy or sore."

"Perhaps he needs to go to the vet."

She snorts. "I can't afford a vet's bill and there isn't a PDSA in Rantersford."

It's almost as if she hopes I will offer to pay. Her poverty is her chief subject of conversation, which is what annoys Keith, and is beginning to annoy me.

Ruth appears just before 7.30, looking tired. Her job as curate of the church on the council estate must be a demanding one, but she still makes time to chair the meetings and organize activities. She puts a sheaf of papers on the top table and we obediently take our places on the rows of chairs. I sidle away from Bright Skirt and sit near the door next to Keith. He looks tired as well, though pleased to see me. He squeezes my hand.

"Hullo everybody," says Ruth. "I'm pleased to say that we have some new prospective members with us this evening. I think it would be best if they introduced themselves and tell us why they have come."

She consults a list and calls out a name. "Tom Arbuthnot."

A stout middle-aged man puts up his had like a boy at school, eager to give correct answers. "I've been a member of CND from the beginning, going on marches and protests. But that sort of thing is a bit out of date, and I've joined the Campaign Against the Arms Trade which covers the production and sale of all sorts of weapons, not just nuclear ones."

Someone shouts "Hear, hear," and someone else applauds.

"Good," says Ruth. "We are aiming to gather together people from various societies which want peace, so welcome." She consults her list again.

"Julia Lucas."

An elderly lady with a long plait stands up. She is unusually tall and thin.

"I write letters about political prisoners for Amnesty International," she informs us. "That is a lonely task, so I would like to meet other scribes."

"I'm sure we all sympathize with that," Ruth assures her. There is a mutter of approval.

More names are read out, and interest increases. We are all pleased that our leafletting has borne fruit.

"This is one in the eye for Naomi," whispers Keith. "She was sure nothing would come of it."

We break for a cup of tea, and Ruth gives details of our meetings to the new members, gathering ideas for future events.

"What about the Gay Rights march in London next Saturday?" asks a shy young man with ginger hair. There is a moment of quiet while people wonder how to react.

Then Naomi pipes up. "Do you mean do we agree with it or are you suggesting we hire a coach and join in?"

At this, everyone talks at once. The subject is controversial enough to reveal a big difference of opinion. Ruth has to call for order.

"How many people would like to go?"

A smattering of hands go up but not enough to warrant a hired coach.

"Perhaps people with cars could offer seats, or we could go on the train." This from new member Tom Arbuthnot.

"Good idea." Ruth is pleased. "See me afterwards and we'll sort it out."

Keith nudges me and raises his eyebrows enquiringly. I can't make out if he is asking me if I want to get involved or if he is joking.

"Good cause, but I can't spare the time," I say quietly. "I could tell Terry and Fernando about it, 'though I don't think it would be their scene."

"What's the Portuguese for Gay?"

I am sometimes irritated by Keith's sense of humour but no doubt there are things about me which annoy him.

At 8.30 we sing, 'We Shall Overcome'. Most organisations seem to use music to bind their members. For example, 'Jerusalem', 'The Red Flag', 'The Internationale'.

We disband with general 'goodnights', uplifted.

"It's Holy Week," I remark as we walk companionably through the dark streets.

"Does that mean we must abstain until after Easter?" There he goes again. Is he joking?

"Well, it's my turn to cook supper this Tuesday, and I think it's a Fast Day only on Good Friday, so we can at least eat."

When we reach Number 16, he puts his arms round me an says how much he enjoys being with me. "I'll come tomorrow about 7.30 and bring a bottle of wine. OK?"

"Of course. See you then." We have an affectionate kiss and he sets off up the hill at his usual run.

In the morning I go round to Susan's to take her Easter egg and talk about Lorna. She is pleased to see me, and laughingly presents me with an Easter egg which she had at the ready. Luckily it is not identical, but about the same size and price. As we both remark, "It's the thought that counts."

"So Lorna seems to have got him under control," she says, recalling Colin's presence at Stainer's Crucifixion.

"Yes, it was good that they were together, but we must keep on the alert and check up if she isn't at the Women's Fellowship."

Susan consults a calendar with scenes of country life on it. "The next meeting is in a fortnight. Perhaps we should have suggested that she phones us regularly for a chat."

Better that than us phoning her, in case Colin answers. I say I'll have a word with James or Gwen when I go to clean the vicarage tomorrow. Maybe they have a plan.

We set off for town together to do some shopping. I need to get Keith's supper but don't want Susan to know, so we part at the fish counter. I wonder what it would be like if Keith and I shared all our meals. Does he have any irritating food fads? I have a regular eating routine, and don't like a cooked breakfast.

Later, while I am laying the table for our supper, I catch myself questioning our future relationship. Now that he loves me, or at least has *said* he loves me, what happens next? At our age, should we be making plans without delay, or should we be taking things slowly, so as not to repeat our own previous mistakes?

When my girls come to stay, how much should I tell them? Is he 'just a friend', or is he more than that? Will they be shocked? I would have been shocked if my mother had told me she was having an affair with an Argos warehouseman, or even a male nurse. But things were different then.

By the time he arrives, carrying a bottle of wine and a bunch of pink roses, I have calmed down, and am able to welcome him in a light-hearted manner, but I still feel the need to know where we stand.

"How's tricks?" I ask.

He looks puzzled. "What does that mean?"

"It means how are things with you. My brother used to say it when he came home on leave from the Navy."

"I didn't know you have a brother in the Navy."

"I don't now. He died of beer and fags a long time ago."

"I'm sorry. I used to drink too much but working as a nurse taught me what harm that can do, so I stopped in time."

I put my hands on his shoulders and look deeply into his face. "I wonder how much we still don't know about each other," I say.

He pulls me close. "I know enough about you to want to marry you," he murmurs.

Can I believe my ears?

"What did you say?"

"I said I want to marry you," he almost shouts, startling Orlando from his place by the gas fire. Then a sudden doubt strikes him.

"Do you want to marry me?"

"Oh yes," I cry, throwing discretion to the winds. "I do, very much," and we whirl round in a joyful dance.

Orlando retreats to the kitchen and sits by the back door. I let him out.

We eat our supper and drink the wine in blissful companionship, a proper couple at last.

After washing up, we speak of the future.

"We haven't got much money, have we?" I say.

"No, but I've got a job as a medical orderly at the hospital," he announces proudly. It starts next month."

"That's marvellous." I give him a hug.

"But I've only got the money from cleaning the vicarage and the Enterprise Grant, and some from my ex-husband which will stop if and when I remarry."

"Perhaps we should go on living in sin for a bit longer then."

"Yes, but where?"

"What d'you mean?"

"Do you move in here, or do I move in with you to the flat?"

"I hadn't thought that far ahead, but I am getting fed up with shuttling up and down that hill."

In the end we decide to wait until my girls have been put in the picture.

"What if they object?"

"They won't when they see how nice you are," I assure him. "They will probably be relieved that I've found someone else."

"What if your husband objects?"

"He's not my husband anymore, and I don't care how he feels about it."

"I've got fewer complications than you, now my Mum's dead. And I haven't got any kids.

"You're my darling orphan," I croon, stroking his lovely hair.

"And you're my fiancée," he whispers. "I'll buy you an engagement ring."

We swoon away until eleven o'clock, when Orlando scratches at the door to come in.

"He doesn't like me, does he?" remarks Keith, putting on his coat.

"He'll get used to you. He's only a cat."

"But a very special cat. I'll have to share you with him."

Is it my imagination, or does Orlando understand how things are. He stands with his tail aloft, inviting a caress. Keith stoops and tickles behind his ears. If Keith had been allergic to cats, which one would I have chosen? Thank goodness that's a question I don't need to answer.

"Good night, darling," we say simultaneously, and laugh. He runs up the hill.

"So now you've done it," comments Maureen as I get into bed. "About time too."

So she approves, but how will other people react. Terry and Fernando will be pleased, I feel sure, but what will Sid and Susan and James and Gwen say?

I'll wait till I have a ring on my finger, and then they will notice and start asking questions. Word will get round.

I fall asleep and dream about my mother. Strange.

Chapter 23

When I get to the vicarage, James has already gone to the hospital and Gwen is still in her dressing-gown. I ask her if she's all right, and she says no, she feels dreadful.

"I keep being sick," she complains. "I hope it's not infectious. Don't stay if you'd rather not."

I assure her I'm not prone to catching things, and I'm certainly staying. I start on the living-room and she retires to the bathroom in a hurry.

In my early married life, 'morning-sickness' was a sure sign of pregnancy. Could Gwen be expecting? When she comes out of the bathroom, I ask her if it came on suddenly.

"Well, I had it yesterday and it went off as the day progressed, but now it's come back.

"Perhaps you should go to the doctor for a check-up," I advise, putting the kettle on.

"Oh dear. I mustn't be ill. James needs me."

I change the subject by asking if Lorna has been in touch.

"Yes, she phoned on Monday and said she was well."

"I'll call on her later this week," I say. "Are you feeling better now?"

"Yes, shall we have a hot drink?"

I make some tea and she gets dressed. "I seem to be putting on a bit of weight," she remarks.

Surely she must put two and two together, but she seems totally ignorant of the signs.

She does some light dusting while I finish the hoovering, and James comes home early.

He is obviously worried about her but she smiles bravely and says she's fine.

I catch his eye. Does he guess?

"I think she should see Dr Flynn," I say. "Everyone in Rantersford swears by him."

"Right. We'll go to his surgery this afternoon." James is very firm in spite of his wife's protests.

I put on my coat and accept my pay envelope.

"I'm sure he'll know what it is." I give her a hug and let myself out.

Fancy that! There will be rejoicing in the parish when people are told that the vicar's wife is having a baby. Woolly coats will be knitted in profusion. Now I have two secrets under my hat. I am engaged to be married and the vicar will soon be a father. I am tempted to tell Susan but think better of it. I call at her house on the way home and suggest that we go together to see Lorna.

"Should we phone first," she wonders.

"No, I don't think so. We must go unexpectedly so he can't put us off."

"We could take her some flowers."

"Women usually take flowers to someone who is ill. How about an Easter egg?"

"That would be a seasonal gift," Susan agrees.

We laugh when we recall that she and I have already exchanged the traditional chocolate offering.

"I'll get another from the supermarket," I say. We arrange to meet at the bus station tomorrow.

———

Keith phones after work. "How's my fiancée?" he asks.

"She's fine, thank you. I think the vicar's wife is pregnant."

There, I have let it out but only a little way.

"Good God," he exclaims. "She's stealing our thunder."

"Both news items are secret at the moment," I tell him. "We can spread the word when I've got a ring and she has seen the doctor."

"Whatever you say."

"Susan and I are going to check up on Lorna tomorrow afternoon."

"What if she's covered in bruises?"

"She won't be. He'll control himself at first, or maybe even for ever."

"Some hopes. They always do it again."

"Not necessarily. We could pray she stays safe."

"That reminds me. I saw a piece in the local paper about a procession on Good Friday. The various denominations join together and march through the town behind a big wooden cross, praying at intervals, and singing hymns. Are we going?"

I am surprised and pleased.

"Yes. Richard did actually mention it after Stainer's Crucifixion but perhaps you didn't hear him. St Stephen's usually steers clear of Churches Together for some reason, but I think we should join in. We can wear our duffel coats."

"O.K. It will be like a historical protest march against those who persecuted Jesus. I wonder if anyone from the Peace Council will be there."

"I'm sure Ruth will, but not many of the others are religious."

"Naomi certainly isn't. She doesn't love her fellow men. What time does it start?"

"Eleven o'clock in the Town Centre. Can you get the day off?"

"Argos is open, but I've got some time owing before I leave."

"Good. See you there." Then I remember his bad eyesight and add, "I'll be outside the Main Post Office."

On the way to meet Susan for our surprise visit to Woodlea Close, I buy an Easter egg containing a little bag of chocolate drops. Lorna can share these with Colin. I picture her gently putting them into his mouth, and then realize that I am thinking of them as behaving as Keith and I would. In all probability, they have never been this intimate.

We catch the bus and sit side-by-side. Susan approves of my choice of egg and insists on paying half. The weather is seasonably spring-like, so she unbuttons her coat. The ride is pleasant, past gardens full of early blossom with the houses standing well back from the road. How much misery is concealed behind this façade, I wonder?

We alight at the right stop and stroll along Woodlea Close. I must admit that I don't know what to expect when we arrive at Number 29. Susan is equally uncertain.

"We are simply calling to see a friend," I say quietly. "If she isn't in, we will leave the Easter egg and come back another day."

The green gate is ajar, and as we walk up the path we can see that the bedroom curtains are drawn back. We are not kept waiting long. In response to our ring at the doorbell, footsteps can be heard hurrying along the passage.

This is a relief. They are a woman's footsteps on high heels. The door opens to reveal Lorna, neatly dressed and with no obvious bruises.

"Hullo," she says brightly, pleased to see us. "Come in do. Colin is at work so we can have a cup of tea and a chat."

How ordinary, and even potentially boring.

We enter, and Susan hands over the Easter egg, which is received with exaggerated appreciation. Our coats are put in a little downstairs cloakroom and we go through to a sun-filled conservatory overlooking the garden.

"How are you?" I ask bluntly, feeling somewhat rude, but she is behaving as if the recent crisis never happened.

She lowers her eyes and edges forward, forced to respond.

"Gladys Grantley comes to visit fairly often. She gets on well with Colin, who is attending a course on learning how to keep his temper."

"Is it working?" Susan asks.

"So far, yes. He really is trying to be his old kind self, like he was when we were first married."

"James and Gwen will be very pleased to hear that," I say. "We have all been thinking of you and are ready to help if things get difficult again."

She gives a watery smile. "You are so kind. I can't thank you enough. Now let me get us a cup of tea. I made a cake this morning, so we can have that with it."

Susan perks up. "That will be lovely," she says. "I like home-made cake, but I'm no good at it."

"But she makes delicious marmalade," I add.

We all laugh and go into the sparkling kitchen.

"I hope you can get to St Stephen's on Easter Day," I say. "Will Colin bring you?"

"He'll drop me off and fetch me back, but I don't think he'll agree to actually attend the service. He's not a church-goer."

Neither was my husband. We often used to argue about religion and, looking back on it, I think that was one of the reasons why we broke up. Let's hope Lorna and Colin can agree to disagree.

Susan and I get ready to leave before Colin comes home, though I wonder if we should have stayed so he could see that his wife has friends.

"I'll tell him you've been," says Lorna, reading my mind. "Please come again when you have time."

"Of course," Susan assures her. We exchange hugs and set off for our bus.

"Well, she seems all right," Susan remarks, "'though a bit nervy. I think we're better off without men."

She settles comfortably on her seat and looks out of the window.

What will she say when I tell her about me getting engaged to Keith?

"Are you going on the Good Friday march?" I ask hastily.

"I've not made up my mind yet. I usually do, but my legs get tired if I walk too far, and some of the other people can be embarrassing."

The word 'Evangelist' is not one she uses, but I can tell what she means. St Stephen's is renowned for being a traditional established church, and its congregation doesn't hold with waving arms and calling on the Lord.

"I'll look out for you if I go," I say when we part, leading her to suppose that I haven't made up my mind either.

———

It's my turn to ask Sid if he is all right this morning. I lean over the fence and see Dolly sitting on the step waiting to be let in. I'm a bit concerned that Sid isn't eating properly or getting enough exercise. He had a brother who died of diabetes.

"Had to have both legs off," he once informed me. "Nearly went blind as well."

Though not obese, Sid has always been hefty, so I hope the illness doesn't run in the family.

Eventually he appears, rubbing his hair with a towel. Dolly squeezes in past his legs.

"Are you going on the march?" he asks.

This is an unexpected question as it has never occurred to me that Sid or Doris would be interested in such an event.

"Yes," I reply, "are you?"

"I'm thinking about it. Doris didn't agree with it but she's not here to argue." Then he adds, "I suppose you'll be going with your boyfriend."

At first, I don't know how to react. The only time Sid has officially seen me together with Keith was at Stainer's Crucifixion, and then he didn't join us at Keith's flat. Could he have observed our recent comings and goings?

"As it happens, yes I am," I say dismissively, but I don't deny the word 'boyfriend'. It wasn't one of the romantic epithets Keith and I laughed about. Rather inappropriate, as it usually applies to the younger age-bracket. The news will soon be out, and of course Sid will be told.

"I'll probably see you there, then."

"We'll look out for you." I don't want him to be on his own.

He goes in to finish drying his hair.

Could it be that Sid is experiencing a soul's awakening? Christian Fellowship is encouraged by James, who runs an afternoon group for older members. Let's hope Sid will join. That would put Eliza's mind at rest.

All the Easter Day hymns are familiar to the choir, so there will be no need for a practice tonight. I understand that on Sunday the choir can leave off their uniforms and sit with the congregation in the body of the church. Richard and is wife will be away on holiday, so the school music teacher is coming to play the piano. At home time, the children will hunt for chocolate eggs in the churchyard – all very joyful after Good Friday's sorrow.

Have I got time to wash my hair before the march? It looks rather a mess, but a good brush will have to suffice.

Keith is waiting outside the Post Office, looking anxiously about him. It must be awful for him having such bad sight.

"Here I am," I say, taking his hand. Relief floods his face.

"I thought perhaps we'd missed each other."

"Well, I'm sure we do miss each other when we aren't together. But I'm here now."

A large crowd is gathering across the road in the Town Square, so we go over and mingle. The various church leaders are there, including James, and Bernard is standing with a group of other strong-looking men beside a large wooden cross which will be carried at the front when the procession sets off.

The Baptists and the Methodists are in the majority, as I expected. Some of the ladies are carrying paper bags full of hot-cross buns, which I understand is customary. They will be distributed to bystanders to encourage them to join the ranks.

I catch sight of Susan's red coat, so her legs must be in good order, and then Sid shows up, his grey hair neatly combed. I half expect Terry and Fernando to be somewhere in the crowd, and then I remember that the Roman Catholics are the ones most reluctant to join in Churches Together activities 'because of the Pope'. I'm not sure exactly what the Pope would object to, but Father Damian is conspicuous by his absence today.

At eleven the procession starts off, following the wooden cross. Some people carry banners saying 'This is Good Friday', just in case the reason for the traffic hold-up puzzles motorists. Several uniformed policemen walk alongside, discouraging dawdlers and controlling road junctions. Shoppers stand on the pavements staring at us, but not many join in, even though they gladly accept the hot-cross buns. We don't sing on the march like some protesters do, but we stop in places such as the Market Place and the big Methodist chapel at intervals to pray and sing a hymn.

Susan and Sid catch us up outside the Museum. They seem to have struck up a friendship. Then I remember that they met at Doris's funeral, where Susan was dispensing the tea and cakes. Two born-and-bred Rantersford folk, same size and shape. Ideally suited.

"Are you matchmaking?" Keith whispers in my ear. He has been watching and is amused. I reply in a discreet undertone.

"Why not? It would be a good thing. Sid deserves a nice lady, and Susan would be ideal. She says she's better on her own, but I used to think that myself till I met you."

"I hope you don't come to regret changing your mind." Poor Keith still suffers slightly from low self-esteem, while my confidence grows.

Maureen intrudes. "Take care not to dominate. You'll drive him away."

"No, I won't. I'm driving my mother away. She mustn't be allowed to spoil things."

"When does all this finish?" Keith has evidently had enough. Susan also wants to know. Her legs must be hurting.

"We are supposed to end up in the Shopping Centre," I say, "but it would be O.K. to melt away now. Shall we all go to the Guildhall café for a cup of tea?"

There is general agreement, so we syphon off, Sid included. We sit at a table for four and share a large pot.

"This is nice," smiles Susan. "I don't get out much these days."

"I can't remember when I last went anywhere except Doris's funeral," joins in Sid, "and that wasn't exactly a treat."

"No, it can't have been." Susan pats his hand sympathetically with her plump palm, much to his confusion.

When the teapot is empty, we stand up.

"Well, if it's not a sin to go shopping on a Good Friday, Clare and I have something to buy now," says Keith firmly.

"I think I've got all I need," says Susan.

"So have I," says Sid, and they set off together for Mill Hill.

Chapter 24

"What have we got to buy? I ask, taking Keith's arm across the road. "I hope they didn't think we were trying to get rid of them."

"I was," Keith admits. "I want to get you an engagement ring."

Goodness me! How could I have forgotten? I am suddenly walking on air, clinging on to steady myself.

There are several jewellery shops on a side-street, including one owned by a silversmith who makes his own stock.

"Let's try here," says Keith, pushing the door open. The inside is soundproof, with a long counter full of trays and stands. No-one else is there, but an elegant lady comes out from the back and asks if she can help.

"I hope so," says Keith, taking my left hand and displaying it for inspection. "We want to choose an engagement ring."

The elegant lady smiles and pushes a tray towards us. "We have a large selection of designs and prices," she says. "I'm sure you'll find something suitable."

She wanders away, but not so far that she can't keep an eye on our movements.

"You do have nice hands," comments Keith as he pushes this ring and that on to my third finger for size.

Some of them are very expensive, and I fear his eyesight isn't clear enough to read the little attached price-tags.

"How about this one?"

It has an opal and is very pretty, but I read somewhere that opals are unlucky because their colour changes, indicating unfaithfulness, so I pick out a modest piece of amber in a stylish silver setting.

The lady approves. "That one was made by Mr Dawlish himself, she says. "They always fit well."

Keith grins. "Good. We don't want it falling off in the washing-up water, do we?"

That is the first chauvinist remark I have heard him make. I hope it's meant as a joke. I know we can't afford a washing-up machine, but I'll see that he takes his turn at the sink.

"Well, if you're certain, we'll have that one."

"Can I keep it on?" I ask. It already feels part of me.

"It has a little box," the lady tells us, "but you can take that separately."

"Right, but I'm not going down on one knee in a shop."

"Do you want to choose a wedding ring as well?" asks the lady, as she wraps the little box.

Keith looks alarmed, so I say, "No thank you. That will have to wait."

When we get outside, I reassure Keith that I don't mind a long engagement, as there are many things to sort out before we actually get married.

He is relieved but says we mustn't wait too long or we might have second thoughts about the whole idea.

There he goes again! How seriously am I supposed to take him? I wish I knew more about his life before we met. He has mentioned a sister, but she doesn't seem to be in contact, and he never speaks of friends in the village.

Like me, he has started a new life in a new place. Perhaps we don't need to know everything about each other. The future is what matters.

We buy a big bag of fish and chips on the way back to his flat and eat them sitting by my electric fire.

Thinking aloud I say, "I'll go round to the vicarage tomorrow and find out if Gwen is pregnant. Shall I tell her about us?"

"What about us?"

"That we are engaged to be married," I snap. "Or had you forgotten?"

We glare at each other. Are we about to have our first row?

Then he takes off his glasses and rubs his eyes.

"Sorry," he mutters, "I'm so tired. I don't seem to be able to talk sense."

Immediately concerned, I put my arms round him.

"It's me who should be sorry," I say. "It's all been a bit too much, hasn't it? You go to bed early and I'll see myself home. Everything will be fine in the morning."

We cling, and gain strength. I stroke his hair and he rubs my back. He sees me down the staircase and, as it's not yet dark, he lets me go home alone. I do not pass a single pedestrian on the way.

Orlando welcomes me, tail aloft, and I turn my mind to Sid and Susan. Did they part after the march, or did she ask him into her nice clean little house? Surely Sid would have had the sense not to let her see inside his squalid abode.

Maureen interrupts my train of thought. "You're getting obsessed with romance. Give it a rest."

So I go to bed but take a long time to get to sleep.

———

Before I call at the vicarage to ask after Gwen's condition, I must write to my girls concerning their coming visit. I can tell them about Keith in time for them to consider my news and maybe discuss it with each other.

Knowing them as I do, I guess Katherine will be amused and then pleased, while Elizabeth could be doubtful and critical.

I find some notepaper and envelopes and sit down at the table but have hardly begun to write before I hear Sid shouting over the fence. I had forgotten that it's my turn to check. I hasten to the back door.

"Are you all right?"

"Yes. Sorry. My routine has gone haywire."

He seems eager to chat.

"That Susan is a nice lady. She asked me in after the march and we got on fine. How did your shopping go?"

Should I tell him about my engagement ring? "Yes," says Maureen," You must spread the word." So I go down the path and show him my finger.

"Very pretty," he comments, not showing any surprise. "I've been wondering. Keith is a good chap. When is it to be?"

"Oh, not yet," I assure him. "We've got to make plans."

"Marry in haste, repent at leisure," he chants, echoing my mother.

"Yes. Well, I must get on." I go back indoors and make another attempt at writing my letters.

After several false starts, I am satisfied, and stick stamps on the envelopes. I post them on the way to the vicarage.

Gwen answers the door. She looks better.

"Come in," she says. "James is writing his Easter sermon for tomorrow. I'm just going to make him a cup of coffee."

For a moment we are silent. Then we both start to speak at the same moment.

"After you," I say, waving a polite arm. Her news will be more important than mine, I am sure."

"Dr Flynn says I am expecting a baby." Gwen seems hardly able to believe this, almost accusing the doctor of having made it up.

"That's lovely," I cry, giving her a hug. "James must be very pleased."

"He is, but I can't take it in. How are we going to manage?"

"Vicars often have big families. That's why Victorian vicarages are so large."

"Yes, but that was a long time ago. How are we going to keep this house clean with a baby? I can't manage without you now, so things will get out of control."

"I can go on helping," I assure her, "and perhaps your mother will come for a while."

James appears from the study.

"Where's that cup of coffee?" he asks mildly. "Hello Clare, have you heard our news?"

I shake his hand and he notices my ring.

"Ah, so you've also got some good news."

Bewildered, Gwen looks at me as if I'm pregnant too.

"I'm engaged to marry Keith," I explain. "We're too old to start a family, so that's one worry less."

We all laugh and James reheats the coffee.

"How appropriate for Easter," he says. "I wonder if I could bring the baby into my sermon. New beginnings and all that."

"Oh no, I will be so embarrassed," objects his wife.

"But everyone will find out eventually, so you might as well break the news while it's fresh."

Then I have a horrid vision of a broken egg, symbolic of a miscarriage. Heaven forbid!

"I presume you don't want me to call the banns yet?" asks James, changing the subject.

"No thank you. We've got a lot of planning to do. My two daughters are coming over next week and I'll have to introduce them to Keith. I don't know how they'll take it."

"I didn't know you've got two daughters," they chorus.

"They are both at University. I'd like you to meet them."

"Bring them round," says Gwen. "Bring Keith as well."

We part with much good will and I go to see Susan.

She is scrubbing the kitchen floor. "Don't slip," she warns, moving the bucket.

I'd decided to confine the news to my engagement, leaving Gwen's pregnancy out of it for the time being but, before I can say anything, she starts singing Sid's praises.

"Isn't he a lovely man?" she gushes. "I wish he lived next door to me."

"Well, I don't think you'd have got on with his wife when she was alive. She could be awkward and so can he."

"You are too particular about men."

"You've changed your tune," I tease. "I recall how we once agreed that we are better off without them. Anyway, I've come to let you know that Keith and I are engaged."

Susan literally nearly kicks the bucket.

"Well I never!"

We go into the living room and, rather to my surprise, she takes a bottle of sherry and two glasses out of the sideboard.

"This calls for a celebration."

She wants to know where we will live, how old he is, has he been married before, has he got a good job. I do my best to enlighten her.

"I hope you don't move far away," she says wistfully. "I would miss you."

I pat her arm. "Don't worry, it will probably be a long engagement and of course we'll stay friends."

We drink our sherry. "See you at church," she says as I depart.

"Of course. Happy Easter."

The service follows the traditional St Stephen's pattern, with lots of excited children and joyful hymns. James saves the baby-news for the coming events items just before the congregation disperses. Everyone is delighted, and poor Gwen is swamped by well-wishers. "How lovely," is the cry.

No one seems to notice my engagement ring, so Keith and I escape unmolested to his flat.

Shall we have a picnic in the park?" he asks. "It's such a nice warm day."

"What a good idea. But have we got anything suitable to eat?"

With a flourish he takes a cloth off a shopping basket to reveal neatly-cut sandwiches and assorted fruit.

"How clever you are!" I give him a big kiss and we set off.

Then suddenly, in the lovely warm spring sunshine, I go cold. Lorna Johnson wasn't at church. If she had been, she would have come up to me and wished me a Happy Easter. Too occupied by my own happiness, I had forgotten all about her constant need for caring friends.

"What's the matter?" asks Keith.

"Lorna Johnson," I say. "Did you see her in church?"

"Can't say I did but my sight isn't good enough to see everybody distinctly."

"Well mine is, and I didn't see her."

"Maybe she's ill, or perhaps they've gone on holiday."

He isn't concerned and doesn't' want our picnic to be spoilt.

"Forget it," says Maureen. "You can phone her when you get back home."

So I do my best to enjoy our treat.

The local park has been smartened up lately and banks of daffodils are in bloom. We sit at a wooden picnic table near the paddling pool.

"Rantersford isn't too bad on days like this, is it?" says Keith rather grudgingly. Sometimes he must miss the village surrounded by open fields.

"One day, could you take me and show me where you used to live?" I say, holding his hand.

"Yes, but I don't care where I live as long as it's with you."

We risk a quick public kiss.

"I suppose we ought to be planning our future," he sighs, "but I'm not very practical. You are the sensible one."

Maureen pricks up her ears. "Strike while the iron is hot. Get down to business."

I take a deep breath. "The first thing we should work out is how much money we've got coming in. Then we will know what we can afford. In the meantime, you could move in with me at 16 Salvin Street, or I could move in with you at your flat."

"True. I'm fed up with going up and down that hill. But what will people say?"

"What people?"

"Well, Sid and Susan, and Terry and Fernando, and James and Gwen. The Peace Group, the choir, my landlady, Father Damian – lots of people."

"But it isn't as if our relationship is a casual one," I protest. "They will all know we intend to get married soon."

"That's another thing. How soon?"

"The sooner the better," mutters Maureen. But I panic.

"Let's consult my girls and your sister before we go any further."

"My sister couldn't care less what I do," Keith remarks. "But your girls are important. Remind me when they are coming."

"Next weekend. They can sleep in the front bedroom."

"Good. Now let's have an ice-cream."

The little café near the bowling green is open, with a group of children pushing to get served. We join the scrum and come away with two large cornets. I suggest that we call on Terry and Fernando this afternoon and tell them our news. I haven't seen them lately and I feel they will be interested.

"Yes, let's do that. We'll need friends and they are an interesting pair."

I like the word 'pair' to describe them. Better than 'same-sex' in my opinion and certainly better than most words used over the years.

We pick up the empty basket and make our way across town. Not having a car means we can take short cuts which drivers wouldn't be familiar with.

"Lucky we've both got good legs," I say.

Keith laughs. "I don't know about my legs but as I've told you before, your legs are exceptionally good."

Terry and Fernando are doing an enormous jig-saw puzzle on a special tray. They are pleased to see us and slide the tray away under the book-case.

"We like to find the right pieces to make a picture," explains Fernando.

"My mother left quite a collection," says Terry. "She didn't use a tray, so half-finished ones got in the way."

"Don't let us interrupt you," says Keith politely.

"We just came to tell you something."

They both look curious, so I show them my ring. Fernando is the first to react.

"Ah, in Portugal that means you will soon be married."

Terry laughs. "It means the same in England," he says. "Congratulations. Let us have a glass of wine."

So we chat amicably for an hour or so and then go next door.

"I suppose Terry won't have to go to work tomorrow. It's Bank Holiday Monday. He's a lucky fellow."

"I'm sure he deserves it," I say, giving Orlando his supper. "Have a sit down while I phone Lorna Johnson."

"Oh dear. I'd forgotten about her." He flops down on the settee with the Sunday papers.

As I feared, there is no answer when I dial the number. "I'll try again tomorrow and if I can't get through, I'll call the social worker."

"Do social workers operate on Bank Holidays?"

"They are on perpetual call. It's a dreadful job."

"More worthwhile than Argos. I'll be glad to leave there and do something important. Only two more weeks to go and then it's Rantersford Hospital."

I imagine him wearing a green overall and wheeling sick people about on a trolley. He will be reassuring and calming like he learned to be with animals on the farm.

"I hope your hours aren't too irregular," I say. "It's bad for people to interfere with their body-clock."

"I expect it will take getting used to, but I'll be having lots of exercise, walking there and back and lifting people on to stretchers."

My father was in the Royal Arm Medical Corps in World War One, and he was an expert stretcher-bearer. But then, most of his patients were past praying for.

We have scrambled eggs for supper and go to bed early.

Chapter 25

I phone Gladys Grantley about Lorna rather than disturb James and Gwen. She answers promptly and I ask her if she has contacted Lorna over Easter.

"I did phone her on Saturday, but got no answer," she tells me. "A holiday away hasn't been mentioned, so if she's still not responding, I'll go round to the house."

"Sorry to trouble you on a Bank Holiday Monday," I say guiltily," but I am a bit worried about her."

"Quite right. It's my job to sort this kind of thing out. I'll phone you or the vicar when I know what's what."

Keith is as impressed as I am by Gladys's dedication.

"When I'm working at the hospital, I'll probably be involved with people in crisis," he speculates. "It won't get me down because I'll have you to come home to, won't I?"

I am touched by this more than I can say, and give him an all-embracing hug.

He decides to go back to the flat today and tidy up, while I get on with my writing. I have been neglecting to earn my Enterprise Grant lately and, while the girls are here next week, I'll be even more distracted.

The phone rings at four o'clock. It is James. I assume he has news of Lorna from Gladys. He has and it is bad.

"I'm afraid she's in hospital," he says. "Colin lost his temper again and had a go at her."

I am horrified. "Oh dear. I should have checked when she wasn't at church on Easter Day."

"So should I, but Gladys seemed to think she would be O.K."

"What did he do to her?"

James lowers his voice. I think he doesn't want Gwen to overhear him.

"Broke her arm and banged her head against the wall. They've operated on her skull. She's in Intensive Care."

"You mean she might die?"

"Could do. The police have been informed."

This is so awful I can hardly take it in.

"What ought we to do?"

"Gladys says nothing can be done at the moment, but I'm wondering if someone should contact her friend Margaret in Liverpool. She gave Gwen her phone number when she was here. I think she feared it might be needed."

I recall Margaret's strong feelings about her friend's decision to return home and guess she will be very distressed to hear what has happened. I offer to let her know, dreading the task, but feeling that James has done enough.

"No, I'll do that. Don't you worry."

He rings off and I dial Keith's number.

"Good God!" he exclaims. "So you were right. Domestic violence is so difficult to understand. How could he have done such a thing?"

"Some men are like that," I say, deeply thankful that he is not one of them.

Bad news travels fast, as they say. When I go to inform Susan, she has already heard from Pat of the Women's Fellowship that Lorna is in hospital but thinks she has had a fall.

"I didn't discuss it with her. Least said, soonest mended."

"That was very sensible of you, but it's about as bad as can be. She's in Intensive Care."

To say that Susan perked up at this would be an exaggeration, but she could not hide the flicker of a thrill which crossed her face. "You mean he tried to *murder* her, like we thought he had before?"

I calm her down. "The social worker says the police are involved, so it seems possible. But we mustn't see it as a Television Soap. It is *real*, with real people being hurt and upset."

"Yes. I'm sorry. Poor Lorna. We should say a prayer for her."

"Yes, so we should. It's all we can do at the moment."

We hold hands, shut our eyes and concentrate on Lorna's hospital bed.

Two letters have come in the post today. One from each of my girls. I presume they have been discussing my news and are giving their opinions. I tear the envelopes open and read Katherine's first.

Dear Mum,

What a lovely surprise! I am so glad you have found someone to settle down with. Keith sounds very nice, but I'm a bit worried about his eyes. You say his sight is bad. Does that mean he could go blind? You should get that checked. Pity he hasn't got much money, but that shouldn't matter if you are happy.

I'm looking forward to seeing you soon,

Lots of love,

Katherine.

I breath a sigh of relief and turn to the other letter.

Dear Mum,

Thank you for your news about getting married again. I'm sure you must have thought very carefully before making the decision, but I can't help being a bit worried about it. You haven't known him for very long, have you, and you don't seem to know much about his past. Some of my friends here have step-parents and they don't always get on. I did not realize that you were lonely in Rantersford, as you seemed so busy with church etc.

Anyway, I'm looking forward to meeting Keith when I come.

Lots of love,

Liz

Oh dear, not so good. She even signs herself 'Liz'.

When I get to the vicarage for the usual Wednesday clean, James says that Margaret from Liverpool has come to Rantersford and is staying again at the Queen's Hotel. She has been to visit Lorna, who recognised her, which the surgeon says is a good sign of recovery.

Gwen appears in her apron and we all express profound relief.

"How long do you think she'll be in hospital?" I ask. "Is she still in Intensive Care?"

It seems that she has been moved to an ordinary ward and short visits are allowed.

"I'll go to the hospital as usual this morning and find her," says James. "She might like to receive Holy Communion."

"Give her our love," we chorus.

When we see him off, I wonder if Gwen has any jealousy left, but I detect only genuine concern.

We get on well with the chores, she avoiding heavy weights.

"Dr Flynn says I must be careful during the first thee months," she informs me, patting her tummy protectively. She has been given basic information about her condition and is following it religiously.

I remind her that my girls are coming on Saturday for a few days and she insists that I bring them and Keith for a meal.

"It won't be any trouble. James is good at entertaining and we'd love to meet them."

I wonder how eager Elizabeth and Katherine will be to accompany me and Keith to the vicarage. Neither of them are religious, but they are mature enough to behave appropriately, so there is no need to worry. I promise to arrange a convenient day.

I see from my wall calendar that it's the Women's Fellowship meeting next Thursday. Pat seems to have taken over while Lorna recovers from her supposed 'fall'. The subject of the lecture is Victorian Rantersford. Should I go? Salvin Street is Victorian, as is St. Stephen's church, so it might be interesting to learn more about their history.

I don't think men are allowed at the WF meetings, so Keith will have to amuse himself. I wonder what his hobbies are. Perhaps choir and Peace Group are all he needs, and when he starts at the hospital, his timetable will make it difficult for him to join anything else.

A lot has been happening lately, and I am rather tired. I put Metatone tonic on my shopping list and vow to devote tomorrow to my writing.

Choir practice has resumed but Keith and I have asked Richard if he will excuse us from being there every week. He understands and says 'Come when you can', but if a concert is planned, we must rehearse or not take part. Fair enough. So this Friday I prepare for the girls' arrival on Saturday morning.

Elizabeth is at Leeds, and Katherine at Hull, so the East Coast Line is convenient for both of them. They will be here for five days. I hope my spare bedroom will be large enough for them. The bed is what used to be known as a 'three-quarter', which is bigger than a single but not as big as a double. Perhaps it was intended for two children, or a mother and child, or one obese adult. Anyway, my sheets and blankets are all double, so they won't be fighting over the bedclothes.

I go to the supermarket to stock up, trying to remember if either of them has any food fads. I envy Terry and Fernando's easy access to eatables. I don't expect they ever run out of anything.

As I'm struggling up the hill, Sid catches me up and offers to carry my heavy bag. I tell him I'm expecting visitors.

"Oh, I thought perhaps you were shopping for two," he slyly remarks.

"No, Keith isn't moving in yet," I assure him. "My daughters are coming for a few days."

"That will be nice for you. I've been invited to Susan's for lunch today. I'm looking forward to it." He smacks his lips enthusiastically.

I smile. "So she's shopping for two, is she?"

"Ah. This is probably a one-off occasion. I don't expect she'd put up with me on a permanent basis."

"I think you would stand a good chance there. She told me you're a lovely man."

Sid stops in his tracks. "Did she really? Doris never called me that."

"Well, she's right," I say, taking back my shopping. "It was lovely of you to carry my heavy bag. Thank you."

He laughs and goes round to his back door.

I unpack the fish and the rest of the provisions and think of Lorna. I wonder if her friend Margaret will stay until she is well enough to leave hospital. Trying to look on the bright side, I imagine a fragile Lorna being taken to live with her friend, far away from Rantersford and all its unhappy memories.

I must confess that although I am looking forward very much to seeing them, I am worried about what Elizabeth and Katherine will think of Keith. Their trains arrive at Rantersford within a few minutes of each other, so I can be there to meet them both. We will come back here, and Keith will join us after lunch. He is owed some paid leave from Argos to be taken before he leaves, so he will be free during their stay.

Chapter 26

As I walk up the hill to the station, I recall that my reason for moving to a town with a convenient rail system was so I could easily get away if I wanted. As it happens, I haven't travelled anywhere on a train since I came here.

Elizabeth arrives first so, after a fond greeting, we wait on the platform for Katherine.

"What an old-fashioned little station," Elizabeth remarks. "It's like something on children's television."

I look round at the fretwork bridge and clearly-indicated toilets.

"It's easy to get to London, and cross-country to the sea-side," I say defensively. "Lots of people commute."

"Ah, then I expect house-prices will go up, as long as the rail-fares don't increase."

Before I can condemn speculation and the current political obsession with capitalism, Katherine's train draws up. We all embrace, and I suggest a cup of coffee at the buffet.

"It's very clean and convenient," I assure Elizabeth, who seems doubtful.

"That would be lovely," says Katherine. "What a nice little station."

We make our way through the swing doors and arrange ourselves at a table near the magazine racks.

They both have those convenient suitcases with wheels, and carry leather shoulder bags. A lady in an apron bustles up and asks us what we would like. I order three coffees and she wipes the table before fetching a laden tray. Biscuits are included free. It doesn't take long for Rantersford to have its relaxing effect.

"This is better than queuing up and fighting for a seat," says Katherine, and my critical Elizabeth agrees.

Only two years separate them but no two sisters could be more different. In appearance and temperament they are opposite - Elizabeth being fair-haired and confident, and Katherine dark and shy.

Right from the start, they have been devoted to each other. There has been no sibling rivalry, no quarrels, no jealousy. They played happily together until school-age and then made friends who competed for their company. "I want to play with Elizabeth and Katherine," was the cry on our doorstep.

Without them my husband and I would not have stayed together for as long as we did. They bound us in a blessed kind of way and seemed not to be adversely affected by our deteriorating relationship. Not until they both left for University did we finally part. They do not take sides, and continue to treat us both with affection and respect. They have each other and seem to be making their way through life successfully so far.

I say so far because now things are different. Keith is on the scene, and I am beginning to fear that they might disapprove.

The area round the station has become my patch. I lead the way along Railway Terrace towards St Stephen's church, past the narrow streets leading to Mill Hill. They follow in a kind of trance.

"This isn't like anywhere I've been," says Katherine. Elizabeth says nothing, taking it all in. I remember how I felt when I first came to Rantersford.

My search for somewhere to live had taken me far and wide. Nowhere seemed right. Then Maureen had suggested trying the 'Midlands'.

I had read a poem at school which described them as being 'sodden and unkind', but respecting my wise friend's judgement, I took a train and alighted at the first place which took my fancy. As I left the station, I raised my eyes and saw a green hill in the distance. This gave me an almost miraculous sensation of freedom and, like a released prisoner, I walked steadily along to Salvin Street. It was as simple as that.

"I'm very happy here," I tell them. "I think you'll like it when I show you round."

Terry and Fernando are leaving Number 17 as we reach home. Armed with large carrier bags, they are off to the shops. I introduce them to my girls who give them charming smiles and warm handshakes.

"They look interesting," remarks Elizabeth when we are inside.

I explain about Terry's mother's death and Fernando being Portuguese.

"Who lives on the other side?" asks Katherine.

"I'll tell you about him after lunch," I promise, leading the way up the narrow staircase.

After further thought about sleeping arrangements, I had decided that the spare bed would be too small for them and swapped the sheets over. I would sleep in the spare bed and they could have my double.

They unpack and have a wash while I put the fish in the oven and lay the table. I must get used to being mother again after months of pleasing myself. This is part of their Easter holiday, and I can't expect them to share the chores. They have been looking after themselves in University housing for nearly two years, and need spoiling.

Orlando, puzzled by upstairs footsteps, asks to go out. I see him jump over the fence to join Dolly on the bench. Sid is not at home much these days. I wonder where he goes.

After lunch we sit on the settee and chat. Both girls seems happy and are doing well with their studies. Elizabeth is taking Geography, and Katherine English Literature. Maybe they will do an Education course after their degree and then become teachers. Their whole lives spread ahead, while mine is about three-quarters gone.

"How's Dad?" I ask. I don't really want to know, but they have seen him lately and I feel I should show interest.

"He's a bit dreary and bitter," says Elizabeth. "He had a lady-friend but she got fed up with him. Tell us about your Keith."

Katherine leans forward. "Yes. How did you meet, and what does he look like?"

I answer her second question first. "Well, I think he is attractive. His hair is like Dad's. He's not as tall as he is, but he's more energetic. He wears glasses."

"How old is he?" Elizabeth wants to know.

"The same age as me. We have a lot in common. He belongs to the church choir and the Peace Group and he likes Jazz."

They both nod approvingly.

"Has he got a proper job?" is the next question.

"He starts work at the local hospital as a medical orderly next week. He was in the Argos warehouse." I am beginning to feel like a prisoner in the dock. "He'll be here soon so you can ask him more yourself."

Elizabeth puts her arm round me. "Sorry, Mum. We only have your interests at heart. We don't want you to be taken advantage of."

We do the washing up and go into the garden. I planted crocuses and they are in full bloom.

Sid comes in his back gate while my green fingers are being praised. I introduce the girls and he apologises for not shaking hands because his are rather dirty from gardening.

"I've been helping Susan with her weeding," he explains to me. "Her back is playing up."

So that's where he has been going.

Dolly follows him in and Orlando jumps back on to our side of the fence.

As the time of Keith's arrival draws near, I find myself getting nervous. What if he is not at his best and makes the wrong impression? I know he's worried, and I have tried to reassure him, but what if I have to choose between him and my girls? Have I known him long enough to be absolutely certain that I am doing the right thing? Maureen seems to have deserted me in this hour of need.

When the doorbell rings we all jump and nervously tidy our hair.

"Please try to like him," I beg. "He's very shy."

They nod and wait for me to let him in.

He is wearing his best jacket and carries a bunch of tulips. I give him a quick kiss and lead him through.

It's all smiles and handshakes but stress is in the air. I take the flowers into the kitchen and put them in water.

When I return they are sitting quiet, ill at ease. Maureen pops up. "What can you expect? It isn't every day that one meets one's future step-daughters."

Squaring his shoulders, Keith asks if the train-journey down was on time.

Elizabeth gets in first with an answer. "Yes thanks. Mum met us both at the station. We walked along past your flat."

Not to be outdone, Katherine explains that they travelled on different trains, but there was only a short while between.

Elizabeth takes her turn. "I suppose living near the town centre means one can manage without a car. When we were little we had an old banger."

Both girls laugh to recall how their childhood had been hampered by breakdowns in country lanes.

Valiantly Keith keeps the ball rolling. "When I lived in a village, the buses were few and far between, so as I don't drive, I had to move into town."

What a stilted conversation! I get up briskly and start to lay the table for tea. Katherine helps but Elizabeth remains talking to Keith. In a somewhat bizarre way, I am reminded of the bit in the Bible when the sisters Mary and Martha are visited by Jesus and one helps with the chores while the other talks to the Master.

"He's very nice," whispers Katherine as we make the sandwiches in the kitchen, "but I'm still worried about his eyes. Has he had them checked at the hospital?"

I am touched by her concern but say we can talk about this later, as I don't want him to think we are whispering about him.

When we return to the dining room, Keith and Elizabeth are deep in a discussion about the Peace Council. "But are you making any difference?" Elizabeth wants to know. "Are you getting anywhere?"

Keith is doing his best. "Well, we did do a lot of leafletting recently, and got some new members."

"And we do plan protests and try to change public opinion," I add, putting a plate of sandwiches and a cake down on the table. "Let's have something to eat now."

We gather round and I ask Keith to pour the wine which I had bought by way of celebration. The girls perk up at this, so I'm glad I thought of it. "Wine maketh glad the heart of man," as my mother used to say. I hope that applies to woman as well.

The conversation ranges from University life to Keith's mother's Multiple Sclerosis. He talks about his time as carer more openly than he has before, and I realize what a large slice of his life was taken up by it. Anyone else would have become resentful, but he went on looking after her for ten years. His sister worked in a solicitor's office and eventually married her boss and left, taking much of the furniture with her. Keith's wife had gone several years previously.

"We didn't have any children, so I only needed Mum's bed and a few chairs. I slept on the settee."

On hearing this, Katherine is quite upset. "How awful for you," she cries.

"It wasn't too bad really. We were renting a council house in the village, so when she died I moved to Rantersford. It's much more convenient, and I've got some good second-hand furniture."

Here I interrupt to say that we haven't yet decided where we will live when we get married, as I don't want Elizabeth to think he might be 'exploiting' me and my home-ownership.

Before he leaves, I remind him that James and Gwen want us all to go to the vicarage for a meal while the girls are here.

"Does your vicar do a lot of entertaining?" asks Elizabeth, surprised at the invitation.

"No, but I know him and his wife very well. She is expecting a baby, but says he likes cooking, so it won't be any trouble. They really want us to go."

"Better suggest Tuesday then, "says Keith. "That's our supper-out day."

I promise to have a word with James after the service tomorrow. We all bid him goodnight and he departs for his flat.

"Do we have to go to church tomorrow?" asks Elizabeth as we get ready for bed. I know my religious leanings have not rubbed off on her, so I tell her to do as she likes.

"Good. Then I'll have a lie in. I am a bit tired."

Katherine says she would like to go with me.

They go upstairs together to use the bathroom while I feed Orlando and lay the table for breakfast.

Terraced houses in Rantersford are not built with strong sound insulation. I used to hear Sid and Doris arguing and, although they don't realize it, I can hear the girls talking in the room above.

"He seems a bit young for his age." This from Elizabeth. "Mum will have to make all the decisions."

"Well, as long as he agrees, that will be fine. Mum usually knows best."

"But they haven't known each other very long, have they? And she doesn't know everything about his past."

"They don't intend to get married yet. They are only engaged. There will be plenty of time to find out more."

"Yes. She can always break it off if things look like going wrong."

I lock the back door loudly and climb the stairs.

"Good night," I call. "Sleep well."

Perhaps the spare-bed mattress is to blame but I myself do *not* sleep well.

Could Elizabeth be right? Maybe I don't know enough about Keith's past. When I parted from the girls' father, I vowed I would not marry again unless it was to a rich widower about whom I knew everything. Keith certainly does not qualify, so why am I even considering him? Maybe I am just lonely and in need of a romantic attachment.

I turn and twist on the unfamiliar mattress, worrying about the future. Then I kneel up and pray for Lorna, and Gwen's baby, and Terry and Fernando, and Sid, and Susan, and for everyone I know in Rantersford. At last I drift off, but wake early.

Chapter 27

Orlando is pleased to see me before my usual time, and eats a good breakfast.

Is it too early to phone Keith? I could have a quick word with him before the girls get up. The bell rings for a long time before he answers. I imagine him groping for his glasses and maybe cursing whoever has woken him so early.

"It's only me," I say reassuringly, in case he thinks it's something urgent or even a wrong number.

"Ah," he mumbles. "What time is it?"

"Seven o'clock. I couldn't sleep and I've got up before the girls wake. Are you all right?"

"I couldn't get to sleep either. I'm afraid I didn't make a very good impression on Elizabeth and Katherine."

"They think you are very nice. You did fine. They've just got to get used to the idea of their old Mum starting afresh."

I assume a practical tone. "Katherine and I are going to the ten o'clock service. I won't sit with the choir as I can't leave her on her own, and Richard has said he doesn't expect us every week. I'll let James and Gwen know that we can all come for supper on Tuesday if that's convenient for them."

"You sound in charge. Is Elizabeth going to church as well?"

"She's having a lie in."

"I'll do the same this week. I expect you will want to show them round Rantersford this afternoon. I'll phone you on Monday to check that Tuesday at the vicarage is O.K."

He sounds unenthusiastic but it might be that I've upset his body-clock.

"Love you," I say and ring off. If I hadn't got his ring on my finger, I would be back in the days of doubt and distress.

"Don't be silly," scolds Maureen. "He's crazy about you."

I make a pot of tea and take it upstairs. The girls are both awake so I pull the curtains back to let the sun in.

"It's very quiet here," says Elizabeth approvingly. "My place in Leeds can be noisy at week-ends."

"What time do we set out for church?" Katherine asks. "Will Keith be there?"

"The service starts at ten. No, he's having a lie in, like your sister."

"I thought you were both in the choir. Don't you have to sit at the holy end?"

"We do sometimes, but I'll sit with you today. My friend Susan will want to meet you."

Elizabeth snuggles down again and I get my Sunday clothes out of the wardrobe while Katherine uses the bathroom. These houses aren't really big enough for more than two people, though when they were built they must have held big families. I expect the Women's Fellowship lecturer on Victorian Rantersford will talk about things like that on Thursday.

"That's right. Forget about him for a bit." Maureen is very evident today. Trying to take her advice, I address Elizabeth's supine form.

"Breakfast is on the table. We'll have ours before we go. Have yours when you feel like it."

"Thanks Mum. This is lovely."

St Stephen's bell is ringing as Katherine and I walk up the hill. We don't have a full peal as the architect didn't include a belfry. Usually Bernard pulls the single rope, keeping it going until the clock strikes ten. He likes the exercise.

Katherine is wearing a black and white flecked coat which goes well with her dark hair. She has gone rather thin since I last saw her. Something else for me to worry about?

I wonder if Lorna will be a subject of conversation after the service. Maybe James will make an announcement.

Susan is in her usual place at the back, and makes room for us.

"Lovely to meet you dear," she says to Katherine. "Where's your sister?"

"Still in bed," I whisper disapprovingly. It feels strange to be in the congregation instead of the choir stalls. I sing up wishing Keith was beside me.

After the service I waylay Gwen, who is looking very well now her pregnancy is progressing, and ask her if Tuesday will suit her. She says "Yes. Come about seven thirty."

James has put a piece in the church newsletter about Lorna's recent stay in hospital. She will convalesce in Liverpool with her friend Margaret. No word about her husband.

When we get home, Elizabeth is washing up. She is wearing an attractive blouse and skirt and seems in a cheerful mood.

"Sid-Next-Door put his head over the fence and asked if you are all right," she says. "He hopes I like Rantersford, so I said I do."

"You did right there. He won't have a word said against the place and refuses to move in with his daughter in Bridlington. She worried about him being on his own."

"Perhaps he'll find a new wife," suggests Katherine. "Is Susan at church the one whose garden he was weeding yesterday?"

"Yes. She fancies him but it doesn't do to jump to conclusions. Would you like to go for a walk this afternoon? There is a pretty park quite near."

This idea appeals to them.

I can't help thinking of last Sunday, when Keith and I went for our Easter picnic.

"Concentrate on your girls," commands Maureen. "Don't let him take over."

We chat happily as we make our way through the town. I have come to love the place and am proud of it when the girls comment favourably on the few remaining Georgian buildings and the Parish Church spire.

St Stephen's church is comparatively new, having been built originally to serve the Victorian slum-dwellers near the Mill. We go through the wrought-iron park gates, to be greeted by banks of daffodils growing beside our little river.

"Is this why it's called Rantersford?" asks Katherine. "Do you have a river-crossing?"

"Oh yes, at least three bridges besides the one you'll see in a minute."

A flock of greedy ducks are assembled. I had put some stale bread in a bag, so we throw tempting bits from an ornate balustrade.

"This is like when we were little and you took us to feed the birds," recalls Elizabeth. "Katherine was in the pushchair."

Those days were happy, with no dark clouds. They came later.

Rantersford is one of the last towns to keep all its public telephone boxes. There is one beside the park gates. I feel in my bag for some coins.

"We could visit Keith on our way back. Then you will be able to see inside his flat. It's in an interesting old building. Shall I phone him?"

"That's a good idea," says Elizabeth. "We'll sit on this seat while you ring to see if he's at home."

I squeeze inside the stuffy cubicle and put some coins in the box. For a moment I can't remember his number. Panic! Then it comes, and I dial. The bell rings seven times, and I am about to put the receiver down when he answers. I press button A and adopt a cheery tone.

"I'm here in the park with the girls. We've been feeding the ducks. Can we call in for a cup of tea?"

He seems taken aback. "The place is in a bit of a mess."

Maureen is indignant. "Lazy devil," she snaps.

True. Suddenly angry, I say, "Tidy it up then. We'll be there in ten minutes."

I put the receiver down with a bang and re-join the girls.

"Come along," I say. "I want you to see as much of him as possible so you can get to know him."

I set the pace at a leisurely stroll to give him time to prepare and am pleased to find him ready for visitors. The kettle is on the boil and a tray laid with mugs and biscuits.

"This is like a student flat in Leeds," says Elizabeth. "A lot of old houses have been converted."

"Yes, it's the same in Hull," agrees Katherine. They make themselves at home on the motley collection of chairs, and I can sense Keith relaxing.

"So you've been feeding the ducks," he says with a smile. "I must admit that I throw my stale bread away, but I must remember to cast it on the waters from now on."

I tell him that Tuesday is fine for supper at the vicarage, and he says he'll call for us so we can all arrive at the same time.

"I've decided to go back to the village tomorrow just for the day. I don't want the people there to think I've melted away."

"They'll be interested to know that you're thinking of getting married," says Katherine.

There is a pause. Then he looks at me and takes my hand. "Not only am I thinking of it," he says. "It is my firm intention."

We all laugh and Maureen joins in.

Keith and I tell the girls about Lorna Johnson's situation, as we are sure it will come up in the conversation on Tuesday. They are both horrified and can't believe that such things happen in a place like Rantersford.

"Domestic violence happens everywhere." I quote the current statistics. "Seven women per month in the British Isles are killed by their partners."

Keith joins in. "And a growing number of men are reporting abuse from their wives."

We all try to change the subject by talking at once. I win.

"It's time we pushed off," I say, gathering our things together. "Have a good time tomorrow and we'll see you on Tuesday. I'll get some flowers for Gwen."

Keith shows us downstairs and kisses us all goodbye.

"Well, I don't think he's the sort to abuse you," observes Elizabeth as we walk down the hill.

Katherine can find no fault with him.

"You must be careful not to boss him about, Mum. Men don't like it."

Did I boss her father about? Perhaps I did. Is that why he eventually left?

We have an evening of memories, looking at old family photos. The girls recall events with pleasure and amusement, so I think it can be said that they had a happy childhood, and judging by overheard snatches of conversation while they are getting ready for bed upstairs, I gather they like Keith and are glad he is to be a member of the family.

"Will we have to call him Dad?" Katherine wonders.

"That could cause confusion," Elizabeth supposes. "People wouldn't know which Dad we are referring to when we mention one or the other."

They giggle. Can I leave it to them to tell Dad Number One about Dad Number Two or should I let him know myself? Maureen says it is my duty. She is right of course. But I will put it off. After all, we plan a long engagement.

The weather is kind for the whole period of the visit. On Monday we go to the museum, which has an exhibition of local artists, and then dine at a new continental-type café in the Market Place.

As I have noted before, Rantersford is renowned for its charity shops, which are opening up everywhere there is a space. Some of the clothes are well worth a try, and I guide the way on a route round town. All three of us are of normal size so are tempted to stock up on summer dresses. I choose garments which show my legs to advantage, remembering Keith's flattering remarks concerning that part of my anatomy. There are plenty of good men's clothes and I am inclined to buy him a blue shirt, but both girls are against this.

"He won't like it if you try to dress him," says Katherine.

"No, he won't," agrees Elizabeth. "He'll think you are treating him like a little boy."

Oh dear, am I in danger of putting him off? I wonder how he is getting on in the village, visiting his old neighbours. Maybe he will phone this evening to tell me.

It is closing time before we reach home, laden with shopping. Fernando is ahead of us on Salvin Street and turns to see us following.

"Hullo," he calls. "Have you had a good day?" If it wasn't for his allergy to Orlando's fur, I would ask him in. I'm sure the girls would get on well with him. As good luck with have it, Terry opens the door of Number 17 and invites us to go in there. We gladly accept.

"You look as if you are in need of a nice cup of tea," he says, indicating our parcels.

"That would be lovely," says Elizabeth. We all sit down in the front room.

As I observe Terry and Fernando, I am overcome by a feeling of delight that they have found each other. They are obviously so happy. Can it be possible that Keith and I will be as fortunate?

Fernando sips delicately at his mug. "Shall we go somewhere nice again soon?"

"Yes, of course," I say. "I'll find out what is on at the theatre and we can get tickets."

Terry is also keen. He says it is his turn to pay.

When we get back home, the girls are full of praise for my neighbours.

"Aren't you lucky having nice people on both sides?" says Katherine. I remember how noisy Sid and Doris had been, but don't go into that.

After supper, I phone Keith. He has not long been back from his village and sounds tired.

"I saw everyone I wanted to, and they are all pleased to hear my news."

"Good. I'd like to see where you used to live. Could we go one day on the bus?"

"O.K. I'll go to bed now. See you all tomorrow."

I call Orlando in for his supper and lock up. There are no lights on in Number 15. I wonder if Sid is already in bed, or if he is staying out late.

Chapter 28

The visit is nearly over. Elizabeth and Katherine will leave on Wednesday on an early train which goes to Leeds via Doncaster, where Katherine changes for Hull. So far they seem to have enjoyed themselves. They both want me and Keith to go and see them for a day soon when they haven't got lectures, so he has evidently won their approval.

Today, Susan would like me to take them to her house for coffee and a chat, and then they can do their packing before we go to the vicarage. My writing is being neglected, I fear.

We arrive at Susan's to find Sid on the point of departure. It seems he has been replacing the electric light bulb on her landing, which was too high for her to reach. He declines the offer of coffee with us as he doesn't want to intrude.

"He is so kind," Susan says. "Nothing is too much trouble for him."

"Have you been invited to his house?" I ask casually.

"No. He doesn't seem to want me there," she complains. "He prefers to come here."

I am not surprised. Knowing as I do the squalor of Number 15 Salvin Street.

I introduce Elizabeth, and the kettle is filled. Susan's house is slightly smaller than mine, with the front door off a side passage which ends in a locked gate. Inside it is spotlessly clean, and smells of hot-cross buns.

"Do sit down, dears, "she says, bustling about with cups and plates. "What do you think of Rantersford?"

The girls have learned how to answer this question with unqualified enthusiasm.

"We've been to the museum and the park," Katherine reports.

"And we've fed the ducks and been shopping," adds Elizabeth.

I join in. "We're having supper at the vicarage tonight, and then they go back to University tomorrow."

"What do you think of your new Dad-to-be?" Susan wants to know. She can be tactless but means well.

"We think he'll do," says Elizabeth with a laugh.

Katherine is embarrassed but mutters her approval. Susan puts a plate of buttered hot-cross buns on the coffee table. "I know these are too late for Good Friday," she admits," but I'm no good at cooking cakes, and these are still within their sell-by date."

We help ourselves. They are delicious.

As we are leaving, Susan reminds me about the Women's Fellowship meeting on Thursday. I say I'll see her there.

"It's good that you have lots of things to do," says Elizabeth as we walk home. "You seem to have joined everything there is to join."

"Yes. I was advised to be active when I moved." I must give Maureen credit where it is due.

Sandwiches are enough for lunch, as a cooked meal will come this evening.

"What shall we wear for the vicarage?" asks Katherine.

"Oh, whatever is comfortable. James and Gwen are informal, and she has to wear loose droopy dresses because of being pregnant."

"We won't have to talk about babies all the time, will we?" Elizabeth asks in alarm.

I become serious. "The subject of conversation is more likely to be Lorna, the poor lady whose husband knocked her about. It's a complicated story and the details are not really our business, but she has a social worker who keeps us up to date so we can help her."

Katherine is concerned. "It sounds as if things go on in Rantersford which would make people less fond of it if they were aware."

Elizabeth thinks perhaps I have chosen the wrong place to settle.

"But I wouldn't have met Keith if I'd gone anywhere else." I look at my watch. "He'll be here soon to escort us, so we'll be safe."

At the last moment, I recall with a shock that I have neglected to get the flowers for Gwen! I had told Keith that I would but they had escaped my mind.

The doorbell rings, and I run to open it. Before I can confess, I see that he is carrying a big bunch of narcissus.

"Thank God," I cry, and give him a big kiss.

"You seem extra pleased to see me," he smiles. "What's brought this on?"

"The flowers," I explain. "I forgot to get some for Gwen, and you've remembered."

"Well, I really got them for you, but we can give them to her if you'd rather."

"Oh yes. That will save the situation. What luck. We are all ready to go."

I call the girls and we are off.

The vicarage kitchen light is on and, as we approach along the garden path, we can see James wearing an apron, checking something on the cooker.

"He looks very domestic," whispers Elizabeth. "I hope they aren't going to a lot of bother for us."

"Gwen says he likes cooking," I say, looking sideways at Keith and wondering if he will continue his previous waiter's skill when we are married.

The porch light comes on and Gwen opens the front door. "Come in," she cries. "It's lovely to see you all."

We troop into the hall and hang our coats on the stand. It seems strange to be an invited visitor instead of a cleaning lady. I am the only one to be familiar with the place, and I observe the others looking round with interest at the Victorian architecture.

"What lovely big rooms." Elizabeth is impressed.

"Too big, really, and rather draughty in the winter," says James, coming out of the kitchen minus his apron. "Would you like a drink of something?"

He indicates the sideboard, which is laden with bottles and glasses.

There is a choice of Guinness, sherry and sloe-gin sent from Wales by Gwen's mother. Keith and James have beer and the rest of us try sloe-gin. By supper-time we are chatting merrily.

The food is delicious. Beef casserole, mashed potatoes and carrots, followed by apple crumble and cream.

"That was lovely," say both girls in one breath.

"Glad you liked it," says James with a note of pride in his voice. "Now let's sit by the fire. I've got two items of news."

"You sound as if you're reading the church news-letter," teases Gwen.

"Is one of the items about Lorna?" I ask, anxious to hear.

"Yes."

We all lean forward.

"She's fit to leave hospital and will move to live with her friend Margaret in Liverpool for good."

I breathe a sigh of relief. "You mean she's divorcing him?"

"Gladys Grantley advised that, and she agreed, though reluctantly."

"It's for the best," says Gwen. "He isn't going to change."

"I only hope he doesn't find another poor lady to beat."

Keith speaks with feeling. He can't understand anyone trying to kill the one they love.

"He'll be getting anger-management advice and be very closely watched," James assures us.

"How much do people at church know?" I ask. "It's Women's Fellowship on Thursday and, as she was the chairperson, there will be speculation."

"I'll put a piece in the newsletter. I'm sure everyone will be sorry she's leaving Rantersford, but people come and go."

At this, Gwen looks at him significantly and clears her throat. "We have another piece of news."

Oh dear! The baby? She still looks pregnant but things can go wrong.

"Ah yes." James is momentarily at a loss for words. "This is confidential," he begins. "I know you will keep it to yourselves for the time being, but when it can be arranged, Gwen and I will be going back to Wales."

I can't believe my ears, as my mother would have said. "You mean for ever?"

"Nothing is for ever except in the religious sense, but we have been here for seven years and, with the baby coming, Gwen will be needing her mother. The Bishop is considering our position, and if no one can soon be found to take over at St Stephen's, there will be an interregnum."

I can't make out if James and Gwen both want to return to Wales, or if he is sacrificing his happiness here for her sake.

Everyone is silent, afraid of saying the wrong thing. Keith is the first brave enough to speak up.

"I'm sure the congregation will miss you very much," he says. "I myself haven't been a member for long, but I get the impression that things are flourishing under your guidance."

Taking Keith's hand, I express my wholehearted agreement.

James blows his nose. "I was looking forward to officiating at your wedding," he says sadly, "but we can come as guests and bring the baby."

"What's an interregnum?" asks Elizabeth. "It sounds somehow unpleasant."

"It can be," admits James. "It means an interval between two reigns."

"But you aren't a king," objects Katherine, puzzled.

"No, but I'm in charge. Someone new will have to take my official place."

"What if the Bishop can't find anyone suitable?" It's my turn to ask questions.

Trying to simplify matters, Gwen joins in.

"I'm sure he will. There must be lots of vicars wanting to come to Rantersford."

"Anyway, it won't be for a while. I will have to find a parish in Swansea which needs a vicar. It will be a complicated business."

Gwen gets up, looking a bit guilty. "Do we all want coffee?" she asks.

Relieved at the change of subject, we all say 'yes please'. I follow her into the kitchen to help with the cups.

"Oh dear. I feel so bad about all this," she says. "He doesn't really want to move, but I can't face looking after a baby without my mother."

I am tempted to tell her to pull herself together but suspect that there is more to her helplessness than meets the eye. The trouble with Lorna Johnson must have taken her confidence, though that was a misunderstanding satisfactorily sorted out. I put my arm round her and she perks up.

"You have two lovely daughters. I hope for a girl, though James would like a boy."

"You could perhaps have one of each," I say. "Your mother can do the washing."

She laughs, luckily not taking offence. "In Wales we all help each other. It's the best place to be."

Maybe she's right, but I can think of plenty of people in Rantersford who would disagree.

Before we go, I explain that Elizabeth and Katherine's train leaves the station at 9.30 a.m. and as I intend to see them off, I will be a few minutes late tomorrow.

As we walk down the hill, Elizabeth wants to know if I really have to keep the cleaning job? She doesn't like to think of her mother as a charwoman.

"There aren't any library jobs here," I say, "and I need the money."

"Don't worry," says Keith. "I start my new job at the hospital on Monday, so I can help."

Katherine has a thought. "If James and Gwen are leaving soon, the place will be empty and not need cleaning till a new vicar comes."

"And if the interregnum thing lasts a long time, you two will be married and living somewhere else," reasons Elizabeth.

I unlock the door of Number 16. "I don't think I want to be living somewhere else," I say. "Not at first, anyway. Rantersford is exercising its charm, even though I wasn't born and bred here."

Keith won't come in as it's getting late. He kisses us all affectionately, says he's glad to have met his new daughters, and turns to run back up the hill.

Orlando is waiting for his supper, indignant at my neglect.

Chapter 29

As I see the 9.30 a.m. train for Leeds disappear, bearing my dear daughters away, I am overcome by a sudden sadness. All things considered, their visit has been a success, but now I must deal with new problems which are piling up ahead.

I make my way to the vicarage, hardly able to believe that James and Gwen will soon be gone. How can St Stephen's function without them?

The choir, the Women's Fellowship, and all the formal parish business need a kingpin to hold them together. Without a vicar, everything will surely fragment.

When I arrive, Gwen is just leaving for an appointment at the ante-natal clinic.

"See you later," she says. "James is writing his sermon. No hospital duty this week."

"Right," I say. "Take care."

I start on the living-room but James comes out of the study before I have done more than dust the chairs.

"Did they catch their train all right?" he asks.

"Yes thanks. We all enjoyed yesterday evening but were upset to think of you moving away. Do you really have to go?"

He runs his hands through his hair. "It seems I do. I've prayed to God about it, and He thinks it will be for the best. I can serve Him anywhere, and there are plenty of churches in Wales. Gwen's happiness is very important too, of course. The baby is due next Christmas, all being well. I'll have to wait till the Bishop speaks to me before I make things official, so please don't tell anyone yet."

"Trust me," I say, remembering how I have in the past had his secrets to keep. "What news of Lorna?"

"She has written to Pat apologising for not having been able to see everyone before leaving for Liverpool. I don't know exactly what reasons she's given but I'm sure people will understand that a permanent change is essential for her health."

I make the coffee and Gwen returns while I am washing the cups.

"Everything all right?" I ask.

"Oh yes. Being pregnant is really very interesting. They do a lot of poking about and can feel if the baby's head is in the right place."

"Yes, but it might move round."

She dutifully dons an apron and helps me finish the chores. This house really is very old-fashioned and draughty, like a Victorian stage-set.

"Does your mother live in a big house in Wales?" I ask.

"No. It's a terrace, but we'll be given another vicarage when James gets a new church."

I foresee a crowded domestic scene, with a crying baby and an exhausted James. How lucky I am to be comparatively unhampered.

"Shall I see you at the WF meeting tomorrow?" I ask as I'm leaving.

A strange expression crosses her face and she places both hands on her stomach as if asking an internal question.

"I'll see how I'm feeling then," she says. "The nurse told me I mustn't get too tired."

Perhaps it would be best if she stays at home with James.

The responsibility of keeping their secret is getting bit much, and I need to relax to fully benefit from the Victorian Rantersford lecture.

When I get home, I phone Keith and ask him to call at the fish and chip shop and get two portions for our lunch. I'm suddenly too tired to cook, and I've not got the excuse of pregnancy.

"Good idea," he says. "It seems a long time since I saw you."

It was only yesterday, but I expect he means saw me on my own.

The fish and chips go down well, and we relax in greasy comfort on the settee.

After a while, he says "I don't like this idea of a long engagement. Do we have to stick to it?"

I gather my thoughts. "Well, now the girls have approved, and you've got a new job, and it's official, I suppose there's no real reason for delay."

My tiredness flies away. I get up and bin the chip paper, eager to follow his train of thought.

"Am I right in thinking that the banns have to be called three times before there can be a wedding?" Keith has evidently been doing some research.

"Yes. If we go to see James quickly and find out a convenient date, he could maybe squeeze us in before he leaves. I would like him to do the service if possible."

He seizes me in his arms and we dance around the room.

"Let's do it," he cries. "Matrimony, here we come!"

Quite out of breath, we flop down again. It is agreed that we will speak to James about it after choir practice on Friday.

"Right, I'll be off now and give my landlady a week's notice before we think better of the whole idea."

"I'm not going to think better of it," I protest indignantly. "It'll be for better or worse, with no going back." I find half a bottle of wine in the pantry, left over from the girls' visit, and we chink glasses in a toast to our future together.

—///—

The speaker at the WF meeting this month is a man. That's unusual, but he is well received by the ladies, some of whom seem to have met him before.

Susan sniffs. "Thinks he knows all there is to know about everything," she whispers.

Actually, he does seem to know quite a lot about Rantersford's past history. There is a projector and screen, and plenty of pictures are met with cries of recognition from the born-and-bredders. I learn that my house was built more than 100 years ago.

Indeed, St Stephen's was erected to serve the growing population in the streets radiating from the nearby factories and railway station.

I wonder who first lived in 16 Salvin Street, and vow to find out by consulting the deeds.

Not much remains of Georgian Rantersford, though that which was spared from demolition still waits to be discovered by historians eager for treasures to reveal to the locals.

Applause is loud and prolonged, and tea and cakes are pressed on the speaker. No-one seems curious about Lorna's absence, so I am relieved until Pat takes me on one side and quietly asks if I would consider acting as secretary of the group while she takes on the chairmanship.

"We need someone who can write reports accurately," she whispers. "I'm sure you could do that. Think about it and let me know."

I suppose I will have time now my book is nearly finished, but I can't say I'm very keen.

Susan says there is something she wants to tell me, so full of curiosity, I follow her inside when we reach her house.

"It's about Sid," she begins. I listen attentively as she confesses to a fondness for him, and he for her.

"That's very nice," I say mildly. "He is a good man and must be lonely on his own."

"He is, and he wants us to join forces and live together."

"You mean he wants to marry you?"

She is shocked. "Of course. I don't believe in the other."

By this, I presume she doesn't really approve of Keith and me. I hasten to enlighten her.

"Keith and I are getting married very soon." I inform her. "We are asking James to read the banns in church on Sunday."

"Oh good." She beams with delight. "Then we can go on being friends as a foursome!"

When I get home, I call to Sid over the fence.

"I hear you are courting," I tease. "I hope you aren't taking advantage of my friend Susan."

He laughs. "Certainly not. My Eliza is coming down to meet her. She thinks I should sell the house to a local builder cheap, so it can be smartened up and sold on. Then I could move in with Susan and share expenses fairly."

"What a good idea. I'll be sorry to see you go but you'll still be nearby. What about Dolly? Does Susan like cats?"

Something tells me that she doesn't but Sid assures me that he can take Dolly with him, so I must be wrong. Orlando will miss his little friend.

I tell Sid that Keith and I are getting married without delay. I wonder who will be first at the matrimonial winning post. Everything seems to be falling neatly into place. Let's hope no impediments arise.

After choir practice, which seems to drag on this week, Keith and I follow Gwen to the vicarage. I ask if James can spare a moment for us to arrange a date for our wedding.

"I'm sure he can. He was unhappy to think we might be gone before he could be involved."

She speaks quietly, not wanting anyone else to hear. I wonder how long the Bishop will take to let the cat out of the bag.

Apparently the rules about banns are rather complicated. They have to be read three times at services where the congregation is present, and if no-one objects, a date can be fixed and preparations made. If we want the choir and flowers at the wedding, it costs more.

"We'll have to start saving up," remarks Keith. "It would have been cheaper to elope."

Gwen is shocked. "You mustn't do that. Lots of people will want to attend. Think of the WF and your girls and neighbours."

We choose Saturday, June 22nd provisionally.

"The weather should be nice and warm by then. You could go to the seaside for the honeymoon." Gwen's enthusiasm knows no bounds."

"I hope she doesn't suggest coming too," says Keith, when we get home.

"We don't have to go anywhere," I say. I believe honeymoons are rare these days. Just a weekend away would do."

I remember my own first nuptials with a shudder. The weather was foggy, and several guests got lost on the way to the church. My husband had refused to have any hymns and wanted as few prayers as possible, being a non-believer. He only agreed to a religious ceremony after pressure from his mother, who refused to attend a Register Office event. My parents privately disapproved of the whole idea of their only daughter marrying 'beneath' her, but did their best to smile for the camera. I can't remember where we went for the honeymoon.

"Let's pretend we're married already," says Keith. "We could be a happy old couple in a play."

I give him a fond kiss. "Yes, let's." And we go upstairs.

Chapter 30

The job at the hospital starts on Monday. I'm sure Keith will do it admirably, but he is less certain. "It's a long time since I had to take responsibility for more than one patient," he confesses.

I try to boost his confidence. "You'll be busy, but you won't be on your own. And I'll be here to cook your supper when you finish your shift. You'll meet interesting people and make new friends."

He sighs. "By the way, according to my diary, it's Peace Council on Monday evening. I fear I will be too tired to go this time. Do you mind going on your own?"

I check my wall calendar and see he is right. Oh dear. I should be here to welcome him home after his first day, but I don't want to miss the meeting.

"I'll think about it," I say. "It's not till after the week-end."

We decide to spend Saturday sorting out his flat. Anything we won't need can be taken to a charity shop and the rest brought here.

"Who do we know with a van," is the next question.

I think of the answer first. "Bernard," I say triumphantly. "He comes to choir in a white van."

Keith pulls a face. "I don't like to ask him," he objects.

"It'll be all right," I say. "He doesn't fancy me any more now he's got Angela."

So we pluck up courage and approach him after church. Our banns are read for the first time of asking this Sunday, and several members of the congregation wish us well. Bernard is willing to help with the move this very afternoon, which fits in perfectly with our plans.

By tea time we are quite worn out, but everything we want to keep is safely stored at 16 Salvin Street and the rest can be taken to a charity shop later in the week. Keith's rent is paid up till Friday, so there is time in hand.

His first shift at the hospital starts at 8 a.m. and finishes at 5 p.m., which sounds reasonable to me.

"It won't always be so convenient," he explains. "Sometimes I'll be on nights, or very early in the morning."

I promise to buy a new alarm clock with a loud bell, and we go early to bed.

Keith sets off for work in good time, leaving me to get on with my writing. We have a shared income now, which will go towards our future lifestyle, whatever shape that takes.

By 5.30 I have an early supper ready, but Keith doesn't get home till 6 o'clock. He's had a very busy day, and I don't like to leave him to go to the Peace Council meeting on my own.

"I'll be O.K. he assures me. "I'll listen to some music on the radio and relax. Give my love to Bright Skirt." We laugh and I realize that it's been a long time since we saw Naomi and Ruth and the rest.

When I arrive at the usual venue, what appears to be a violent argument is going on. Naomi is at the centre of it.

"You're all idiots," she shouts. "People will leave in droves if we don't change our tune."

She catches sight of me and continues. "Keith has obviously been put off, as Clare is here on her own."

Everyone looks at me. I can't let that pass.

"No, he's not. He's just started a new job at the hospital and is too tired to come out tonight. He sends his apologies."

At this point Ruth hurries in with her usual bundle of papers. "Time to settle down," she says firmly. "We've got a lot to discuss."

Her training in the Church has taught her how to calm troubled waters. Miraculously, the majority sits down and studies the agenda.

To my embarrassment, Naomi comes across to sit beside me. She sees me as an ally, though I've never given her particular support.

"I thought perhaps you and Keith had split up," she whispers. Something in her tone leads me to suspect that she is disappointed we are still together.

"We are getting married next month," I whisper back. She gives a kind of little shudder, as if the idea is repugnant to her. We are not listening to Ruth as she goes through her report, but I cannot resist taking Bright Skirt down a peg.

"Unlike you, I find loving cats is not enough."

Someone says 'shush', so we shut up.

Ruth has asked a question and is waiting for an answer. Unfortunately, she is looking at me.

"Sorry," I say," I didn't quite hear what you said."

She clears her throat and raises her voice.

"Julia wonders if the Good Friday March is the kind of thing we should be supporting."

"Oh yes," I say. "I went with some friends but didn't see many people from the group. We are supposed to be protesters and, in a way, we were protesting against the crucifixion of Jesus."

Ruth looks pleased. "Good." She makes a note.

"I don't agree," says a little man in a woolly hat. "I'm not religious, and I don't think religion or politics should come into things."

"Rubbish!" This from a young man with a ponytail who works at the museum. "If you go into it, Religion and Politics control everything. This group should see to it that they don't get too much power."

"Hear, hear," shouts Naomi. So she does agree with someone.

Ruth reads a letter from Oxfam asking for volunteers to help in the local charity shop, and the tall lady with long grey hair wants people to sign a letter demanding the release of a Tibetan political prisoner. The Campaign Against the Arms Trade is planning to blockade a big arms fair in London. I feel I should go to this but fear I have too much on at the moment.

Over a cup of tea, Ruth tells me that she has heard that Keith and I are planning to marry.

"I'm friendly with James and Gwen of St Stephen's," she explains. "Rantersford is a small world, as you've no doubt discovered. News travels fast."

I am tempted to mention the baby and even to hint at the interregnum, but refrain.

"Do you have a family?" I ask.

"Yes, I have two children. My husband died of cancer last year, so I don't get much spare time. He was a teacher." She consults her watch and we resume the business.

Poor Ruth. How awful for her. My mind wanders away from the crowded room to St Stephen's vicarage. James and Gwen have gone, and Ruth and her two fatherless children are there instead.

"Shall we share a taxi?" Naomi brings me back to earth with a bump. The meeting is breaking up. Maureen says. "Tell her 'No'. She won't pay for her half share." Keith would add his weight but he isn't here, and I can't think quickly enough.

She takes my arm and bears me along to the nearby taxi rank. "You can drop me off first," she says. "I've got further to go than you."

I should have broken free and said I would prefer to walk, but it's getting dark and Keith hasn't arranged to meet me. So we get into the first taxi and I do mental arithmetic on the contents of my purse. "Tell her you can only pay half," nags, Maureen. "Make her give you the money now."

But I am soft. Poor Naomi seems to have few friends, and she likes me, so I ask after her cats, and she sings their praises till we reach her address in a cul-de-sac.

The taxi driver turns back on to the main road and remarks that all his mates know her because when she uses them she always argues over the price.

"It's a flat rate," he says. "We can't undercharge or we'd get the sack."

"I think she has a low income," I say, trying to excuse her, but he says no-one has much money these days. He draws up at 16 Salvin Street and I give him a tip for which he thanks me profusely and calls me 'Duckie'.

Keith is dozing on the settee. He rouses himself and asks how the meeting went.

"I'll tell you tomorrow," I say. "Time for bed now."

I feed Orlando, lock up, and soon we are both fast asleep.

—⁓—

Keith's first few days at the hospital exhaust him, but he does not complain. He's not actually involved in nursing. It's mostly lifting people on to trolleys and transporting them here and there. Sometimes they are going to have an operation and he must be cheerful and tell them they'll be fine.

"They don't often look very fine," he admits.

I hope he isn't reminded too much of his poor mother.

Sid spends most of his days at Susan's but always comes back home to sleep. Suddenly Eliza is there, full of plans.

"I'm not going to clean the place," she declares. "The builder will strip everything down. I'll just put clean sheets on the spare bed and stay until the sale has been agreed. I don't expect we'll get much, but he'll make it nice and find someone respectable to move in. You won't want riffraff for neighbours, will you?"

I am grateful that she includes us in her plans, as next-door neighbours can be a pain.

With Keith at work, I have more time for my writing. 'My Granny's got a Handbell' has nearly covered a full school year, and I am running out of material. It will need reading through and polishing, but to me it seems both interesting and amusing. I'll have to get it typed and then look for a literary agent in the Writer's and Artist's Yearbook at the Public Library. How exciting it will be if I actually get it published! Not many people know I have been writing a book, so they would be surprised and maybe buy a signed copy.

I break off to make a list of wedding guests. June 22nd will soon be here. It will have to be a modest occasion as we can't afford much. I think back to my first wedding, and how friends wanted to know what we needed for presents. This time we don't really need much except good luck.

I'll phone my girls and give them the date so they can make arrangements. I suppose they will tell their Dad, but I hope he doesn't want to come. The idea of him putting in an appearance makes me suddenly upset. It took me a long time to get over our parting, and now I am reminded of the miserable years which led to it. I blow my nose and make a cup of tea which I take into the garden to drink.

Orlando and Dolly are sitting on Sid's bench in the sun. Rather to my surprise, Sid opens his back door and issues forth to join them. I lean over the fence.

"You all right?" he asks.

"Not really," I reply. "I'm feeling depressed."

"Had a row with Keith?" He is sympathetic but his imagination doesn't go further than his own emotional experience.

"You've got a lot to look forward to, like me." He goes on. "It doesn't do to worry. Things will work out."

What a kind man he is! He deserves to be happy. Maureen joins in.

"So do you. You've come a long way. Just cast your mind back. When you came to Rantersford, you didn't know anybody here. You joined groups of likeminded people and made friends. Everything has fallen into place. Your future is secure, as far as it can be. Well done!"

I laugh aloud. Sid scratches his head.

"You've cheered up quick."

"Yes, you've done me good. Where's Eliza?"

"She's gone for a takeaway. She won't cook in my house. Says it's full of germs. The builder's made a decent offer so she's going back to Bridlington tomorrow."

"When are you going to marry Susan?"

"End of June. You are both invited of course."

"We've beaten you to it. Our date is 22nd of June."

We shake hands enthusiastically over the fence while Orlando and Dolly look on.

"I'll bring you some beetroot from the allotment tomorrow. It's fine if you boil it long enough."

I remember our first meeting nearly a year ago, when Sid asked me if I was 'stopping' in Rantersford. I said I would stay if I found that I liked it.

And like it I do, so here I will stay, among my kindred spirits.

The author was born in Nottingham in 1932. She worked as a librarian in that city, sharing a flat with her friend Elizabeth who later became the wife of the writer Malcolm Bradbury.

She herself married a mature student in Oxford. They had two daughters, but separated after eighteen years.

After making a fresh start in a strange town, she wrote three collections of poetry which were well-received.

This is her first novel, based on a new life where she seeks kindred spirits who share her way of looking.